A Duke For Dessert

A Billionaire Dukes Novel

Miriam Allenson

Publishing History

Print edition published by MS Allenson & Associates,
© 2019
Cover design by Jamie Banta at JamieBeeDesigns.com

ISBN13: 978-1733850117

What People Are Saying About Miriam Allenson's Books

"Miriam Allenson writes characters that leap off the page and into your heart, bringing love and laughter with them."
–*Nancy Herkness, best-selling author of the Wager of Hearts series*

"By the time I reached the end of the book, I knew that this was one that would be going on my re-read shelf."

–*Karen Laird, Shade Tree Book Reviews*

"Hilarious, sexy, heartwarming…a fabulous debut! Miriam Allenson hits it out of the park in her debut novel FOR THE LOVE OF THE DAME. Sofia and Car are proof that when opposites attract, sparks fly."

–*Lisa Verge Higgins, author of Senseless Acts of Beauty*

Other Books By Miriam Allenson

FOR THE LOVE OF THE DAME

CHAPTER ONE

Charlie Camville never took meetings without an appointment. His assistant, Louisa, made sure of that. When his office door crashed open and a woman rushed toward where he stood calmly reading a letter, he turned, one eyebrow raised in surprise. Shock took over when she threw handfuls of weeds and dirt that hit him square in the sternum.

"What the hell, woman!" Dropping the letter on his desk, he took a step back and looked down. Dirt splattered his starched white shirt. Bits of dried-up leaves dotted his trousers. He fixed his attacker with a black look and she returned it, eyes huge with some kind of emotion he damn well had no desire to understand.

"Hell? That's where you belong," she said, her voice fierce and low.

"I am so sorry," Louisa said from the doorway. "I couldn't stop her. Shall I ring security?"

Not taking his eyes off the little witch, Charlie began to brush away the mess. "Yes Louisa. Tell them we have a problem."

The problem raised a quivering chin. "You have one hell of a nerve."

"I have a nerve? It was you who hit me." He shook his foot. Dirt had gotten into one of his shoes.

She took a shuddering breath. "I wish I could do more than hit you."

"More violence. Lovely." He kicked aside a particularly large clump of dirt. "Rather than wait for security, I believe I'll throw you out myself."

The ruffle on her pink blouse trembled with the rise and fall of her chest. "That's exactly the reaction I'd expect from somebody like you."

"Somebody like me who's opposed to assault by topsoil?"

"Somebody like you who ordered the destruction of the garden we just planted for Bisby's kids."

Charlie frowned. "What garden?"

"Like you didn't know…" She was breathing in spurts.

For a moment he was afraid she might be hyperventilating. "I don't know. In point of fact, that's why I asked." He reached a hand out and touched her shoulder. "Are you all right?"

She shook him off. "I'm fine. But the garden that was at the entrance to of the Manor isn't." She jabbed a finger in the direction of his chest. "That's Melbury Manor. *Your* property."

Wondering if perhaps he hadn't heard right, he waited a beat before he said, "How and why would you plant a garden on my property?"

"Because your estate manager, George Swynford, said we could."

As her words sank in, Charlie's pulse jittered. His damned estate manager and loose cannon of a brother-in-law, George. What had he done this time? Stepping back, Charlie reached across his desk for his phone. "Louisa, tell security I don't need them."

He placed the handset back in its cradle, never taking his eyes off the short—and now that he had a moment to note it—curvy woman. "Perhaps we should begin again." He indicated one of the two Biedermeier chairs in front of his desk. "Please."

She didn't move.

He raised one eyebrow. She exhaled a sharp breath and took the chair he'd offered, which allowed him to take his. Looking down at her still-swirling ankle-length skirt, he had a sudden urge to needle her. "Come from another century, have you?"

"Try for a better quip." Her exotic, long-lashed black-brown eyes narrowed. "Charlie."

A muscle knotted in the back of his neck. Charlie's mother, a stickler for tradition, called him Lindsey after the dukedom he held. He didn't mind when others called him Your Grace. No one but his friends called him by his Christian name. This ridiculously-dressed woman was not a friend, not even an acquaintance. "I beg your pardon," he said in his coolest tones.

She looked daggers at him. "Sure, beg. I don't mind."

Irritated, he folded one leg over the other and made a business of brushing flecks of dirt from his trousers. "How did all this come about?"

"Which part? The planting or the bulldozing?"

"Both." He held up a hand. "But before you go on, tell me your name. I'd prefer not to address you as madam." Or *shrew*.

She clasped her hands together in her lap. He supposed it was to keep herself from taking a swing at him again. "It's Annie. Annie Lukin."

"Lovely. Now if you don't mind, please start at the beginning."

"I'll start with a question. Why did you do it?" She leaned forward and her blouse gapped enough for him to see she was wearing a black bra edged in lace.

Before he spoke, he took a moment to clear his throat. "Destroy your garden? Until moments ago, I wasn't aware of its existence."

"Good try. Before I left Bisby this morning, I spoke to George and he said it was you who gave the okay to bulldoze it. He said he was only following *your* orders."

A pulse throbbed its way across Charlie's forehead. George had indeed called yesterday. He was keen to tell him about an idea he was working on with a consortium. It was an idea he was sure Charlie would think quite brilliant. "I don't suppose George mentioned he wants to turn Melbury Manor into a hunting lodge and develop the property for grouse hunting." Infuriated as Charlie had been at the idea that George would make such plans without checking with him first, he no doubt heard nothing more of their conversation. Certainly he heard nothing about a garden.

The woman popped up out of her chair. Because he'd been raised a gentleman, Charlie came to his feet, as well.

"I was never told about any of that. The deal I–" She bit her lip and began to pace around his office as if it were hers, past the long windows out of which he often looked down on the Thames just below. She trod across the deep blue Axminster carpet he'd purchased at Pentreath & Hall in Bloomsbury, and around the Louis XV carved walnut desk he'd snagged at auction at Sotheby's in celebration of selling his multi-national security firm, The Rotherforde Group for billions.

She was quite an energetic thing for being so tiny. Now that he'd gotten over the shock of being attacked in his own space, he could take note of her many delightful features, which included the shining, black curls that flowed across and halfway down her back. They framed a face with glowing skin, arched eyebrows, high cheekbones, pointed chin, and a small nose with a bump in the middle. He'd not have been surprised to learn she'd indulged in a career in pugilism.

He clasped his hands behind his back. "You were saying…?"

"The soil is rocky everywhere in the village." Her arms swung wide in synchrony with the skirt that accentuated a pair of rounded hips. "Except at the Manor."

He frowned. Were those combat boots she was wearing? As she circled his desk and came toward him one more time, he saw they were, indeed. The skirt, the pink blouse, the boots, the combination was so comical he had a bit of a time suppressing his smile. "There was a kitchen garden somewhere in the back, I believe, decades, perhaps a century ago." He tried not to look down at her odd footwear. "However, in the time the Manor has been an entail of the dukes of Lindsey—three centuries at least—I don't believe there's ever been a garden of any kind at the entrance."

She made one more turn around his desk and came to a halt in front of him. "What's an entail?" She held up a hand. "No, don't tell me. What's your point?"

He glanced down again at the ruffled blouse beneath which her full breasts swayed. "Only that perhaps you misunderstood George."

She reared back on her heels. The giant hooped earrings, worn in her neat little ears, danced back and forth. "I misunderstood nothing. George promised me we could have use of that one piece of your property for the growing season. In return, he got the thing he wanted. The community did, too."

"My dear lady. What was it George wanted?"

She looked away. "Reservations."

An odd thing, that. Charlie exhaled a weary sigh. But what else, after all, could he expect? More and more he'd come to realize how unfortunate it was that he and George Swynford were related if only by marriage to his sister, Viola. Since he loved Viola too much to sack her husband, he had to suffer George in as much silence as he could muster and hope the bloke didn't often make a botch of things. It looked like now he had. "What type of garden was it? Flowers? Or vegetables?"

"It was a *vegetable* garden. We planted it so the children of Bisby could learn how to grow things they could take home and eat." She flung herself back into her chair. "That seems a capital idea," he said and sat, although he did no flinging.

She leaned toward him and the ruffle at the edge of her blouse trembled again. "Just so you know, there were a lot of angry people in Bisby this morning. A lot of tears, too." She hesitated and then in a quieter voice said, "Especially from the kids."

He flinched. "My dear Miss Lukin." He rather hoped she was a miss. "I don't like to think there have been any tears shed in Bisby because of something you say I've done."

"You did. Do it, that is." She had clutched her fists so tightly together the knuckles showed white. "Those kids? They're poor children. Unlike some people, they weren't born with every advantage."

She was quite good at tossing verbal grenades, wasn't she? But if Charlie wasn't mistaken—and he didn't think he was—her eyes held the glisten of unshed tears. He wondered. Had they been there from the first?

"All those boys and girls were excited about picking the lettuce, radishes, and peas that were just beginning to come up," she went on. "When you had the garden plowed over, you took all that away from them."

His gaze touched on her hands as she clenched and unclenched them. "You know I might well have given you my permission to plant your garden on my property had you addressed your query directly to me."

"If I had addressed—" She gasped. "You might have—" She took a breath. "You are one piece of work."

"A piece of work, am I?" He had wanted to throw her out when she'd burst in upon him. But he hadn't and now he wouldn't. By her actions—and the unshed tears—it said she cared about the children of Bisby. More than cared. Coming all the way from Bisby to London said to Charlie that she'd made herself their champion and as their champion, she'd come to do battle with the villain of the piece. Him.

She intrigued him. She was a fighter, this fierce gypsy-like girl, odd and appealing with her peculiar, even bizarre, outfit, her disordered hair, her glinting gold earrings and flashing black-brown eyes, and her passion. "If you have to call me a name," he said, trying to tell himself he didn't want to soften in any way toward her, "I prefer it not be a piece of work. Perhaps you might call me something that's more appropriate."

Her nostrils flared. "How about Your Royal Highness?"

"Ah, a truly American mistake." Said with cheek. He ground his jaws together to keep from grinning. "You can't refer to me as Your Royal Highness. There are, of course, some dukes for whom you can. Wills, and Harry. Charles, Phillip, and the uncles."

She leaned forward again, the edge of the blouse moving lower as she did. At last he gave himself permission to look.

"So sorry, but I haven't had much personal experience with…" She paused and then, with undisguised distaste, added, "Dukes."

"Ah." He stood. "About your garden…since you say it is—I beg pardon—*was* on my property, and I stand accused of being responsible for its destruction, I'd like to see if I can make it up to you."

He held out a hand to her. She looked at it as if it were a rabid animal. But then she relented, took it, and let him raise her to her feet.

Wrinkling her expressive eyebrows, she said, "I don't suppose you can make time go in reverse."

"I've many talents. That's not one of them." He picked up his mobile from where it lay on his desk and slid it into the holder on his belt. "I'd better call to have this mess you made—" She looked away—"cleaned up. While it's being done, let me treat you to a coffee—I assume you'd rather it be coffee instead of tea as you're an American—and we'll decide together how we're going to get the issue of the garden sorted."

"I don't drink coffee because so much of it is over-processed and not responsibly sourced."

"Ah, I see. Then perhaps you would like a cup of tea after all."

"As long as the tea is responsibly sourced."

"I don't think I can confirm that the lovely tea shop just down the street sources its beverages responsibly. May I suggest, instead, we indulge in a scone whilst there?"

"Your tea shop probably serves scones made with non-GMO flour but thank you, no. You can buy me a bottle of spring water, however."

"Right." He motioned for her to step in front of him to the door. "I assume you left a coat in the anteroom—or perhaps to go with your outfit, a cape? We can only hope Louisa didn't toss it out when you were in here having your violent way with me."

Urging her on with a hand set at the small of her back, he said, "Let's walk rather than take a cab. One wants to do everything one can to maintain a healthy body. Walking, as you know, is good for one's health. Just as is avoiding GMO flour." He paused for effect. "One tries, doesn't one?"

She slid wide, startled eyes up at his face and—who would have thought her capable of contrition—colored.

She wasn't a witch at all.

The tea shop was what Annie had come to think of as a typical old English dining establishment. The interior, a little dark, with small tables and a wooden floor that was probably laid in the reign of Elizabeth—the first one—the clink of china and subdued talk. That she would be walking into such a place with a man she'd just clobbered seemed right out of some TV comedy. Without the laugh track.

"Do you come to London often?"

Annie ventured a glance sideways. It was obvious, the way he carried himself that he was comfortable in his body and his clothing, the suit custom-made, as was typical of a man of his class, dark gray with a barely-seen white stripe. If she'd learned nothing since she'd come to England three years ago, she'd learned about class.

"Not very often, no."

A hostess hurried toward them. She led the way past any number of tables, set close together in the center, to one that was more secluded, and seated them. The woman all but curtsied. Oh, yes class.

As he ordered a tea and a scone for him, water for her, from the server—who likewise rushed to take care of them—Annie played back the last embarrassing half hour. She wanted to kick herself. Fury, panic, and her reaction to the children devastated by the destruction of the garden had driven her to drop everything and take the midday train from Lincoln to London. But to have allowed those feelings to stay with her while the train ate up the miles to the capital city, even heat up further as she barged into the man's office, for that she deserved not one but many kicks.

On the train she'd done a Google search about the man she was about to confront. She found very little other than the fact that he, Charles Camville was the sixteenth Duke of Lindsey, thirty-five, and a businessman. The article referenced something called The Rotherforde Group, an online security company, which he'd just sold. There'd been mention of his father, the previous duke, who had died a mere six months before. From a little reading between the lines, Annie suspected Duke Number 15 had been as useless as tits on a bull, and done a great job of ignoring the business of the dukedom, running it into a big red hole, his reputation along with it. As with the son, there'd been no other details.

If it weren't for an article Annie had read in the *South Lindsey Chronicle* on the occasion of Charlie—

and hadn't she gotten under his skin when she'd disrespected the whole duke thing and called him Charlie—becoming duke, she wouldn't have known he had multiple middle names to go along with his first and last, and they were a mouthful. Charles David Hugo Montagu Camville, the Duke of Lindsey, it said, was in the process of making plans to restore the family's image and its finances.

Well, part of what she was doing these days was restoring *her* finances, so they had that in common.

As the server left with their order, the duke smiled. "And so. Shall we talk about our garden?"

She was worn out from emotion, but she wasn't about to give in. "*My* garden."

He raised one of those damn eyebrows. He'd been flipping them up so much she wanted to take some tape to them.

"On my property. *Our* garden."

Point to him.

Within what seemed like mere moments, his tea, scone, and her water came. Well, of course. He was an aristocrat, and the server knew it. While the woman fussed with the placement of the cream and sugar bowls, Annie took advantage of the distraction and stared at the man. Funny that he didn't look like what she'd come to think of as a typical English patrician, the kind that was always red-faced from too much drink, with pale blue eyes, light brown hair on the thin side, an overbite, and a long, aristocratic nose that he would look down at her from. Or with. Or whatever.

This duke? He was no pale, overbred blueblood. He was southern European dark, his skin olive-tinted, his black hair with a natural wave that would tend toward curls if he didn't corral it with product. His eyes glowed deep black. The nose? He had a seriously not thin nose. The Duke of Lindsey's nose could lead a phalanx of soldiers across a battlefield. She was fascinated by that nose. As, unfortunately, she was with the rest of the man.

When the server left, he said, "I am sorry that we quite carelessly plowed up your garden. There was a reason—not a good one I must assume—but that reason is yet to be confirmed." He moved. The chair creaked.

Eyes on the chair, which seemed too small for his tall, rangy body and doing her best to tamp down the sarcasm, she said, "I'm sure, now that the deed is done, the kids will appreciate hearing that."

He raised one eyebrow. "I assume we're still speaking of the human offspring of adults as opposed to goats."

She hoped it was an act, the whole cool, plummy, upper-class attitude and speech. And the cluelessness. Otherwise it would be too depressing, thinking this was what was coming from the mouth of one of the most stunning males whose presence she'd ever been in. She wanted him to be better. She wanted him to fix what he'd done.

"The children of Bisby. Not goats, Your Highness. Their parents are chronically unemployed. In case you didn't know the unemployment rate in Bisby and its surrounding area is higher than in any other part of Lincolnshire."

There was a flash in his eyes of something besides cluelessness.

He put down his cup. "I am quite impressed that you, a foreigner, would know about economic conditions in England."

A foreigner? So, that flash of something was a trick of what little light there was in this precious tea room. He was a total smart-ass and a condescending jerk, and she wasn't sure she could sit here much longer without heaving her water in his face. "Because I'm a foreigner doesn't mean I don't know things. I've been in England more than three years and have made it my business to find out as much about the country as I can."

"Admirable." More eyebrow raising. "The children's parents. You were going to tell me?"

"Yes, them. Their dads lost their jobs when the shipyards up north closed at the start of the latest economic disaster. But a man of your station wouldn't have an interest in the lives of people who are obviously not your kind. You wouldn't know about shipyards closing. No doubt you were otherwise occupied at weekend parties at country houses, hanging out at Wimbledon and Ascot."

His black eyes took on a sulfurous glow.

"I beg your pardon?" He uncrossed his mile-long legs and set both feet on the floor. Leaning forward, and with exaggerated care, he placed one hand on the table. It was a large hand. She eyed it with trepidation. Those long fingers looked more than capable of wrapping themselves around her neck.

A thrill of fear—or God help her, sexual awareness—rushed through her. Eyes fixed on his hand, she said, "That was uncalled for. I apologize."

He sat back, sliding his hand onto one firm-muscled thigh. The chair creaked again. "I wonder, Miss Lukin."

She risked a glance up at his face. The light in his eyes had cooled. "Yes?"

"What is it you do for a living?"

All right, then, change of subject. No chopping block at the Tower of London for her today. "I own The Ocular."

Once more with that eyebrow. Oh, for a roll of adhesive tape.

"The restaurant that has put Bisby on the culinary map? I am impressed."

She felt a rush of warmth she shouldn't have felt. Not now. Not from this man. "Thank you."

"What, then, is the purpose of having the garden on my property? Did you plan to supply your restaurant with fresh vegetables? Perhaps I should charge you a fee." His lips twitched.

Okay, so he could tease, could he? Well, she could, too. "Good Lord, Your Majesty. It was only moments ago I told you the garden was for Bisby's kids, and you've already forgotten."

His lips curved upward in a real smile. Gorgeous lips they were too. What would he do if she reached up and— She slipped her hands between her knees and squeezed.

Pushing his tea cup away, he said, "My sister, Viola—you know she and her husband live at the Manor—tells me she dined on a sublime risotto at The Ocular the other evening. I do so love a good risotto."

"Come to Bisby the next time I serve it. You'll have to make a reservation, though. I don't take walk-ins."

"Yes, I'd heard. The Ocular is the place to be. But I'm curious. Where, in regard to Bisby's young, does The Ocular figure?"

"It doesn't. Not directly, anyway. I came up with the idea of planting a garden because nobody's doing enough for Bisby's kids. My plan was for them to work in the garden as it grows, which would help them learn discipline and teamwork. Those are good character traits to hone if you're going to make it in the world."

"That's an honorable initiative. Teach a man to fish and all that. Or a child to harvest a vegetable. But what do you get out of it, since it's not mushrooms for your risotto. You do include mushrooms in the risotto, don't you?"

She gripped her water bottle hard. He might be so hot that she'd broken out into a sweat; he might be good at teasing. But he was better at being obnoxious. "In fact, I do. And I have local suppliers for my mushrooms. But the kids often eat meals with low nutritional value. If they could take home just harvested peas, or tomatoes and zucchini—courgettes to you—later in the season, they would see that fresh food is better than what comes out of a tin or box."

"My dear Miss Lukin, I'm intrigued. And I believe I want to see the spot where your garden was."

She could feel herself tremble. Even her hair was vibrating with the— God, she didn't even have the word for whatever emotion it was she was feeling. "Why? Do you get a kick out of seeing what destruction looks like?"

"Your cynicism is showing. No, no, it's to make things up to the children of Bisby." He leaned close. Too close. Her heart did a backflip. "And to you."

CHAPTER TWO

Her eyes had gone wide. Placing both hands on the table, she lifted her face to him. "Really?"

As with everything else about her, Charlie didn't know if she meant it or if, with that innocent blinking of her eyes, she was having him on. "I always mean what I say, Miss Lukin. It is miss, yes?"

"Yes, it's miss."

"I'm relieved."

"Relieved in what way?"

Right. As if he could explain the need to keep teasing her even after she'd infuriated him by suggesting he didn't care about the widespread loss of jobs in Bisby. He did care. He took it as his responsibility as duke to ensure there were jobs in and around the village and on his properties. He'd not been able to do that to the extent he wanted to until he'd sold The Rotherforde Group. Now he was able. "It's of no matter. What does matter is the garden." And restoring morale among Bisby's adults and children alike.

He stroked his chin. "I wonder, though, perfect as you no doubt think that parcel of land is, if there isn't another, perhaps a better spot."

"Like I said. There isn't one, Your Holiness."

Your Holiness. He rather liked this one more than *Your Majesty,* although that one was spot on too. He motioned for their server to approach. "You've convinced me. I'll ring George and make sure he's available to bring me up to speed on the unfortunate turn of events that brought you down to London to accomplish your quite spectacular"—he rubbed his chest— "goal."

Her face colored. Ah yes. Contrition, again.

"When? I want to be there when the garden is restored. Just to make sure you mean what you say."

Perhaps not too much contrition. "We can re-plow the garden as early as Monday, perhaps Tuesday, weather permitting. I'll drive up tomorrow, take care of my business with George, and then you can show me what needs to be done in the garden. If you would be so good as to give me your mobile—rather, your cell phone number—I'll text you when I have a better idea of my time."

"Let's do it differently. You give me *your* number, first."

Ah. She wasn't convinced he'd follow through.

"I'll text you mine," she continued. "That way I'll have your number and you'll have mine."

Whether she knew it or not, he rather thought he already did.

Just as they finished their exchange of information, her mobile buzzed. Her lovely arched eyebrows came together in a frown. "Do you mind if I take this? One of my staff at the restaurant is texting me."

While she bent her head to tap in her response, Charlie gave his credit card to the server and thought about what plans he needed to rearrange. Louisa could take care of rescheduling tomorrow's appointments. He would have to ring Samantha—Lady Samantha Carberry—and cancel the plans they'd made to go to Paris for the long weekend.

A vision of Samantha drifted into his head. All blonde and blue-eyed, she was tall and thin with perfect posture, perfect diction, perfect face, perfect long, straight hair cut just so.

There was nothing *just so* about the gypsy girl who sat in front of him texting away, head bent to her task. A long, black curl fell over her shoulder and across her breast, part of it just at the edge of her pink blouse and its fetching ruffle. His fingers twitched. Oh, to be that curl. Or the ruffle.

The server came back with Charlie's credit card. With a flourish he signed the check. "Thank you, my good woman."

She gave him a half curtsy and melted away.

"It must be nice to be a duke," his companion at table said.

"It has its moments." Not as many as she might think.

"You nod at a server and she appears at your royal side just because it's you. It's amazing. You snap your fingers and it's all done."

"I didn't snap my fingers. And as I believe I've already told you, I'm not a royal."

"All figurative, Mr. Duke."

An idea came to him. "Once we return to my building, I could snap my fingers and ask for my car to be brought 'round. Rather than you having to put up with the inconvenience of public transportation—can I assume you didn't drive, instead took the train?"

"I don't own a car."

He raised an eyebrow at that curiosity. What person who lived outside a metropolis didn't own a car? "Well, then, you took the train," he went on. "I could ask and you could accept a ride with me the entire way to Bisby." He paused. Had he just offered her a lift to Bisby this afternoon when he had no intention of leaving London for the north until tomorrow? What was coming over him?

She rose from the table, all poise, despite the long skirt that might have tripped her up. "Thank you, but no. I bought a round trip ticket. No use letting it go to waste." She gathered up her things and gave him a canny look from beneath her ridiculously long eyelashes. "Besides you might snap your fingers at me."

There was the suggestion of a dimple on one side of her mouth. The deep black- brown sparkle in her eyes, the sweet oval of her face made her look less like a gypsy and more like a pixie.

He came to his feet. "And risk your fury if I did? I think not."

She looped her handbag by its long straps over her shoulder. "Please remember to text me with the time we're going to meet." She paused. "Oh, and I just remembered I'm more than usually busy tomorrow. Can we make it Saturday in the afternoon around two o'clock?" Not waiting for an answer, she turned toward the door, tossing some of her splendid hair over her shoulder. "I'll be waiting."

As she closed the door behind her, Charlie sat down, puzzled. Annie Lukin was a prize-winning chef of national repute. He remembered reading about her restaurant online on a Best in Britain list. What a surprise it had been to discover The Ocular was in Bisby, the village where he'd grown up. What he might have thought of her personality, what he'd seen of it, today, didn't gibe with what he read on that list. The woman he'd met today had insulted him, repeatedly. She'd assaulted him with garden detritus. She wanted to use him. He was quite sure, despite that last spectacular smile she'd given him, she didn't like him. Why, then, did she fascinate him so?

He looked at his plate where the remainder of his scone sat. He did know one thing. He, Charles Camville, Duke of Lindsey, had been dismissed. Out of hand. By an American and a commoner.

At which point he realized there was nothing common about her at all.

Annie was still shaking when she skirted around the side of the brick building that stood at the corner one block up from the cafe. She collapsed against the wall before her rubber knees could give out. What had tempted her to sit at a table with the duke of Lindsey when all she'd wanted was his agreement to repair the damage done to the garden?

She looked down at the bottle of water he'd bought her, still clutched in her hand, and grimaced because she knew the answer to that question. Much taller than she'd imagined, much more fit, too, he of the gorgeous Henry Cavill hair was frighteningly handsome, almost too much to look at without fainting. Way more than all his names and titles, he was hot and totally appetizing, an exotic dessert to savor at the end of a satisfying meal. Or the night afterward.

Much as she loved dessert, she needed to remind herself that this particular dessert—man—was too rich, too much for her. She looked at her watch. The whole confrontation and cafe-ing had taken more time than she'd planned. She could not keep wasting it thinking about Mr. Oh-My-God Gorgeous. She could run, she supposed. But she'd have to be Usain Bolt to make it to Kings Cross Station before the five-thirty train to Lincoln pulled out. Much as she didn't want to spend any of her otherwise-committed pounds and shillings on such a luxury, a cab it was going to have to be.

It was after midnight when Annie got back to The Ocular. She'd been stuck for endless hours on the train, which had been stopped cold on the tracks with some electronic malfunction just outside Peterborough. Calling the restaurant more than once, she'd spoken to Molly, whom she'd left in charge, and Molly had not only assured her that first seating had gone off as it should, but second seating was well on the way to being as problem-free. Annie called the last time as the train pulled into Lincoln, and Molly told her to stop worrying. The last table was bussed and she was closing up.

Hearing Molly's confident tones, Annie breathed a sigh of relief. She'd spent months building up Molly's self-confidence and would have hated to hear that some unforeseen pressure had her coming undone.

After the ride share driver dropped her at The Ocular, she unlocked its front door and entered. It was quiet inside. She eased past her VIP table, sitting square at the entrance to the kitchen. When The

Ocular had made it to the top ten of the Top 100 *Sunday Times* Best Restaurants in Britain was when Annie had decided to add the table as an element of exclusivity.

She'd grown to like her VIP table, not for the sometimes snobbish members of the upper classes who sat there, but for how it helped pay the salaries of the dozen people in Bisby she'd hired as staff. It paid for other things, too, things she wanted to do to help them. And it paid for her debt.

A single light glowed over the cool stainless-steel surfaces and on her burnished pots hanging all in a row next to her six-burner stove. There was the sweet, clean scent of mint in the air. Somebody must have brought in some from the pots out behind the restaurant where she grew all her herbs—basil, oregano, rosemary, thyme, and the mint.

"Is that you, Annie?" The voice came, disembodied, from downstairs.

Annie slapped a hand on her chest. "Molly! I thought you went home."

Molly pushed open the door from the basement, her arms laden with cloth. "I was counting the serviettes to see if we had enough for tomorrow."

"We don't have enough napkins?" As many years as she'd been in England, Annie still couldn't call them serviettes.

Molly angled her chin in the direction of the napkins in her arms. "We used more than the usual tonight. Even with these from the supply closet, I won't have enough for tomorrow. I'll just nip over to the launderette in the morning and do a quick wash." A grin wreathed Molly's plain face. Still, she kept her lips pressed together over what Annie knew were misshapen teeth. "Aren't you proud of me? I never lost my cool tonight."

Nothing in Molly's background—a single-parent home where she was left to grow up any which way—said she'd be able to work in a fine-dining restaurant. That hadn't stopped Annie from training Molly up so she could. "I am proud of you. Now I want you to go home. It's after midnight."

Molly grimaced. "We had a cancellation at the VIP table for tomorrow night and then two jiffs later I took one from someone else."

Annie's exhausted mind began to creak into gear. "Who?" If the guests had eaten at the restaurant, she could start planning what she'd make, because she always wrote down what her VIP guests liked. Figuring out the best menu for repeat guests was so relaxing, it put Annie to sleep when she had bouts of insomnia, which was often. "When was the last time they ate here?"

Molly's eyes shone with anxiety. "Well, one of them has never. I've got the collywobbles thinking about him and what he might say about The Ocular."

Annie took Molly's hand and gave it a comforting squeeze. "C'mon, Moll. Remember. Everyone puts their pants on—"

"I know. One leg at a time." Molly eased her hand out from under Annie's. "But it's him." She took a deep breath. "The duke of Lindsey."

Annie sagged down on one of the chairs at the VIP table.

"I know I should be happy he's coming," Molly continued. "He's a real toff, a duke, and there aren't so many of them anymore. But…" Molly's voice trailed off. "I heard it was him what wrecked our garden."

The duke of Lindsey. Hadn't Annie hoped the only time she'd have to see him up close and personal ever again would be when they met at the garden? A few minutes, maybe a half hour is what it would take for her to point things out to him and be done.

Now she was going to have to be within feet of him—her experience with VIPs told her they liked to linger over their dinner—for three hours or more. What would happen if she had to brush past him when she visited other diners, as she usually did, at their tables?

In the narrow pass-through between the kitchen and the front of the house, she might stumble. Perhaps the duke would steady her with one of his big, long-fingered hands. She needed steadying right now thinking about his hands on her shoulder. Or the back of her neck, or— "Don't worry about that, Moll," she heard herself declare. "He's promised to restore the garden."

"Gosh, Annie. You don't have to talk so loud. I'm right here."

Annie shot to her feet. She'd raised her voice. And didn't that say way too much about how the man who would be showing up at The Ocular tomorrow night had her all messed up tonight? "Sorry. How many in his party? And do we know who?"

"I think four. Or maybe three. It's him and you know who."

Of course. George and Viola Swynford. What had she thought? In the village of Bisby, population 440, how many people were there of the duke of Lindsey's class who he would be socializing with?

"So, Molly, if we're entertaining royalty, I think I'll serve crostini with beef tartare." She thought for a moment. "Maybe a risotto." Yes, the risotto His Majesty said he loved. With mushrooms. "For the rest, I don't know yet." There were no menus at The Ocular. Diners got what Annie decided to make for the day. If they didn't like it, they didn't have to come back.

"Oh, Annie. Not royalty." Molly put a hand over her mouth. Molly didn't know it but Annie had almost saved enough to pay for a big London dentist to fix Molly up so she never had to hide her beautiful smile again. "Royalty's the queen and the princes and their wives."

And hadn't His Majesty explained that difference? "Well, he speaks like royalty." Yes, in that upper-class, through-his-nose way.

Once, Annie thought she could be friends with some of the upper classes. Emily Torquil for one. Even Ross. All she wanted to do now was avoid the one member of the upper classes who'd come into her life, today…no, yesterday. If she couldn't avoid him—which it seemed she couldn't—after the garden was restored, she'd make sure she had nothing to do with him ever again.

CHAPTER THREE

In the morning, when he eased out of traffic onto the A15, Charlie remembered that he *might* actually have known the garden had been plowed up. "Bugger," he muttered.

During yesterday's talk, George had said the people from the consortium would wonder at an unkempt garden at the entrance to the Manor when they came to inspect the property. Only half-listening to George's ramblings and to get him off the phone, he might have said something like 'take care of it.' George no doubt decided that meant plow it up.

Charlie stepped harder on the gas pedal and the Jag ate up the macadam with a throaty roar. Charlie should have paid closer attention to George's nonsense. Oh, and his bragging about how he could get a reservation at The Ocular with a day's notice, of all things. He stepped even harder on the gas pedal and the car surged forward. Speed would get him to Bisby sooner, but it wouldn't fix the garden. There was one thing that would, though. He engaged his Bluetooth system. "Call Andy Prescott."

Andy picked up on the first ring. "You miserable git. Just found your phone, did you?"

"What? Who'd want to have a conversation with a wanker like you?" Charlie said and grinned. He hadn't talked to Andy in weeks.

"Wait for it, mate." Then there was the sound of a loudspeaker in the background, words unintelligible. Andy's voice came muffled, his hand over the mouthpiece, just as unintelligible. It was March. Lincolnshire's gardeners were no doubt getting ready for the planting season, and making their purchases at Prescott Nurseries.

"What's up, old man?" Andy was back. "Time is money. Chop, chop. And how are you by the way?"

"I'm fine, thank you for asking," Charlie said, as a MINI Cooper Countryman passed him like it had been shot from a cannon. "I'm on my way to Bisby."

"Finally. How long has it been since you've been here? I believe I've forgotten what you look like."

"Ah, the dementia sets in at last. You do remember coming down to London a couple of months ago with Jane that lovely wife of yours. Or perhaps not." Charlie's grin widened. It had been too long since they'd spoken and he'd missed the verbal wrangling that marked his friendship with Andy.

"For that memorable dinner, yes. With your Serena."

"Not my Serena, thank you. As for my coming to Bisby of late?" He swallowed his sudden emotion. "Andy…the funeral."

"Yeah. I know." Andy sighed. "I still can't believe it's six months. Right up to the end he was a force, wasn't he?"

It was a curious thing that Andy's father and Charlie's had died within days of each other, Ian Prescott first, and then Freddie Camville…Charles Frederick Averill Montmorency Camville. Charlie mourned Andy's dad. He would never mourn his own. "How's your mum?"

"Still grieving." Andy's voice was soft, without its usual mockery. "She's not gotten over it yet. I wonder if she ever will."

Charlie's heart squeezed. *He'd* barely gotten over Ian Prescott's passing. For a time, growing up in Bisby, Ian and Gertie Prescott had been his substitute parents. They'd provided him the stability he didn't have with his own. He blinked away the sudden moisture in his eyes and cleared his throat. "I know exactly how to cheer your mum up. Before I drive on to Lincoln to check into my hotel, I'll stop by for a visit and entertain her with stories about you. For the shock effect, you know."

"Best be careful, mate. She might not love you as much if I told her some stories about *you*."

"That's bollocks. But don't distract me. I made a cock-up of something, and I need some help from you to put things right."

"Name it, Charlie. My shop is your shop."

Prescott Nurseries had been Charlie's first client, back when Ian Prescott had almost lost everything to a cheesed-off former employee with mad hacker skills. The bastard had come close to bringing the business to its knees.

"No, thank you." Charlie engaged his blinker to switch lanes and avoid being stuck behind an oversized lorry that was lumbering along at 25 mph. "I'm a fair hand at cybersecurity. My gardening skills are nil. What I need from you is help with a garden that George had plowed up at the manor house. At my direction unfortunately."

There was a long pause. Charlie could swear the line had frozen over. And then Andy said, "You were the one who had the garden destroyed."

"Yes. It was my fault. I didn't have the entire picture in my head. I do now."

"What do you need me for, then?"

"I'm going to have the garden restored," he said with caution. Andy's voice had cooled. He'd dropped all of his jocular insults. "I'll need to know what kinds of seeds Annie bought and then buy whatever she needs as an equivalent."

"Annie, is it? Using her first name, are we?"

Charlie felt a strange, quite ridiculous spurt of jealousy, which he made himself ignore. His best friend from childhood—his *married* best friend—and Annie Lukin were obviously friends, if the turn in this conversation told him anything. That would be all, wouldn't it? "One falls into a pattern of American informality, doesn't one, when associating with them. Can you replenish her supply of seeds?" He paused. "Or must I go to another source?"

Andy made a scoffing sound. "Give over, Charlie. I'll get you whatever Annie needs. Since you're paying, I'll make sure whatever it is, it's the most dear."

"I hope we're not speaking of seeds for herbaceous plants grown on the Vietnamese archipelago." Annie Lukin struck him as someone who'd make it her business to plant something as different and unusual as she.

"That's a real laugher, Charlie. Think again."

Charlie sighed. "Are you willing to help me? Or are you going to keep after me as if I'm some daft prat?"

"Oh, all right." His friend was back. Charlie let go of a breath he hadn't known he was holding.

"The problem we're going to run into is the seeds Annie wants don't come through normal channels. Sure, I can get all the non-GMO she wants, and believe me, that's what she wants. But she ordered seeds for greens, for example, that used to be grown in this part of the UK that we haven't seen for decades, and for that I have to go to a specialty supplier."

"Why is that?"

"Our Annie, her restaurant aside, likes the idea of teaching kids all kinds of English history, including agricultural."

On an impulse Charlie said, "Meet me for a pint at the pub tonight? You can tell me more about this project of hers."

"Done. By the bye, it's more than time you told me how you plan to use some of the billions you made from the sale of that little company of yours for Bisby's benefit."

If that was the pretext his friend wanted to make the reason for them getting together, so be it. Charlie didn't have to tell Andy he wanted to find out, not about the garden, but more about Annie Lukin. The gypsy girl, herself.

That night, sitting at the bar at the Strangling Duck, Bisby's only pub, Charlie told Andy about his afternoon visit with Gertie.

"She seems smaller in stature since your dad's death, an odd thing for me to suppose, don't you think?"

Andy nodded, his hazel eyes turned down at the corners.

Charlie twisted his glass around and around on the bar's scarred surface. "The first time you invited me to your house, do you remember? I was already taller than your mum."

Andy snorted. "That's not saying much. My mum was always pint-sized."

"But mighty," Charlie said.

A slow smile creased Andy's mouth. "Do you remember my mum's wooden spoon?"

Charlie snorted. "How could I forget?" He'd been all but living with the Prescotts, things being so terrible at the Manor. It was a cold afternoon before Christmas. He and Andy had been horsing around in the kitchen. Over Gertie's protests, they'd shoved each other from one end of the room to the other.

They'd avoided disaster up until the moment Andy pushed Charlie into the table where Gertie had set out a mince pie to cool. The table squealed and lurched. They stopped what they were doing, but it was too late. The pie took off like it had been shot from a catapult, flew off the table, and smashed into bits of glass, fruit, and crust on the floor. Gertie took the wooden spoon with which she'd been stirring a pot of stew and, brandishing it like a saber, smacked him and then Andy on the bum.

"You nitwits! Look what you've done!"

They'd made their escape, more terrified of the vengeful mother figure than sorry they weren't going to have mince pie for dessert.

"We were more than a pair of nitwits, weren't we?" Andy and Charlie laughed over the memory until the tears stood out in their eyes. Charlie took a swig of the dark brew he favored and when he could speak again said, "Your mum and dad saved my life."

"I have faith you would have done well enough."

Perhaps or perhaps not, if the only model he'd had of what family was supposed to act like was his own. "I told your mum about the plans I've begun to make to get Bisby back on its feet. She was pleased. She said it was about time. As you might imagine she did not shy away from reminding me how my father ignored the village's needs, and how he refused to make repairs to the leases on duchy land."

Andy made a noncommittal sound.

Charlie took another swallow. "It was common knowledge, perhaps not with us, but that older generation. He spent thousands on the purchase of exclusive club memberships, travel and cars, and extravagant clothing and jewelry."

He couldn't think of a term bad enough to describe his father. It had him looking sideways at Andy. "The latter was for his mistress, mind you, not my mother."

"I hesitate to speak ill of the dead, but even when you were a kid, you had more heart and integrity than that maggot."

Charlie had never forgiven his father for destroying everything there was to be proud of about the Camvilles—the history, the land, and the name. He'd barely endured the shame of his father's personal corruption. "I should take exception to you calling my parent a maggot, but we both know I won't."

"Sorry for it, old man," Andy said. "That was a bad time when he left you to fend for yourself. And you still at university."

Charlie swirled the beer in his glass. At the grand age of nineteen he'd taken on head-of-the-Camville family responsibilities. In the years after, working as hard and smart as he could to support his mother and his sister, he'd never been sure it was enough. "I mentioned the repairs I've already begun to your mum on some of the duchy's lease-holdings up towards the castle as well. She said concentrate on Bisby."

"It ought to be easy for you to do both."

Charlie raised an eyebrow.

"I read in *Forbes* that you're one of the twenty richest people in the UK. So, yeah, easy. And if I can do something to make it easier, I'm ready and willing to order you about and give you advice on how to spend your billions."

Charlie's mouth dropped open. "You want me to take your advice?"

Andy gave him an elbow to his upper arm, reminding Charlie of all the times when they'd given each other more than an elbow.

"I'm feeling a certain level of frustration that I've not been able to come up with a solution for what will work best in Bisby. People need jobs. I want to do my part to help provide them."

Andy raised his mug. "I'll drink to that."

"I suppose it's a step in the right direction," Charlie continued, "That I've been able to begin the restoration at Rotherforde Castle into what it must have looked like in the fourteenth century. If only the National Trust were not mired down in their bureaucratic details, we might actually be able to proceed before the end of this century. Thank goodness I can keep them from mucking about in the research my people are doing for the book I want written on Camville family history."

"Well, that's one book that will take one person working no time at all to get done."

Charlie's shoulders tightened with displeasure. "I beg your pardon. There's quite a lot of material to work on. Camvilles have been center stage at every turning point in English history."

Andy made a dismissive sound. "Get off your effing ducal horse. You want to research your family's reputation? Have at it. But don't give me that look that tells me you think your lofty Camville name means your shite don't smell."

Charlie stiffened. "You, of all people, know I don't feel like that."

Giving him a rueful look, Andy said, "What I know is every so often, you get a look on your face that says we're back in the fourteenth century, you live in that damn pile of rocks you call a castle, and everyone has to take a knee to you."

The thought that he might, in some way be like that embarrassed Charlie as not much else embarrassed him. In the moment of silence that stretched out between them, he grabbed a handful of peanuts and searched for an alternative subject. "You know the Hewitt boy, Eddie?"

"Yeah. He went to school with my cousin, Jenny."

"I hired him as a favor to my mother. Clarice, Eddie's mother, is my mother's assistant."

Andy swiveled on his stool and pointed to a table in the back of the pub where a lone man sat hunched over a pint. "Speaking of which, there's Eddie's dad. Our Clarice divorced him, you know. Not the happiest bloke, Tom is. Pissed as a fart all the time. Misses his wife, he says. That makes him barmy, I say, as much a bitch as Clarice is. But make Tom happy, why don't you? Go on over and tell him what a nice young man his Eddie is."

Charlie eyed the man who, hunched over and still as he was, had the look of an angry Rodin statue. "I'll pass on that one."

"Andy!" John Bracey, proprietor of the Strangling Duck, appeared from out of a door behind the bar, his ample belly leading the way. "Maudie's made a fancy steak pie in honor of His Grace coming back home to Bisby as he should." He gave Charlie a look. "At least for one day."

Charlie had been hearing quite a number of sharp remarks about him coming back home. Bisby was a place where he had property, but it wasn't home.

Andy pointed to a chalkboard, complete with a list of offerings, above the bar. "Has Maudie decided to expand the menu?"

"Maudie's always reading those American food magazines." John angled his head in the direction of the door behind him. "They go on about what's served in pubs. Gastro pub food they call it." He preened with his knowledge. "She figures if people come up to Bisby to have a bite over at Annie's, they might want to try out the Strangling Duck, as well. So yeah. Steak pie."

"Well, then." Charlie glanced at Andy. "Let's have some of Maudie's steak pie."

As John trod back behind the bar into the kitchen, Andy murmured, "Maudie's food doesn't hold a candle to Annie's."

At last the conversation was turning in the direction Charlie had wanted it to go. "What's the story on how Annie ended up here?"

"Came with Ross Stoughton. He was in the estate business over in the States; real estate the Yanks call it. His grandfather, the earl, put up the money, but the thing failed anyway, no surprise knowing Ross. When he came back, he brought Annie with him. Then?" He shook his head. "Arsehole… Annie caught him in their bed shagging some silly cow."

"Hmm." Charlie took a swallow of his beer. He didn't like thinking about any man in bed with Annie, even if it was a thing of the past. "What's Annie's restaurant like?"

"Brilliant. Small carbon foot print she calls it, locally sourced and all that. It's Italian, but not like any Italian you've ever eaten."

Charlie turned that one over in his mind. "Her kind of Italian."

Andy cracked a laugh. "Hadn't thought of it that way, but why not? People come from all over to eat at The Ocular. You have to reserve weeks in advance. Jane and I dine there now and then. But I have to make a reservation far in advance like everyone else."

Reservations was what George wanted in exchange for locating the garden on the Manor's property. "I'm curious. How is it my brother-in-law can get a reservation on short notice?"

"Can he? That's news to me."

Charlie pondered that. "What's the best thing on the menu at The Ocular?"

"It's all the best, but the best of the best is her Mt. Etna Cake. If you're lucky, and she's in the mood, she'll make it for you."

John shoved the kitchen door open with his shoulder. With a flourish, he set two plates of piping-hot pie down in front of Charlie and Andy. "Dig in, mates." He stood back to watch, an expectant smile on his face.

Andy cut into a piece, chewed, and waved his fork at John. "Tell Maudie this is some pie."

John gave him an ear-to-ear grin. "Well, I'll go tell her. She'll be that chuffed." He turned and disappeared into the kitchen.

Leaning toward Charlie, Andy said, "Maudie fancies herself the Gordon Ramsay of the East Midlands."

With a grimace, Charlie said, "Is it me or is this pie…?"

"Dog's dinner, Charlie. It's dog's dinner."

The door from the kitchen swung open, and John was back. "Maudie's made a Banoffee pie for afters and wants to know if she can serve you a dish."

Andy held up both hands. "Sorry. I can't. If I do I'll not be able to get myself round the shop."

John's smile faded. "If you change your mind, you say so." And he disappeared back into the kitchen.

"I assume Maudie's Banoffee pie is not in the same category as Annie's Mt. Etna Cake."

"Nothing Maudie could make—or any other baker in the kingdom—would measure up to Annie's desserts." He laid his fork down. "Back before Annie opened the restaurant, she baked in her flat—not that dump she lives in now; the place she lived in with Stoughton. She gave more of it away than she sold. She even delivered to the homebound, like my aunt Nancy, God rest her soul. Some of the other old ones, too." Andy raised his glass. "That girl is saintly."

Charlie had been using words like *sharp* and *sarcastic* to describe the gypsy girl. He turned this new word over in his mind.

"Speaking of Annie..." Andy shifted around. "I took delivery of the seeds she wants."

"That's quick," Charlie noted, his mind on how he could ask Annie to make that cake Andy was going on about.

Andy patted his chest. "They like me."

Charlie snorted. "I'll bring Annie out tomorrow."

Andy frowned. "I can come and get her. No need for you to bother."

"But I'm paying, old man," Charlie said, doing his best to ignore that odd pinch of jealousy come back again. "I want to be there when you make up the invoice."

The door to the pub swung open, and three men entered. John stuck his head out of the kitchen. Eyeing the new arrivals, he said, "What'll it be for you lot?"

The tallest of the three, said, "Did Maudie make some of that steak pie? We was hoping she did."

Andy swiveled on his stool back toward them. "She did and the duke and I think you should each have a piece."

All three heads swung in Charlie's direction. Eyes wide, each gave a jerky nod. Charlie nodded back.

"I'll just go tell Maudie to cut some slices. You take a seat," John said.

Charlie leaned in toward Andy. "I recognize them. I don't remember their names, though."

"That's because that lot, if they're not home sitting in front of the idiot box, they're for hanging out here. If you recall, when we were boys my mum frowned on us doing the same."

Charlie's mobile buzzed. It was Samantha. She wanted to know why he'd cancelled their holiday in Paris. He tapped out a response, apologizing for having had to make the unexpected trip to Bisby and how, after a quick dinner at The Ocular tomorrow night and a task Monday, he'd be back in London and then he would call her.

The frown on Andy's face disappeared, replaced by curiosity.

Before Andy could ask, Charlie said, "It was Samantha."

"Ah yes, Lady Samantha." Andy smiled. "Not a rocket scientist, but perhaps I don't know her that well."

"In fact she is quite lovely. And sweet."

"I'll give her that. As your oldest friend, I'll take the liberty of telling you, though, she isn't for you."

Charlie couldn't respond with more than a noncommittal sound, since of late he'd begun to think Andy could be right.

"I'll give the girl this. She's better than some of the other lovelies you've been with these last years. Like…what was her name? The one with the high, squeaky voice?"

Charlie grimaced. "That would have been Callista Sands-Willoughby."

"It seems Callista's mum never told her to modulate her tones."

"Be fair, Andy. It wasn't how she spoke. It was her laugh. So sudden and startling."

"And as I recall, she cut quite a fine figure." Andy held up his hands and sketched the shape of a robust female. "Almost as fine as…what was the name of that woman you dated for a short time? Oh yes. Lady Mary La Zouche."

Charlie looked at Andy askance. "What has Mary to do with it? Not that we should be talking about her either, but she was rather slender."

"But her horse, Poopsie, wasn't."

Charlie had picked up his beer to take a swallow—a mistake.

As he coughed into a napkin, Andy gave him a series of hard knocks on his back, and said, "Yes, and doesn't that bring us to Lady Serena."

Charlie stopped coughing.

"Now Lady Serena had the looks. She was smart, and yes, she spoke in the modulated tones she'd have needed to make a perfect duchess."

"She wasn't *that* smart," Charlie said and remembered how, the night he'd introduced her to Andy and Jane, he'd had the engagement ring, worn by every duchess of Lindsey for the last 200 years, in his pocket. During a long, revelatory evening at a top London restaurant, Serena had proceeded to treat

Andy and Jane with barely concealed disdain that bordered on contempt.

When Charlie confronted Serena later about her bad manners, she'd shrugged. *"What could I have possibly discussed with them? I have no idea what kind of little lives they lead."* Then she turned and left. Days later, he found out where she'd gone. A photo appeared in one of the worst of the tabloids, the *Daily Prime*, showed her stepping out of star footballer, Fizz Barclay's Kensington flat.

"You're right, not smart," Andy agreed. "Daft cow… Getting caught by paparazzi at seven a.m. wearing the same dress she wore when she went out with us the night before… What could Lady Serena have been thinking?"

"Perhaps she thought monogamy and loyalty were too middle-class."

"Perhaps one day you'll find a middle-class kind of woman, the kind who wouldn't mind that every once in a while you get a stick up that noble arse of yours."

Charlie gave him the kind of salute for which Gertie would have given him a hard whack with her wooden spoon. "My noble blood has nothing to do with who I associate with."

Andy held up his hands in protest. "I was kidding, Charlie. Besides which, you're obligated, now, to start looking. You're a duke, you know. If your mum hasn't already decided it's your duty to get married and produce the heir and spare, she soon will."

Charlie grimaced. "That's rubbish. Although I'll acknowledge you're right. My mother, who doesn't care what I do with my life as long as I stay out of hers—except, of course, when she needs something from me, like more money—has now decided to be my social secretary."

"Nip that one in the bud, old man. Otherwise she's going to find you another Serena."

With a warning look, Charlie said, "Believe it or not, I don't take my marching orders from my mother."

"Good to hear, because the way I remember her, your mum can be quite insistent once she's on to something. Oh, wait for it." Andy picked up his mobile. "Jane's calling."

While Andy spoke to his wife, voice a murmur, Charlie thought about the women he'd been with the last few years. Perhaps they weren't as good a sort as Jane. It depressed him to think many of them had been like Serena.

Now, Annie Lukin, he wasn't sure if he would describe her as a good sort, she of the sharp tongue. She was forthright, however, and there would be, he supposed, never a question about what she was thinking. He suspected she would never play a trick on a fellow like Serena had, either.

At last Andy finished his call.

Turning his glass round and round, Charlie said, "You're a lucky bastard to have a woman like Jane. She saved your bacon."

"Jane saves my bacon every day. Why don't you be on the lookout for someone to save yours?" Andy took a swig and set his glass back down on the bar. "Give one of those dating websites a go."

Charlie stood and pushed away from the bar. "Not for me, mate."

Andy stood as well. "Take a chance, Charlie. Do something. I'd like to see you happy."

CHAPTER FOUR

By ten o'clock the next morning Annie had started her routine, prepping for what she intended to serve that night. As she worked on some stuffed Jerusalem artichokes, she heard the front door open. She looked up and sighed as Ross Stoughton swept in. "You are up way early today, at least way early for you." She made no attempt to hide the snide from her voice.

"Annie, my love," he said, ignoring that opening salvo. "You're looking particularly fetching today."

Even though they were no longer together, Ross continued to greet her like they were one of those couples that had parted on friendly terms. She looked down at her black clogs, already white with flour, and the tomato-sauce-splashed apron she wore over her long, black skirt and short-sleeved tee. She wondered what Ross' mother would think of her outfit. As if

Annie cared. "What did you want, Ross? I'm kind of busy."

His facial features tightened up. "I know you're meeting with Lindsey tomorrow. About your garden. Perhaps for it to be reestablished."

"Lindsey?"

Ross's gaze darted up, down, and sideways. "Duke of."

Like she didn't know. "How did you find out about the meeting? Did you plant a bug on him?"

With indignation he said, "That's an awful thing to say."

"At the risk of repeating myself, why are you here? I know you didn't come by to make nice to me."

She wasn't sure what she liked less about Ross: his myopic worldview, in which he was the featured star, or his allergy to the truth. With his black, black hair and his blue, blue eyes, he was good to look at, though. The combination of that, and his then charm had her following him all the way from New York to Lincolnshire. Where his black, black hair, his blue, blue eyes, and his charm palled, especially after he belatedly figured out she wasn't good enough to associate with his aristocratic family.

He drew himself up as tall as he could, which, given his Brit-with-Viking forebear genes, was tall. "I know I disappointed you, Annie. I wish I hadn't done it. But it would be awfully good of you not to act toward me in such a hostile manner. Perhaps you could even find it in your heart to forgive me."

"Forgive you? After you brought that brainless bunny into our bed and screwed her on the sheets I'd just bought on sale at Marks and Spencer?" She took a step away from her cutting board and the knife she'd just laid down. Not that she would use it on Ross. She'd hate to dull the blade. "I had to throw them out."

He got a prissy look on his face. "That's what I mean, Annie. All that ill will is quite over-the-top. It's what drove me to it, if I'm being honest."

"If you were being honest…" She raised an eyebrow. "Really?"

"I admitted I was the weak one, didn't I?" The look on his face spoke of his grievance and an attempt to pair words with conscience, which was impossible for Ross, since he didn't have one. "But it's over, isn't it?"

To Annie's mind, the bunny in the bed had been Ross's way of telling her he wanted out of the relationship that he'd all but said was beneath him without having to summon up the guts to tell her straight out. "Yes, it's over."

"Well then, all I ask is for you treat me with a modicum of decency when we're in public."

"Making sure I treat you with the deference due you, the grandson of an earl, right?"

Like a gladiator facing a lioness, Ross began to breathe in and out through his nose. Annie dialed back because she knew he was never going to leave until he said what he'd come to say. "Okay. Tell me what you need from me."

He patted his blue and red rep tie. "When you meet with Lindsey about the garden, how do you think the conversation will go?"

"Well, I think we'll be polite to each other for starters." She narrowed her eyes. "C'mon. Out with it."

Ross shifted from one foot to the other. "I have a client who has expressed an interest in purchasing Melbury Manor."

"I've heard George Swynford is talking to a developer who's thinking of turning it into a hunting lodge. Are you two working together?"

A look of disgust flickered across Ross's face. "Certainly not. George Swynford is not the type of person one wants to do business with."

There it was, the latest installment in the tale of the pot and the kettle.

"The thing is, Annie, that garden is a dreadful eyesore. It could destroy any deal I might negotiate."

"Assuming you can negotiate it, aren't you counting your pounds and shillings before there's a signature on the bottom line? Maybe your prospect will change his mind about Melbury Manor, whether the community garden is there or not."

"I suppose that's true. However, if you would let me find you a different location, I–"

"No."

"You do know it's not really your property, that you have no right to say no."

"Then why are we having this conversation?"

He opened his mouth and closed it again. Even in the beginning, when she thought she might be in love with him, his handsome face, and what she thought of as his winning personality, Annie knew Ross wouldn't be asked to join Mensa anytime soon. Looking back, she wondered what she could have seen in him. She'd been in recovery mode, true, from Joe and Carne and all that. With his English charm Ross had convinced her that the UK would be a warm and welcoming place for her wounded self, which should have been beside the point if she'd been thinking clearly. But she'd gone with it anyway. And now here she stood in her restaurant with that very man and she was tired of having a fruitless discussion with him. Her artichokes awaited. "Ross, go away."

He held out a supplicating hand. "Annie…"

"No, really. Please go."

Without another word he started for the door. Before he reached it, he turned back. "You should try to be more accommodating. That's what one does when with those who are better."

In the loud silence that followed him closing the door with a bang, Annie realized she'd begun to breathe fast. She hated how way too many of the "better" people thought they were that because they'd been born into the lucky sperm club. If she could, she'd have nothing to do with them. They were, however, some of the people who dined at The Ocular. When they did, she grinned and pretended. And this morning she wasn't going to let anything Ross Stoughton had to say about being better bother her.

Charlie looked at his watch. It was ten o'clock. As eager as George said he was for Charlie to meet the fellow from the consortium, he was late.

He tapped his fingers on the desk and gazed around the space he'd leased for George in Bisby's only two-story building. As an office, it was small but adequate, one filing cabinet, shelves along one wall, two chairs and the desk on which were strewn file folders and papers everywhere.

A quick rap and then George cracked open the door and leaned in. Charlie could see the bulk of the other man behind him. "Sorry, we're late."

Charlie stood, nettled. "Good morning."

George waved in the burly but well-clothed man with him. "Lindsey, won't you say hello to Lance Parrish. Parrish, this is His Grace, the Duke of Lindsey. Lance is with Stanford, Mellish, and DeWart, representing the consortium."

Yes, the consortium that would facilitate the plans George was making, plans Charlie had known nothing about before the other day.

"A pleasure to meet you, Mr. Parrish." He shook the man's hand and turned to George. "I suppose we can, at last, speak about the shoot. Shall we?"

"Yes, indeed." George rubbed his hands together. "And you were right, Lindsey to insist we wait to be face-to-face when we sign the agreement." George reached across the desk and began to rummage through the papers. "The agreement... I've got it somewhere."

"George," Charlie said, "I've been thinking. Perhaps we're moving too fast."

George straightened. "But Lindsey, I thought the decision had been made. I thought—"

"Sorry, George. I believe we need to wait before making any decision that concerns the disposition of the house and the land."

"Apologies, Lindsey," George said. "Poor choice of words. I meant should you and I decide Melbury Manor should become a hunting lodge and the land a property for grouse hunting, Parrish and his colleagues will make it quite the best in all of England." George's gaze swiveled from Charlie to Parrish and back again. "And as Viola and I will be in possession of the Manor and—"

"Ah yes," Charlie interrupted. "That other, the entail. Your concern about breaking it. Perhaps we should save that for a discussion between us, as well."

Parrish leaned forward. "Your Grace, my company will work with you at any pace you require."

"Thank you, Mr. Parrish." Charlie had kept his eye on George, whose face had reddened when Charlie, as circumspectly as he could, had closed off discussion of everything.

Parrish nodded an acknowledgment. "I've long been a great admirer of your business acumen, Lindsey."

Charlie sighed. He hoped that observation was not the beginning of a long, boring paean. There were too many people who thought because he was a duke, he would expect one. "Thank you, Mr. Parrish."

George cleared his throat. "Perhaps, Lindsey, you can give Parrish, here, a hint—that's all it would take—of when we might finish negotiations."

Charlie wondered how he was going to answer that without embarrassing George further, which little as he liked him, he didn't want to do. He was saved by the ding of an incoming text. "Pardon me," he said to the two men. The text was from Samantha, the third he'd received from her today. She was thrilled about his intentions to have dinner at The Ocular and was going to join him.

Could he meet her at the six thirty train, after all she'd never been to Lincoln, really it was such an out-of-the way place, and she wouldn't know where to find a car to hire to take her to what was the name of that town where The Ocular was located? Samantha had a way of writing a text that was as breathless as her speech. He'd once thought it, and her, adorable. It wasn't quite so adorable now. He'd begun to recognize hers was a single note in a personality that was short on notes.

"Well, chaps. I really must go." Charlie stowed his mobile and turned to George. "Let's save that conversation for the next time we three meet."

"Perfect," George said, although from the look on his face, Charlie knew his comment was, for George, the furthest from perfect.

Charlie moved toward the door. "We'll see each other later, then. Seven thirty at The Ocular, right?"

"That's right," George said and turned to Parrish. "At the VIP table, you know. A hard reservation to get, but I do have influence with the owner." He slid his gaze toward Charlie. "I think that speaks to my ability to negotiate."

Charlie ignored George and held out his hand to Parrish, who proffered his. "I look forward to seeing you again, sir." Charlie raised an eyebrow. Thank goodness the man turned out not to be a sycophant.

Watching the two men walk away, Charlie wondered again how George was able to get reservations at The Ocular on short notice. Now, though, his interest was more for getting a look at the garden planted at the entrance to the Manor. He could think about George another time.

Charlie pulled up to the Manor and got out of his car. With slow steps he walked up to what was left of the garden, an obscene gash in the earth. He kicked at a clump of dirt, shoved his hands into his pockets, and looked down at the shriveled leaves lying about, a slaughter of young growth left to wither under a gray March sky. Whenever the garden had been plowed up it was done just as it had begun to bloom.

He turned from the garden to gaze at the Manor. The path led to the bulk of the building, dark, red brick, four stories, slate roof, and dormer windows. Three shallow steps led to the front door, which was bordered by shrubbery on both sides. Even from a distance he could see that Viola had not had the repair done to the top step, where the bricks had come loose.

The day his father left, Charlie had stood and shivered just there. He'd been home for the Christmas holidays. *"Why Istanbul? Can't you find somewhere closer to run away to?*

Busy supervising the cab driver who had been loading up the boot with his luggage, his father had said, *"Don't dare to suggest I'm running away, Thorne."* Thorne, as in Earl of. Charlie's courtesy title.

"Maria has a lovely villa overlooking the Bosporus and I need time to rest after the latest brouhaha." The so-called brouhaha had been the public announcement in all the tabloids of a duke of the realm involved in a financial scandal of his own making. *If everything I've done to shield your mother from the worst of it hasn't been enough, well, really. Why would anyone expect me to do more?"*

"But Father, what are we supposed to do? How will we pay for Viola's school and mine?"

Still his father hadn't looked up, and Charlie grabbed him by the sleeve of his heavy, sheepskin-lined jacket and pulled him around. *"You can't leave us alone to figure it out by ourselves."*

His father yanked himself away from Charlie's grip and with long-perfected haughtiness said, *"We, Thorne? I refuse to be part of your we. As for your schooling? I'm confident you'll sort it out."*

Charlie had. Though he made sure Viola could go back to her school, he did not go back to his. Instead he went full bore into the business that had been a hobby up to then, him playing with code in his dormitory room at Cambridge, all the time figuring out how to thwart hackers bent on malice. And succeeding.

It had been a rough eighteen months until his business began to take off, until he had clients enough to make a real go of things. He didn't sleep much. He grew thin because he didn't have much appetite. What food he did eat was limited to pot noodles and Fray Bentos pies.

It took him years to undo all the damage his father had done with bad investments and poor land management, not to mention the bankruptcy. He shivered and not from the cold. He hated even to think *that* word.

As his own wealth increased, Charlie bought back the properties his father had lost until he'd bought back almost all of them.

He looked down. After smoothing the soil underfoot with the sole of one shoe, he started toward his car. Later this evening, he was to see Annie Lukin at her restaurant. He did not want to wait. He wanted to see her now, alone, in that place that was part of what defined her.

It wasn't far, the distance between the garden and the head of High Street, a matter of one hundred yards or so. The Ocular should have been easy to find. It should have looked like a palace, given its reputation. There should have been bright lights over the door, an elegantly appointed awning, and the restaurant's name, scrolled in big letters across expansive glass. Instead Charlie had a problem picking out its location from among the sad-looking, abandoned storefronts that had, at one time, housed busy retail establishments. That is, until the scents drifting in the air found him and he knew it was the place directly across, with the door ajar.

He started to cross the street as a well-dressed man exited that door. The features on his face, marked by a frown, cleared as he noticed Charlie. Holding up a hand in greeting, broad smile on his face, the fellow said, "Lindsey isn't it? Stoughton, here."

So this was Ross Stoughton, the gypsy girl's erstwhile lover, perhaps not so erstwhile if he was coming out of her restaurant. Charlie decided on the spot he didn't like the man. "It's been a while."

"Quite." Stoughton grabbed Charlie's hand and pumped like he was attempting to shake something loose. "At Eton, I believe. I was three years behind you, what? I recognize you from a picture I saw of you in the *Daily Prime*."

Gossipy trash… It was the worst of the tabloids, filled with half-truths at best, lies almost always… Charlie hated it. He removed his hand from Stoughton's grasp. Tilting his head in the direction of the gypsy girl's restaurant, Charlie said, "Making a reservation at The Ocular, were you?"

A pained expression came over Stoughton's face. "No, Lindsey. Not a reservation." But then his face cleared and with a crafty slant in his eyes he said, "I'm with Lincoln Homes. An estate agent, don't you know. What luck, meeting you here. I have a client who's interested in the Manor."

Charlie raised an eyebrow. "To buy it, do you mean?"

"Well, of course, old man."

Charlie clasped his hands behind his back. "It's not for sale."

Stoughton's face fell. "But I thought…"

"If at some point I do decide to sell Melbury, you would talk to George Swynford first. He's my land manager."

A look of disdain curled Stoughton's lip. "I'd rather do business with you."

"As I say, there's no business to be done. If your client has it in his mind to purchase an old manor house, I would suggest he look elsewhere. And now I really must go. Business with Miss Lukin." Charlie skirted around Stoughton and made for the door Stoughton had exited.

Hand to the doorknob, Charlie paused. He could tell Stoughton was watching him. From the look on his face, whatever the reason for which Stoughton had been visiting The Ocular, it had not been an amusing one. Altogether pleased, Charlie opened the restaurant's door and, breathing deep, took in the tempting scent of spices and herbs curling in waves through the air around him.

Closing his eyes, he let the seductive fragrances of garlic and onion, sharp, peppery olive oil, and basil bathe his olfactory nerves. If the food Annie Lukin made was anything like what this captivatingly perfumed air suggested, dinner tonight was going to be superlative by miles to any dinner he'd ever had.

Opening his eyes, he took note of where he was standing. Under his feet, intense, gleaming dark wood flooring. Walnut? Oak? Teak? He didn't know; he was no expert. To one side a brick wall, whitewashed, standing in contrast to dark wood paneling covering the other three walls, just a touch lighter in color than the flooring. Above him, hanging between exposed wood beams, clusters of hand-blown glass globes extended downward on delicate, silver chains. Each light cast warm circles across the floor.

The tables were clothed in white. Small clay pots sat in the tables' centers. The pots were filled not with flowers, as one would expect, but herbs. He recognized sturdy parsley in one, feathery dill in another, corrugated-leafed mint, and best of all, deep-green basil.

From across the room, on the other side of a trifold partition, came the sound of singing, a warm voice, a lot off-key. He knew the melody. It was one of Charlie's operatic favorites, Deh' vieni ala finestra, o' mio Tesoro, or in English, Come to the window, my treasure, from Mozart's *Don Giovanni*. There was also a lot of banging of what he presumed were pots. Not quite so melodic. He took a step past the table in front of the partition and jostled a chair. Its legs made a scraping sound on the floor.

The pot banging and the singing stopped. "Is that you, Ross?" came the disembodied voice. "Because if it is, you can go. I've said everything I need to say to you for the next century and a half."

"It's not Ross."

There was a deafening silence, then a clang of a single pot and steps. Around the partition she came. She was in a long skirt, just as she'd been the other day, this one some black gauzy thing. Over it, she wore a bright yellow t-shirt, and a white apron. Yesterday she'd worn boots. Today she had on a pair of black shoes he imagined a Dutch boy would wear if he were holding his finger in a hole in a dike. Yesterday her hair had been loose. Today all those curls were scraped back into a braid that lay over one shoulder. He wanted to ask her to slip out of those shoes so he could see her feet. Bare, he hoped. He wanted to do something to that braid. Unravel it, perhaps.

Her eyes widened. She held a spoon with a long handle, the business end pointed in his direction.

Dropping his gaze to the spoon, he allowed himself a small smile. "Should I be frightened?"

She jerked the spoon down to her side and bit her lip. "What are you doing here?"

Eyes on that lip, he said, "A lovely greeting, that."

She squeezed her eyes shut, opened them, and then huffed a sharp breath. "Hello, what are you doing here?"

"I was curious. I wanted to see what The Ocular looked like before tonight. I understand my party is to be seated at the VIP table."

"This is it." She pointed to the table and the chair he'd just banged into.

"It's not I with the reservation, however. It's my brother-in-law who has it. I'm his guest." He watched her closely. "I wonder how it is that he, alone, can get a reservation with short notice."

She narrowed her eyes. "Do you want to know why *you* can't or why everyone can't?"

"Knowing why I can't would do," Charlie said.

Folding both arms across her chest, the spoon dangling down from one hand, she gave him a cool look. "I bet it would."

Into the silence, that followed, Charlie realized he wasn't doing a very good job if what he wanted was to have the gypsy girl get over her dislike of him. He smiled. "If the scents coming from your kitchen are any indication, no matter who has the reservation, I'm quite sure I'll feel like a VIP tonight."

"Everyone who eats at The Ocular is meant to feel like a VIP."

Regarding her still watchful eyes, he said, "I have a feeling all of us, no matter where we sit, will enjoy our dinner. That's what I've heard from everyone I know who's dined with you. Which makes me wonder why the VIP table?"

She shrugged. "Pure marketing. You superior types think you're better than the rest of us not so superior types. Your serfs." The words were more of the same, but she'd given him a half smile as she said them, which he decided to regard as progress.

"I assume, then, I can expect to be treated like the superior type I am."

"The dishes I serve you won't be like those I serve the other diners. Not better, just different." She cocked her head to the side, as if she were changing her mind about him—he hoped. "How do you feel about sampling something I'm experimenting with and thinking of serving? Not tonight, but maybe soon. You can tell me what you think."

He raised an eyebrow. Of all the things he might have expected her to say next, this was not it. He was charmed, though he still had no idea where he stood with her. "Would you do that for me?"

With a diffident shrug, she said, "You're here. I need a taste tester." She turned toward the kitchen and looked over her shoulder. "Are you coming or not?"

"I would have to be a fool to turn down the generous invitation, Miss Lukin."

"Yes, you would." She whisked around the partition, her skirt fluttering behind her. "If I'm going to feed you, I think you'd better stop calling me Miss Lukin. My name is Annie."

He let go the breath he was holding. Somewhere, somehow, she had at last decided to accept his presence. "Annie it is, then. Would I be able to get you to call me by my name?" He followed behind her and stepped around the partition.

"You mean I can call you Your Royal Highness?"

The kitchen was small but ruthlessly organized. An industrial-sized stove with six burners butted up against stainless steel work spaces on either side. Pots polished to a high shine sat on wire shelving, and knives in sheaths sat at the ready. He was so fascinated with the look of the kitchen that he almost didn't catch the tease in her voice calling him that ridiculous name. "Only if you add 'mighty.'"

Her dimple made a quick appearance. "Should I curtsy at the same time?"

"That would be a sight I'd enjoy." He let his gaze travel the length of her lush figure, her breasts straining against the t-shirt, just hidden by the apron she wore over it. Her waist was tiny by comparison, and the flare of her rounded hips had his fingers twitching. "But no need," he added, with a warning to control himself. "Just call me Charlie."

"Okay." She let her gaze slide away. "Charlie."

She'd done it. Called him by his most private name. He felt oddly pleased. And he wished Stoughton could have heard that.

She cleared her throat. "So, how do you like pasta?" She hefted a pot from the rolling flame on her stove, and transferred it into a deep sink.

"What red-blooded Englishman can turn down pasta?"

She shot him a glance over her shoulder as she poured the water out of the pot. Small, round noodles dropped into a colander. "The kind that pronounces it wrong. Poh-stuh. Can you say that instead of paa-stah?"

"Poh-stuh," he said, watching to see if she would react as he mimicked her.

But if Annie Lukin was going to react to anything he said, he was going to have to up his game even more. She was too focused on his mispronounced pasta. Steam rose in curlicues as, with efficient movements, she transferred some of the pasta to a bowl and ladled on a pale, creamy sauce. The luxurious scent curled up into his nose. "That is not tomato sauce."

"Pronouncing it toe-mah-toe I suppose is better than calling what it's covering paa-stah." She set the bowl down on the counter with a click. "Because it's pasta doesn't mean the sauce has to be red."

He knew all sauces weren't red. And yes, he knew how to pronounce the word, *pasta*. But Charlie had discovered that he liked teasing the gypsy girl. He liked seeing her react to his supposed English refusal to pronounce foreign words. It was a thing to be savored.

His mouth beginning to water, he stared down at the pasta. "Won't you satisfy my curiosity and tell me what you call this sauce?" He reached for the bowl.

She narrowed her eyes to slits and stuck out a hand. "Don't even think about it. You're not going to pick up a plate of food and take it out of my kitchen like this is a buffet." She grabbed the bowl. "Go. Sit. Then I'll tell you what it is."

He skirted around the partition and stopped at the VIP table. "Here?" Where he was shortly to be a VIP of one. He liked that idea.

She was right behind him. "Yes, here." She placed the bowl on the table and grabbed the dark wooden cylinder she'd secured under one arm. "Pepper?" She didn't wait for an answer, instead began to dust his pasta with a rhythmic grr-grr of the mill. As she did, he breathed in the lovely, sharp scent of the sauce. He glanced up at her, once, and then, because he couldn't wait, shoved his fork into the pasta with a violence that would have done a spear fisher proud. The taste exploded on his tongue. He closed his eyes against the sensation. "It has a tartness, with just the right amount of salt. I don't know that I've ever tasted anything quite like this."

"It's safe to say you like it." A half smile marked her face.

"This is ambrosia." He grabbed her hand. It was rough with calluses and cuts. He didn't care, though, and lifted it to place a kiss on her knuckles. "Tell me what I'm eating."

She snatched her hand back and rubbed it against the other. "Don't get crazy on me. It's just pasta." But she kept her eyes on him and watched, expectantly, as he ate.

"There's no just about it." He waved his fork at her. "I repeat. This is ambrosia."

She blushed and looked away. "It's a tonnato sauce."

He blinked. Could the woman who had thrown dirt at him not two days ago be the same woman who now hovered over him, seemingly anxious about whether he would like what she made? This brilliant and highly successful chef...was she shy about the quality of her food? With him? He grinned, triumphant. He might well have won her over. "Truly. I love it." He started to take another bite and stopped. He put down his fork. "Wait. Tonnato? As in tuna?"

However shy he might have thought her, she recovered quickly. "Don't curl up your aristocratic lip. It's a sauce made with capers, anchovies, seasonings, and yes, tuna. It's usually served over veal. Only thing is you'll never eat veal at The Ocular because I don't serve meat from animals that have been tortured. But I do like the sauce and I decided to experiment with using it in other ways. I don't know that it works on this pasta, which is called *rotelle*. That's 'little wheels' in English."

"It works." He took another bite. "Make me a promise."

"What?"

"Don't serve this to anyone but me."

Her eyes widened. She pressed her lips together and blushed again. He told himself he could get accustomed to her blushes. "That's insane. Besides, it's an experiment."

"Hah. Some experiment."

She gave him a sidewise smile. An even deeper color stained her high cheekbones. "I might try it with a pork tenderloin."

Oh, she was a darling girl each time she showed her shy side. "How can I be invited to that dinner?"

She answered his grin with one of her own. "Make a reservation." And she left him to eat by himself.

Into the quiet of her absence, he raised his voice and said, "Why do you have this partition? Don't your

VIPs want to feel they're special because they can see you cooking up close while they eat?"

"I take the screen down during service," came her voice from the kitchen.

"Can I ask you another question?"

She stepped back to the table. "You're full of questions."

Yes, he was. The more he knew about her, the more he wanted to know. "How does your Italian heritage influence the food at The Ocular?"

"What Italian heritage?" She frowned. "I'm an American."

"Good Lord! I never would have guessed."

She gave him a squinty-eyed stare.

He laughed. "No, really. You have that gorgeous Italian look about you."

"You do, too. And yet you're an English duke."

"I come by it quite honestly. My maternal grandfather emigrated from Sicily, I'm told, by the only relative on that side with whom my mother has deigned to have a relationship. It's said that I look exactly like him."

"Is that why you asked? Because *I* look Italian?"

He leaned back in his chair. "I'm fascinated with that part of me I know so little about. I thought I might find something we had in common."

"My ancestors came to the United States from Russia. They were subsistence farmers in the old country. I don't know what your maternal grandfather did, but I assure you whatever it was, my people had nothing in common with yours."

Said like a gauntlet thrown. His gypsy had a chip, and wouldn't it be interesting to brush it off her shoulder into oblivion. "My Sicilian grandparent was a poor boy just off the boat from Palermo after World War II."

"My grandfather, who raised me, worked as a printer at a newspaper. He's retired now, living in a one-bedroom house on the west coast of Florida. All the upholstered furniture is covered in plastic. What about your grandfather? Where does he live? In a townhouse in Knightsbridge?"

Another gauntlet. "My grandfather was a sculptor. He worked in metals. He had a studio, and eventually made a name for himself and a fair amount of money, although he didn't live in Knightsbridge. He's dead, a long time now. I didn't know him."

"But he was a man of means, right? I rest my case."

He ignored her interruption. "His sculptures were sought after. He became famous. In fact, that's how my parents met."

"Your father bought one of your grandfather's sculptures?"

"No, he met my mother at one my grandfather's shows. One of the stories my father told Viola and me, when we were little and he was still a presence in our lives, was how romantic that meeting was. She a commoner and he a lord. Love at first sight and all that rot."

"Oho, Mr. Duke. You don't believe in the whole aristocrat-falling-in-love-with-the-commoner business? You're not that kind of romantic?"

Odd that she would think that kind of thing didn't happen. It did, these days. All the time. "I've seen too many romances end in bitter divorces, that one in particular."

"We have that in common, at least."

"Were your parents divorced as well?"

"No. They did something equally irresponsible. They got killed in a car wreck. But I'm like you. Not a romantic."

He winced. She tossed that off as if it didn't matter. "How old were you?"

She began to rub one hand against the other. "I was twelve, not such a good age to lose your mother and father."

Charlie would have been good losing his parents, cruel as it was to say, at any age. But her? Before she'd turned away, he'd caught a glimpse of sadness in her eyes. He ignored it because it was apparent she didn't want him to notice. "A relationship brought you to England. That's romantic."

"What of it? That relationship is done, a case of an aristocrat's failure to appreciate the value of a commoner. I've got other things on my mind now. Like making this restaurant the best it can be, maybe even providing more people in Bisby with jobs. For sure it doesn't include looking for the man of my dreams, if there is such a thing."

"Planting a garden. It includes that."

"Oh." She held up a finger. "Can we put off meeting at the garden until tomorrow? I'm unexpectedly short-staffed today."

Meeting tomorrow agreed with him. It meant him spending more time in Bisby. And potentially more time with her. He patted his mouth with the napkin and placed it on the table next to the now empty bowl. "Well, then. Tomorrow we'll look at the garden. And then I'll take you out to Prescott Nurseries to pick up your seeds."

"Thanks, but no need for you to bother. I can take myself out to pick them up."

"I recall you telling me you don't have a car. Does that mean you're going to walk?"

"It's not that far, only a couple of miles." She lifted her chin.

He held up a hand. "It's done. Andy has ordered the seeds, and I've paid for them. All you need to do is come along for the ride." He stood. "I've also arranged for John Peele to come out to Melbury Manor on Monday and re-plow the garden."

"Thank you." She bit her lip. "When I think of how we started out…"

Those teeth, that mouth. He felt a stirring. "Think nothing of it," he said and ignored his body. "How we started out was you accusing me, quite forcefully, of being responsible for the destruction of the garden. All I'm doing is correcting the situation."

She ducked her head and again rubbed one hand against the other—a nervous affectation, he thought.

"If Andy hasn't ordered everything you need, you'll be sure to tell him what else you do need and I'll make sure he gets it for you." He leaned forward. "May I make a request?"

With a look of wariness in her dark brown eyes, she said, "You may."

"I'm partial to rocket. Would it be too much to ask you to plant some?"

She looked down as if she were checking to see if he had dropped a *rotelle*—or if it were one, would it be a rotello? Was she thinking he'd made a muck of his meal? She picked up her head, and there on her pretty lips lurked another one of her charming half-smiles. "How come you're not talking in your usual hoity-toity, snobby Brit way?"

He didn't know he wasn't. "My dear lady." He cut the words with precision as if he were in the presence of someone from College of Arms. "I can certainly revert to my hoity-toity, snobby Brit speech if it would make you happy." He placed a hand on his chest and pretended a bow, which wasn't easy from a sitting position.

She smacked his arm.

"Am I your punching bag?" He grabbed his arm in pretended affront. "You may be the most violent woman I've ever met."

"I'm trying to get your attention so you'll give it the right name." She leaned into him, smile full-out, eyes shining like beacons, the dimple making a no-holds-barred appearance. "It's not called rocket. It's a green that's pronounced ah-roo-guh-lah, with the accent on the roo."

"Arugula," he said, surprised he could speak considering how that smile and her beautiful eyes had knocked him arse over elbow. "Although I prefer calling it what I and everyone else I know calls it: rocket."

"I'll plant rocket for you. And I'll even let you harvest some of it if you stick around. That's if you're willing to put your hands in dirt."

"I love a good handful of earth." In fact he had 52,000 acres of it and counting.

She swept the bowl off the table and made shooing motions. "Now go. I have work."

Without a whimper he went. As he got in the Jag, he remembered something Andy had said to him last night. *I'd like to see you happy.*

How odd that he should think of it now. Charlie began to press the ignition button and then dropped his hand back into his lap. He turned to stare at The Ocular. Was Annie Lukin the kind of woman who could make him happy?

CHAPTER FIVE

Annie watched fifteen-year-old James, her newest hire, beat a soubise into submission, a look of intense concentration on his face. He'd arrived not a minute after the duke departed—school was out, one of those British half-holidays. James was special to her. He was in foster care, now, having escaped a brutal home life. She pushed away the image of how she'd first seen him, black and blue marks everywhere.

"Annie, I've got your chickens. Where do you want them?"

She turned toward Arthur Entwhistle who held the box with the birds in it as easy as if it were just feathers. "Put the box right here," she said, looking up into his sun-reddened face. She patted the table's surface.

"That's good then, love." The table shuddered when he plunked the box down. "Is that side of beef I've got on the lorry going down to the cooler?"

"Yup. That's right." But Arthur was already out the door on his way to retrieve the beef that came from one of the grass-fed cows Henry Eames had been raising for her.

"Annie, I need to print up the menus." Molly came traipsing up in her red clogs. "Have you decided what we're going to have for afters?"

Oh yes. The question of the day. What was she going to serve the duke of Lindsey for dessert? She might have been able to decide if only she could get him out her mind. How he'd looked at her, head to toe, and how she'd wanted to faint, thinking how much better it would be if it were his hands touching her, not his gaze. Or the lure of his smile when he teased her about tonnato being tuna. And how much he loved it. Loved. How freighted *that* word was. She hunched up against a sudden shiver. "Give me fifteen minutes."

Molly sighed. "No longer than fifteen minutes, mind. If you keep on dithering, I won't have time to drive up to Market Rasen to the quick print and back and change into my togs before service starts."

"Fifteen minutes. I promise." There was more traipsing about and a slam of the door. Annie winced. She kept trying to get Molly to stop slamming doors.

"My goodness, what is that about?" said a new voice, one Annie recognized instantly.

Ordinarily Annie would be happy to see Lynette Leslie, her best friend in the world, who must have slipped in as Molly made her way out. Annie had met Lynette when she'd first come to Bisby with Ross. *"I could have told you Ross was the worst kind of tosser,"* Lynette had confided in Annie just after she'd told Ross to beat it. *"But if he hadn't brought you to Bisby, we wouldn't have met."* She'd hugged Annie. *"That would not have done."*

Annie was so behind she had no time to chat. "Just what happens in restaurant. Why aren't you at school teaching?"

Lynette stepped into the kitchen and leaned against the prep table Annie was working on. "School holiday."

"Oh yeah." James had just told her that.

"I wonder if you would satisfy my curiosity."

"What curiosity?" Annie didn't look up from her prep.

"There's a man sitting in a lovely black Jaguar across the street. Why?"

Annie resisted the urge to rush over to the front window. "I wouldn't know."

Lynette snickered. "What a fib. You know why. And you know who. As do I." She slanted a knowing glance at Annie. "The word is out that you're to serve him tonight."

Serve him? Annie broke out in a sweat thinking of the many ways she could "serve" the damn man. She smacked her wicked mind into submission. "And your point would be?"

"No point, really."

"I'm happy to hear that because I've served all kinds of high-profile types in my career. Why should I care that a measly duke will grace—oh, bad word—my restaurant tonight?" She turned toward Brandon, her newest server, who was setting the VIP table. "No, Brandon. Forget the herbs. I need the turquoise vase and then some primroses—the yellow and white ones. Make sure there are no broken petals."

Brandon nodded and headed down to the cooler.

Annie could feel Lynette's eyes on her. "Really?" Lynette asked. "It doesn't matter?"

"It really doesn't," Annie insisted.

"You know the duke is unattached."

Annie swiped an arm across her forehead. "Are you suggesting—what is that quaint phrase—I should set my cap for him? His Majesty, I'm-just-a-regular-guy-but-don't-forget-I'm-a-duke, Charles David Hugo Montagu Camville?"

There was a prolonged silence. "You're not even the teensy bit attracted to the man, but you know every one of his names?"

Annie rolled her eyes and hoped she wasn't blushing. "I think the guy's hot, okay?" She snatched up her knife to continue slicing lemon for the broccoli sauce she was making. "He has no interest in me." Because now that she thought of it— because she *was* thinking of it—if he did, he'd lose that interest once he found out about what had happened in New York at Carne three years ago.

"The evidence seems otherwise." Lynette waved one hand in the direction of the front of the restaurant. "He's there, across the street. Just sitting." She shrugged, the impish smile fixed in place.

Annie laid her knife down and ambled over to the window. And yes, there it was. A sleek, black, powerful car. Her insides went all liquid. She glanced back at Lynette. "He's probably making a phone call."

It was Lynette's turn to roll her eyes.

Just then the car roared to life, and the person behind the wheel drove off. "See? He's gone. I told you he's not interested."

Lynette grimaced.

"Okay, so maybe he is." Annie went back to her prep. "It's only because I'm unconventional. I work for a living. I dress in an odd way." She remembered how hard it had been not to laugh when he'd wondered if she'd left her cape with his assistant.

She set one lemon aside and started on another. "Think, Lynette. He was raised an aristocrat, totally upper class. I was raised in a working-class neighborhood in New York City and not even one of the good parts. What world could you imagine us inhabiting together? What kind of future might we have when we have nothing in common?"

Lynette pursed her lips. "I was thinking a date or two. You were thinking of a bridal shower?"

"No," Annie protested, all vehemence. "That would be idiotic." She waved a piece of lemon peel speared on her knife in Lynette's direction. "Enough, now. I have work to do and I can't afford to be dilly-dallying with my bestie."

Lynette snickered. "Tomorrow, your bestie is going to want a report on the evening's activities and you'd best be prepared not to leave out a single detail." She waved a hand and left.

It took Annie a minute to recalibrate her brain because it was filled with too many thoughts of Charlie Camville touching her. Like in his office when he'd placed his hand at the small of her back in order to steer her toward the door.

She picked up another lemon, and began to make quick cuts.

Like before, when she'd placed the pasta in front of him and his fingers brushed against hers.

She dropped that lemon in a container and picked up the last one.

Like when he'd taken her hand in his and kissed it and her skin began to throb with the feel of his thumb caressing her knuckles as he'd drawn her hand to his lips, the moist heat of his breath bathing her skin.

Like…

She nicked her finger with the knife.

"Dammit," she muttered. Reaching for a paper towel to press against the small wound, she stanched it and then snapped on a glove to keep from contaminating her lemons. She had no business thinking about Charlie Camville or Charles or whatever she was calling him. She had a restaurant to run; he had a… well, she didn't know what he had.

Before her imagination could veer off in another unproductive direction, she put her cut-up lemons in her under-counter cooler and reminded herself of the differences between her duke and her. His blood was aristocratic blue and hers, peasant red. Whatever spark of interest might somehow grow between them could only be that. Anything further than a spark would be a fire that would burn her to a crisp.

By the time Duke Charles David Hugo Montagu arrived—God, she had to stop thinking of him with all his names—along with his sister and brother-in-law, Annie had a raging headache. Two tables of guests who were coming up from London and had reserved tables four and five, had called to say they'd be a half hour late. Ordinarily late diners lost their reservations, but she was too nervous about her VIP table to be her usual stickler self.

Even worse, standing in the safety of the kitchen, she could see that one of her other tables was not satisfied with their appetizer. She was trying to decide what to do when the door opened and in they came. First, Viola and George. Then came the duke and a tall blonde, who as soon as she was through the doorway, wrapped one possessive arm around his.

And just like that, Lynette's dream of being the bestie of a duchess evaporated. Hers, too. Except Annie hadn't had one, she reminded herself.

"Annie," Molly said, breathing hard, "table ten didn't like the artichokes."

Of course they hadn't. For one of the few times since she'd opened The Ocular, Annie hadn't paid full attention to her work. The reason why was approaching the VIP table with the blonde, who was still in cling mode. "Give them my apologies, and tell them I'll be comping them their dinner."

"But Annie, they haven't complained about the food they haven't eaten yet."

His Majesty, the duke, held out a chair to seat first his sister and then the blonde, who was decorative and expensive in all the obvious ways. "We don't need people saying they had a bad experience at The Ocular." Annie couldn't help seeing how the blonde stared up with puppy-dog eyes at Mr. Duke and how he—

Was staring at *her, Annie Lukin,* a smile curving the corners of his lips, sharing the joke. Like he knew what was in her mind.

Annie's pulse did an Olympic high jump. "In fact," she said, jerking around so fast it was a wonder she didn't get whiplash, "why don't you tell them they'll be my guests next time they come back to The Ocular."

"Wha-at?" Molly was so surprised she forgot to cover her mouth and the gray stumps of her teeth.

Then she sighed. "Okay." It didn't sound like Molly thought it was okay, but she went back to the table with Annie's message.

With a hard exhale, Annie ducked her head and bent to the insalata di carne cruda—beef tartare—she was making for the VIP table instead of the rotelle tonnato, which he'd said he didn't want her to make for anyone but him.

What was it with her and this man who was so far out of her league? How many times did she need to tell herself not to think of him as something divine and delicious? Like a dish of fully-ripened strawberries with a zabaglione sauce? She eyed the top half of her double boiler and wondered what her staff would say if she picked it up and gave herself one good bonk on the head. She pushed aside thoughts of the duke as dessert and concentrated on deciding what to make for table ten as a substitute for the artichokes they didn't like.

Molly was back. "I gave them your message. They said no need to do that."

"That's very nice and please thank them. But my restaurant, my rules. They're getting comped."

Molly sighed. "I guess it's me that will have to make sure they don't make too much of a fuss, then." She dashed away, muttering a "sorry" to Brandon as she almost knocked him over.

"Annie, I'm ready to serve the VIP table," said Brandon, frowning with disapproval at Molly.

"Give them this for starters." With deft hands Annie slathered bruschetta with cremini and a touch of truffle oil she'd just whipped up, onto four oval toasts, and placed them on a white plate with scalloped edging. She handed the plate to Brandon and added, "Be sure to make eye contact with everyone. You have nothing to be ashamed of."

He ducked his head, took the plate, and left.

She went back to her beef tartare and thought it was time to call that dermatologist in York. She needed to see how much he would charge for laser treatments, if she paid him in cash. She'd just about convinced Brandon to let her do it for him. Whatever, it was going to be expensive since they were talking about something the NHS didn't cover.

"Annie, you want to check the quails? I'm going to baste them now," said Davey, her line chef, newly arrived from the London culinary school classes she'd paid for.

She eyeballed the nicely browning quail. "Go ahead. I need to do my meet and greet." Which she should have done already if the arrival of His Eminence hadn't distracted her. She looked down at the front of her apron, hoping it wasn't soiled, and stepped out of the kitchen and up to the VIP table.

The Swynfords had taken the seats farthest from the kitchen. The blonde had taken the middle and was whispering in His Majesty's ear. She was dressed all in spring pastels, and she was smiling with a wide, pinky-red lipstick-slicked mouth, all white teeth, and a perfectly made-up face. Did the woman not know how all that lipstick made her look like a clown?

He had taken the seat closest to the kitchen. As Annie stepped up to the table, he came to his feet. Oh God. He towered over her. She felt tiny. Precious. Pulled into his big, delectable body.

"Miss Lukin, how lovely to see you."

She opened her mouth to respond. Nothing came out.

"May I introduce my friend, Samantha Carberry?" His voice was a caress. Low, magical, all bedroom cajolery.

"Nice to meet you," Annie said, happy she could form the words.

"Nice to meet you as well," Samantha responded in a breathy voice.

Annie nodded. and acknowledged Viola and George Swynford before turning her gaze, once more, on… Well, he'd told her to call him Charlie.

He was dressed to kill. A dark navy tie with some kind of abstract design on it in yellow and red, and baby blue shirt, a suit of some lustrous navy, almost black wool. His jaw was clean-shaven. It was crazy to think she could smell his after shave—its citrusy notes—with all the competing restaurant smells eddying around them. But she fancied she could.

His midnight-black hair was slicked back, not a single curl in sight. Annie found herself wanting to reach up and burrow her fingers underneath all that control and spring them free. "Char—" She clutched her hands into fists at her sides.

"You can say it, you know. I asked you to," he murmured and leaned down toward her. "Charlie."

"Okay." And yes, that was a citrusy scent he wore. For a scary moment, she thought she was having an attack of vertigo.

"Annie, what's different about our table arrangement? You've done something." Viola was looking at Annie with a too-wanting-to-please smile.

"Only thing is the flowers." Annie forced herself to concentrate on Viola, a hard thing when he— Charlie—had insisted she get all intimate with his name. "Ordinarily you'd see pots of herbs on your table. I thought I'd treat you to some early primroses from Prescott Nurseries. Andy knows I'm always on the lookout for the prettiest blooms, and today he sent me some."

"Annie, I know you believe in supporting the local economy," George broke in. "It's quite admirable. I applaud you for that." He made little clapping motions. "I do wish, though, you'd let me introduce you to Rodney Ashburton in Sheffield. He'll give you a better price than Andy does on flowers and such, but also for the seeds for your garden."

George dared to bring up the garden he'd destroyed? Annie would never forget the look on the children's faces when they saw the carnage. "Oh, George," she said, feeling the hate-on she had for the worm rise. "You dug up the garden because I didn't buy my seeds from your friend? Seems a little extreme."

It took George a moment to recover. But then he threw his head back and laughed. No, a bray. Like the ass he was. The diners at the other ten tables paused. George cut the laugh. His eyes, a washed-out blue, bore into hers. On his mouth there was a tight, forced smile. "I do so love your American mockery. But really, why not give old Rodney a try? I think you'll be pleased with the results."

"I didn't know Ashburton had a retail establishment, George." Charlie who'd seated himself again, spoke in a quiet tone, although his black eyes were not quiet. "But really, why are we talking business when Miss Lukin is about to serve us what promises to be extraordinary fare?"

In The Ocular's dim lighting, the rise in color on George's face was easy to see. "Too right."

Charlie turned away from George. His eyes warmed when they touched Annie's face. "I've been looking forward to this evening. I understand we'll be served dishes you've made exclusively for our table."

"That's right. Tonight, for the first course you'll have my take on beef tartare."

"Won't that be raw?" Miss Blonde Samantha's voice wasn't just breath, but high and girlish. "Perhaps we should worry about trichinosis."

"My dear Samantha, no need to," Charlie said. "Trichinosis might affect our swine population. It won't our bovines."

Samantha wrinkled her handsomely penciled eyebrows. "Bovine. Do you mean a bull, Charlie, because why would anyone eat Ferdinand?"

Charlie patted Samantha's hand. "No one wants to eat Ferdinand. That said, I believe you'll quite enjoy the beef tartare. The ingredients are locally sourced and quite safe." He cast a sidewise glance at Annie. "Isn't that right, Miss Lukin?"

Annie's heart did a backflip. Somehow he must have found out she bought local from Lincolnshire farmers and approved. The vertigo was back.

"Sorry," murmured Brandon, plates in hand, as he inched by Annie on his way to table two in the far corner by the front window.

Annie stepped aside and to Samantha, said, "If you feel the beef tartare isn't to your liking, please tell your server and I'll make something else for you." Beating a retreat to the protection of her kitchen, she called out in a voice higher than Samantha's, *"Buon Appetito!"*

After Annie assured herself that her lungs would work the way they were meant to when not in the presence of a man with four first names, she checked the prosciutto Davey was wrapping around asparagus for table ten's substitute appetizer. And told herself to stop thinking about *him*.

She watched Sally, her pastry chef, finish the meringue for the Mt. Etna Cake that she planned on serving to her regular diners for dessert. And uttered a frustrated groan because she was still thinking about *him*.

She checked on the sauce for the quail. She eyed the risotto made with the mushrooms grown at Smiler's Farm because Charlie had said he loved mushrooms in risotto, and the rhubarb tart Annie had in her cooler to serve to her VIPs. She was pairing the tart with vanilla ice cream that was so rich if you overdid, it could put you into a food coma. None of this, however, served to get His Majesty out of her mind. He was there, like a burr she couldn't unstick from her brain. By the time Molly came rushing back into the kitchen for the millionth time, Annie was fed up with herself.

"Annie, table ten wants to thank you. They loved the asparagus."

"Good." She hated thinking one small thing could impact the restaurant's reputation. She did have her pride—but she also had a responsibility to be the best for her employees. When Davey dropped a pan on the floor with a clang that disturbed everyone, she cursed herself up and down. She still couldn't stop thinking about *him*.

"Lady Viola wants to know if you'd mind speaking to her," said Brandon coming into the kitchen a half hour later as Annie was putting the balance of the lush vanilla ice cream back into the freezer.

Without turning around, Annie said, "Okay. I'll be right out."

She wiped her hands on a towel and then stepped up to the VIP table. His Eminence was chatting with Viola. The blonde was leaning against him.

"Oh, here you are." Viola interrupted her brother, who took that moment to disentangle himself from his blonde. Annie wanted to do a jig of satisfaction.

Viola came to her feet. "Can we talk for a moment?"

Annie nodded and stepped to the front of the room, which was the only space in the restaurant where they could stand without others hearing them.

"George is sorry he ordered your garden to be plowed over."

"Apology accepted." What else could Annie say?

"Excellent." Viola held herself in unnatural stiffness. "George and I are expecting some very important guests to visit us Wednesday next. I'd like you to prepare a luncheon for six at the Manor." She fixed Annie with an unblinking stare.

"What did you have in mind?"

With a nervous twitch of her head, Viola glanced at the VIP table, where her husband was leaning across Samantha, the blonde, and whispering in Charlie's ear. "Can you make it a hunting theme?"

"You mean wild boar? Or birds?"

"Birds, yes. Brilliant!" Viola took Annie by the hand. Annie noted how cold Viola's was. "The men coming to see us are from a consortium who are considering Melbury Manor for a hunting lodge and the property for a grouse shoot."

"Oh?" The consortium in whose name George had destroyed the garden. Had Annie known who the luncheon was for, she would have said no.

Her gaze unblinking, Viola said, "They think the house and the property are perfect."

For Annie, this wasn't a surprise. Melbury Manor, in front, including the space where the community garden had been, was flat. But behind the manor house, the land, which seemed to go on forever in every direction, was hilly and yet easy to tramp over. She'd done it once with Lynette before George and Viola moved in. It would be good exercise, Lynette had insisted. Annie had enough exercise, tramping around her kitchen and said, *Let's not do this again.*"

Annie tilted her head to one side. "I thought you just said the consortium considered the property perfect. What's keeping them from making a commitment to you?"

Viola made a face. "There's another property they're considering. Melbury Manor is ahead, but not by that much." Her gaze went once more to the table, where George was looking off into mid-distance. "There is one more thing."

Annie stiffened.

"The garden's location at the entrance of the Manor. If you insist upon it being restored, it will look awful to the men from the consortium. It might be just the thing to tip them in favor of choosing the other property." She squeezed Annie's hand.

"Viola…"

Viola's grip on Annie's hand hardened almost to pain. "It's for Bisby. Should they choose us, it will mean jobs for dozens of men from the village."

Jobs for some? Or the garden for the children? Annie's stomach twisted in knots. In Viola's scenario no matter what Annie decided, someone was going to be hurt.

She took a deep breath. "Let me think about it, Viola. At least for a day."

Viola let her go. "Please try to make the right decision."

CHAPTER SIX

Somehow Annie made it through the remainder of dinner service with the smile on her face intact. Her diners loved her Mt. Etna Cake, which was nothing more than a classic genoise with wild, slightly browned meringue peaks, a dusting of confectioner's sugar and toasted almonds scattered across the peaks. She knew her VIP table loved her rhubarb tart with vanilla ice cream because Viola asked Annie to make it for the luncheon.

Annie peeked out, but all she saw was Charlie and Samantha, heads together. She'd bet Samantha was from a family the duke of Lindsey would think appropriate to marry into. Annie put a slice of rhubarb tart in a to-go box for Viola. "Get over yourself. He's hers, not yours," she muttered. And after she showed him the garden tomorrow he wouldn't be in her life at all.

The evening done, unable to stop thinking about the garden and the decision Viola wanted her to make, she locked up and walked the short distance to her apartment, opened the door, headed up the narrow flight of stairs, and flopped onto her bed. Exhausted, worried, she closed her eyes, thinking of how she needed to take her shoes off and get undressed and she'd do it in a moment. The next thing she knew, the sun was shining on her face, she was tangled in her blanket, and someone was banging on her door.

She jumped up and almost knocked herself out on the skinny floor lamp standing next to her bed. With one hand, she grabbed it before it could go over, and with the other rubbed her forehead.

"Coming," she yelled. Still half-asleep, she staggered down the stairs to the door to the street. She snatched it open to see the last person she wanted to see after she'd slept all night in the clothes she'd worn in the kitchen: Charles, the Duke of Lindsey. There he stood, as immaculate as the first time she'd seen him in his bespoke suit. This time, as a complement to his intense black eyes and hair, he was wearing a heather-black wool sweater with a white tee beneath just peeking out from the collar. His jeans were so neat they might have been pressed.

A smile lit his dark Italian eyes. He looked at the door and back to her. "Your door is painted pink? Why?"

"Who knows?" She pushed the strands of hair that had come loose from her braid off her forehead. "My crazy landlord likes the color."

"Ah." He looked at his watch and then up at the pale sun, which was high enough in the sky that Annie knew it was mid-morning. "Had a late night on the town, did you?"

"Maybe you forgot? I was making your dinner." She bit her tongue. "Sorry."

"Don't apologize. I've gotten used to your—shall we say—unceremonious speech. And I was teasing. Obviously I knew where you were."

"Um." She looked around him. There sat the shiny black Jaguar, crouching at the edge of the street like the beast it was; affirmation that yes, it was the car that yesterday had sat across the street from the restaurant. She blushed, remembering her conversation with Lynette.

Walking past the Jaguar were two of Bisby's residents, Evelyn Prideaux and her twin sister, Emma Thurley, age eighty at least, on their way to church. Just behind them came two of the younger ones, Martin and Nell Capes, who Annie knew were both seventy-five. Nell waved, and started across the street, still slow but so much surer of foot since her hip surgery. Annie waved back.

"Annie, love, those biscuit things you brought me were lovely," Nell called out. "Thank you, my dear." She kept coming.

"Think of them as a get-well gift," Annie said, voice raised. She sidled back toward her door. "I'll come see you next week and bring you some more."

Annie thought it was not such a good idea for the residents of Bisby to see her, the disheveled American owner of The Ocular, together with the scion of local nobility. She reached out, yanked the scion into the hallway, and slammed the door behind them.

He raised an eyebrow again. "What a nice invitation, Miss Lukin."

Unsettled, up-ended, she swiped more strands of hair that had straggled onto her face. "Quit the Miss Lukin crap. My name is Annie. I said you could use it. And what are you doing here anyway?"

The stairwell leading up to her apartment was narrow and dark. In the half-light seeping down from upstairs, the apartment door's wacky color dulled to a muddy pink. "Dinner last night—" He shook his head in awe. "It was everything everyone said it would be. Fantastic."

She smoothed her hands down her sides and wondered if the remains of said dinner were slathered on her trousers. "Thank you."

"I was a bit jealous that our table wasn't served your Mt. Etna Cake, because I'd heard it was so special. Your rhubarb tart, though, was lovely, and I very much enjoyed it." A half-smile lurked at the edges of his mouth and in the glow of his black eyes. "I particularly enjoyed the beef tartare."

"Made to please your party of four. Some *other* poor bovine—"Annie couldn't keep from grinning—"suffered death so Ferdinand could live on if in no other place than imagination."

"Some of us have wonderful imaginations."

"Is that what you call it?"

He shrugged. "I must." Shifting in place, he said, "But enough said about that. I came by to take you shopping." And then he did a terrible thing. He gave her a true and full smile and the light of a thousand suns in a thousand galaxies lit the inside of her hallway.

"You did?" Her heart flung itself up against her lungs. Or at least she thought that was what had happened. Since all of a sudden, she couldn't breathe.

He leaned down and she was caught in his light, citrusy scent. "How soon they forget," he murmured.

She clenched her hands together at her waist to keep from reaching out to grab a handful of his sweater and pull his big body even closer to hers. His face was near enough to hers that she could capture his tempting lips with her own, and... Her breath caught. "Oh."

He raised an eyebrow. "Is that all the comment you plan on making to explain your amnesia? Oh?"

Annie could feel herself coloring. "I...um..."

"Right. I didn't specify a.m. as in ten a.m. when we arranged our time to meet, did I? Foolish me."

She took a breath to steady herself. How convenient it was that he thought that was the reason for her *um*. "I'm sorry. I fell asleep without setting my alarm."

"A woman of your discipline falling asleep without setting your alarm, forgetting about a time made to meet," he said, the smile growing rueful. "I find that quite fascinating."

His continued teasing was doing terrible things to the color of her skin. She hoped the subdued light in the hallway disguised how red it had to have turned. "What does that mean?"

"You're quite young to be running such an extraordinary restaurant."

"I'm not that young. I'm twenty-nine."

"My mistake. Ancient." He waved the words away. "You've accomplished so much. And as I know from my own experience, you're willing to speak up and act when you see the need to. The consequences don't seem to matter. I admire you for that."

If he knew what she'd said and done before she'd come to Bisby, he wouldn't think there was so much to admire in her. But then, no worries there. There'd be no reason to tell him. "All in a day's work, Your Highness." She rubbed her thumb over the scar on her right hand.

"There's the part about how you support the people of the village as well. That fascinates me."

She relaxed marginally. "It's about competence. Forget the fascinate part."

"That's not what I've heard. People rave about what you've taken upon yourself to do. Nell Capes, just now. It proves my point. In my mind, when it comes to cooking—and life—you either have the heart for it or you don't."

She felt herself melt like a warm caramel sauce. "That's laying it on pretty thick, Your Highness."

His mouth quirked up on one side. "Not very good at accepting compliments, are you."

She wasn't, but she wasn't going to admit it. "My restaurant's reputation is what matters to me." And a reputation was a hard thing to regain, once you lost it.

"You seek perfection."

"I always seek perfection."

"Is that what they taught you in school?"

"They taught me technique. They taught me what might have taken me years to learn on my own. Graduating from that school gave me entree to my first job." With Joe. At Carne. Where good deeds went punished.

"It's no small thing, either, that you've gone to bat for Bisby over a community garden. How many would who hadn't been born here?"

"I know all about small-town syndrome and how people think of you as a stranger unless you were born in the place. But that's not what happened here. I got taken in. Made to feel like I was home. That's part of why I campaigned for the garden, and because it was the right thing to do."

"Bisby was home for me when I was a kid," he said, looking away.

She wondered why it wasn't now. Unlike his sister, for which it was. Or at least had been for the last four months. Which made Annie remember her conversation with Viola and how she didn't want to talk about it with him. Right now. "I better take a shower." She took a couple of steps backward up the stairs. He followed, his one matching her two. And now he was in too much of her personal space.

"I think you should." His eyes began to sparkle again, and a smile tickled one corner of his mouth. "Get ready and all that."

It dawned on Annie that the duke of Lindsey had been not so much teasing as flirting with her and not in a subtle way. This was dangerous on so many levels. Even if she was attracted to him—which she was—allowing herself to be flirted with was to be avoided at all costs. Whatever he thought he wanted from her would be for the short term. She couldn't afford to let him in, even for the short term. Hadn't she told herself this man could hurt her?

"I've been thinking," she hedged. "Maybe we should put this off until I figure out how much shade we'll have to contend with for the garden and what we should plant."

He placed a hand on her trailing shoulder and turned her to face him. "There are no trees near your garden. What's this about shade?"

What to tell him… But there wasn't a choice, and much as she didn't want to, she had to tell him. "Viola says George is working with a group of investors who they hope will choose the Manor and develop it into a lodge and the land for shooting birds."

"I know that." A look of assessment cooled the light in his black eyes.

"Viola's afraid the garden will convince them to choose the property in Hampshire. She wants me to consider moving it somewhere else, and I'm thinking of it because it might mean more jobs."

"Might?"

She nodded.

"Do you want to move the garden?"

She shook her head. "I've told you. Where it is it's in the best place."

The planes of his face hardened. "I've only begun my conversations with George about what the consortium wants. In the end, what matters is what I want."

"I worry about—"

"Any worrying to be done will be on my part." He held her by both shoulders. She could feel the heat of his palms through her shirt.

How ducal he was. She felt sorry for George and Viola. Almost.

The irritation in his eyes faded. His hardened jaw softened. "I've a besetting sin called ignorance. Other than eating what comes out of them, I don't know a thing about gardens and I want to. Please, can we at last get on with our seed-buying expedition to Prescott's? And remember. My name is Charlie."

He was all alpha male with sweet edges. Without doing a thing but smiling, his brilliant black eyes daring her to look away, he was becoming more dangerous by the second. "Charlie," she whispered.

"Yes." His fingers flexed against her skin. Gaze sharpening with intent, he took a step closer. His thigh brushed against her knee. His lips parted and she felt the whisper of his breath.

She held hers.

He frowned and slid his hands down her arms, and let go. The skin on the balls of her shoulders tingled where his hands had been. He cleared his voice. "I've asked Andy to set out an array of seeds for us which means there will be no need to worry you'll be late for the restaurant."

"How managing of you," she said with hardly a tremble in her voice.

"It's one of my best qualities. Now, go on and brush your teeth, take your shower, and do whatever it is gardener-chefs do to get ready for a day of wild spending when someone else is paying."

Hands once again on her shoulders, this time all business, he turned her and urged her upward. She had a moment of complete panic. What did her room look like? Was yesterday's underwear draped over her one rickety chair? She dug in her heels, forcing him to stop. "Maybe you should wait down at the bottom of the steps. Or better yet, go on outside to your car. I'll only be a few minutes."

He propelled her forward again, this time both hands on her hips, all but taking her off her feet. One small part of her brain noted that Charlie had some serious muscle power. "My dear woman, if you think I'm going to stand at the bottom of a dark stairwell—your fascinating pink door aside—you're off your trolley. And I do not wait for anyone in my car." He tugged on her falling-down braid. "Besides." He leaned forward, his breath tickling her ear. "The good people of Bisby will wonder why I'm sitting outside your flat like a lover scorned become a stalker. I can't have that."

She turned. His face was inches from hers. His warm, toothpaste-scented breath bathed her nose and cheeks and mouth. She could see how beautiful were his thick-as-brushes eyelashes. Even this early in the day there was the merest onset of stubble on his cheeks. It would take one little step forward for her to be in his arms, to satisfy her curiosity and thwarted need. And kiss him at last.

Breath catching in her throat, she took a hasty step backward. "Well, come up, then." She resisted slapping a hand across her chest to calm her foolish, racing heart. "But don't make any comments about what my place looks like." She turned and thumped up the steps. He came behind her, a hound of hell on her tail.

Bursting into the apartment, she hastened into the bathroom. And burst back out. She needed clean clothes. Otherwise she'd have only two options after her shower: get into the disgusting clothes that belonged in her hamper. Or come out naked. She ripped through her dresser for underwear, a pair of worn but thank God, clean jeans, and a white, peasant-looking blouse with a loose hem that would hit at her hips. She scooted into the bathroom, slamming the door behind her.

Eyes closing, she slumped against it. She'd almost kissed Charlie Camville. And then what would she have done?

How, Charlie wondered, had that happened? One moment he was teasing her. And yes, teasing her was perhaps the most fun he'd had in months, if not years. The next moment, there in her dark hallway— with the scent of last night's dessert leaking through the wall from the restaurant two empty stores down—he was seconds away from taking her in his arms and kissing her.

He heard the shower begin to run. He looked around the flat to take his mind off his incomprehensible behavior. It was one step up from being condemned. And a mess. Clothes puddled on the seat of an old wooden chair, bed sagging in the middle and unmade, the sheets and one thin blanket pushed to the side in an untidy heap. He eyed a smallish, round table that belonged in a trash bin—all her furniture belonged in a trash bin—and wondered why she didn't replace it with something decent. The restaurant was wildly successful. Surely she could afford some new furniture, a new and better flat, too.

Baffled, his gaze lit on a scalloped-edged round dish on the table, a haphazard pile of papers next to it. The dish was overflowing with safety pins and pens and one pair of earrings, the hoops that had swung from her ears the day she accosted him in his office.

Remembering them with fondness, he poked at them with one finger. The pens, which hadn't belonged in the dish to begin with, fell out onto the uneven pile of papers, which then slithered onto the floor. He bent to pick them up. One was a glossy advert. He heard the shower shut off. The gypsy moved fast, did she?

Placing the papers back on the table, he lay the advert on top. In large point, the title screamed *Chemical Peels That Will Work for You*. He picked the advert back up. Idly he looked on the reverse side. No doubt it had been mailed to her by mistake. But there was her name and address. "No, my dear girl," he murmured. "I hope you're not considering doing something so dangerous." She was perfect as far as he could see. Not a blemish. She—

The door from the loo swung open. "Give me that!" Annie stalked across the floor in her bare feet, snatched the advert out of his hand, and slapped it onto the table.

He looked down at her feet. They were slender feet, with high arches, delicately-boned ankles, little toes, nails trimmed neatly and painted black. He remembered how he'd wanted to see them bare. And he forgot about the advert as an urge came over him to push her down into the chair next to the table, pick up one of those lovely feet, run his fingers across that high arch, encircle the ankle, kiss the pale skin, and lick her neatly trimmed toes.

She'd put on a shirt—white with lace at the hem—and hadn't pulled it all the way down in the back, exposing an interesting swath of pale skin. Placing both hands on her shoulders, he turned her to face away from him.

"What are you doing?" She stiffened up like an angry kitten and scowled at him over her shoulder.

Her curly hair flowed down over her back halfway to a tiny waist. For a fleeting moment he let himself study her curvy bum. He took hold of the shirt's hem and eased it down over her wonderful hips. He let his fingers linger to make sure the hem was lying flat. Before his imagination could get altogether out of control, he turned her back around. "I'm making sure that when we go out, you don't look like a half-dressed vagabond."

"I don't know if you can imagine this, but I can dress without your help."

He wanted to silence her. With his mouth. And then he remembered the advert. He picked it up once more. "What's this?"

She snatched it out of his hand. "None of your business."

Irritation jittered through him. "What an awfully grown-up thing to say."

"Why are you so interested?"

"Explain to me, please, why you're going to have a chemical peel done. It's a dangerous and yes, painful procedure." One it frightened him to think she would put herself through, and for what? It would— A disturbing thought floated into his mind. "Do you need it done? Is there some medical reason—"

"I don't and no, there isn't."

"Then why do you have this?" Puzzled, he took it back from her.

Her beautiful—unblemished—skin flushed. Her mouth took on a mulish look, and somehow he knew. The advert wasn't for her. He thought he knew, however, who it was for. Charlie placed the card back on the table. "That young man who served us last night… What's his name?"

She folded her arms over her chest. Lifting her chin, she turned away from him. "Brandon."

He sighed and, one hand on her shoulder, turned her back around to face him. Her brown-black eyes smoldered. "What's wrong?"

"I'm tired of everyone telling me what I shouldn't do. If I want to help someone out because I have the money to do it, then what's the big deal?" She batted his hand away.

Eyebrows raised, he said, "Are you paying for the procedure?"

"So he can stop hiding from the world when he's a wonderful person and shouldn't have any reason to hide? Yes. And what's it to you?"

He stared down into her eyes burning with defiance because she thought now *he'd* tell her what others had been telling her. "Daft woman, you know it's going to cost you the earth."

"Yes, I know." She squared her shoulders. "But the damned NHS doesn't cover the procedure, and what's he to do? Walk around all disfigured from a childhood disease because they don't?" She swiveled on her heels and stalked the few feet to stare out the window across from her bed.

Charlie let his gaze drift down from the black curls that, post-shower, were going every which way across her back.

Now he understood. The wretched flat and her falling-apart furniture. Neither buying better furniture, nor living somewhere with proper amenities was high on her list of priorities. Not when there was a world out there to fix.

Charlie closed the gap between them and took her in his arms. Startled, she made a little squeaking sound. His heart took up a steady, fast beat, and he turned her to face him.

"Annie." He took her face in his hands and leaned down to press his mouth to hers. It wasn't much of a kiss. A scintilla of breath across skin. He picked up his head and stared. Her beautiful brown-black eyes had grown large, her mouth formed a perfect O. He didn't say another thing. He didn't have to. Because he knew. That touch of his lips to hers changed everything.

CHAPTER SEVEN

Her eyelids fluttered downward and Charlie took in the sum of her features, the dewy skin along her high cheekbones, her minimalist nose, her sulky mouth. He pulled her flush against his body and filled his hands with her splendid bum. He angled his head to one side and then the other, and then brought his mouth down to hers.

It took a microsecond for her lush body to melt against his. In the next second she became the aggressor. Only the smallest part of him found it startling because he should have expected the fascinating girl to take matters into her own hands.

In the silence of the room there was only the sound of their deep, concentrated breathing. She wound her arms around his neck. She licked the inside of his mouth. He returned the favor. Then it was no more favor for him but the meshing of his tongue with hers and then his lips pressed to hers and a sudden, desperate need to get closer. He shoved his thigh between hers and pressed against her. She moaned and wound one leg around his thigh, opening herself further to him.

He worked his hand beneath her blouse and smoothed it against her hot, damp skin. His fingers found the clasp of her bra where it lay against her spine. He began to fumble with it, and she stiffened. "Charlie," she said, low and insistent.

On an intake of breath, he took one fitful step back and stared. She stared back, her eyes wide, her wet, swollen lips, parted. She brought a trembling hand to her mouth. "We can't do this."

His brain was caught in the maelstrom of pure emotion, his body raging with need. He forced himself to regulate his breathing. "Indeed? Why did we?"

She looked around as if searching for an answer. "I…" Her voiced faded away.

"Annie." A pulse hammered at his right temple. "You have a way of slipping past all my reserve. I should not have done that."

Her eyes glistened with some emotion too equivocal for him to parse out. "I didn't exactly push you away."

No, she hadn't. He barely stopped himself from stroking a finger across her smooth-as-silk eyebrows just so he could, once more, watch her ridiculously long-lashed lids flutter down over her eyes. "There's a reason why it happened."

Her eyebrows came together in a ferocious frown. "Do you plan on sharing? Or are you keeping it all to yourself?"

"No." He ignored her sarcasm—since he was beginning to realize it was her defense mechanism. "There's an attraction between us."

The frown disappeared. It was followed by the sarcastic curl of her top lip. "I think you're full of it, Your Eminence."

"I don't think so."

A shadow chased itself across her expressive face. "Then what do you think?"

"Acknowledging it would be the adult thing to do."

She threw up her hands. "I had a feeling that's what you were going to say. Let me clue you in to what would happen if I admitted to having a thing for you. It would be insanity. In case you never read anything about female psychology in that fancy university you went to—"

"Cambridge."

She huffed a breath. "For us women, we're very much into our emotions. You start something with us, we eventually want it to be more than just wild monkey sex."

He folded his arms across his chest to keep himself from doing what he wanted to. Take her in his arms again. Hold her until she sorted it all out.

Although talk of the wild monkey sex caught his attention.

"Think about it," she continued. "Except for the garden, we never would have met, and we definitely wouldn't be part of each other's lives. What this really is? It's kind of like a thing from an old-time movie. A chance encounter."

"So, we need to get past it. Is that what you're saying?"

She took in a deep breath. "Totally."

"Well, then. We should get started on our outing to Prescott's," he heard himself say. Like nothing of note had just happened.

Her gaze flitted away from him again. She lifted a handful of her hair. "I'll get this mess fixed. Give me a minute." She stepped into the loo and closed the door behind her.

He let out the breath he'd been holding. She was attracted to him, was she? Now there were two of them caught in this craziness. He put his hands on his hips and stared down at her bed, the ratty blanket thrown to the side and falling off the mattress.

He'd not acknowledged it then, but with that kiss, he could now. He'd wanted her from the start. From the moment she'd stormed into his office, with her Boudicca come-to-do-battle attitude, and wide, dark brown eyes ablaze with righteous passion. He'd wanted to do to her what he'd just done and he wanted her to do to him what she'd done.

He didn't know what she could possibly be to him. But he would think about it. Explore it. With his emotions engaged—and *yes*, he'd wanted to howl, *we men do have emotions*—it was best to leave it for when they weren't. With an adjustment to his jeans, he brought his John Henry to order.

She took that moment to return. Her silky black hair was wrenched back in the unforgiving braid she'd worn yesterday. She'd put on a pair of sneakers, white, and laced up tight. They showed off her tiny feet, unlike the Hans Brinker footwear she'd worn last night at the restaurant. "It's a bit chilly out. Do you need a jumper? If you don't have one, I can always give you one of mine."

"Relax." She dug through the pile of clothes heaped on the chair. "I've got one here, only I call it a sweater." She held it up to show him. "The differences between us range from the unimportant— like what you call things we wear—to the differences that are about who we were born. What we just did was a mistake, Charlie. Let's not do it again."

"If that's what you want," he snapped, the emotions she'd dismissed making him feel altogether out of sorts.

As she scooted in front of him, he added, "No need to turn on a light. The glow from your charming pink door will light our way."

With a flick of her head, she tossed that braid back so it lay arrow straight down her back. He made a fist and pressed it hard against his side.

"Maybe you want to depend upon the door, but I know from experience, better to do it electronically." She put words into action, and flooded the stairwell with light from an ugly wall fixture. She hurried down the stairs in front of him.

The kiss was behind them. The day loomed ahead. Charlie took a deep breath and gave himself directions on how best to behave over the next hours. He rubbed his chest just above his heart and followed his gypsy down the stairs.

Annie burst out of the stairwell and onto the street. The skin up and down her back, from shoulders to heels, tingled knowing he was just behind her. What had happened? One moment she was totally pissed off with him, and the next she was all over him like he was strawberry shortcake and she was hungry for something luscious.

She reminded herself that she was in a lot of danger with a man like the duke of Lindsey. She could never ever let him get close to her. Because truth was, if she did and he ever found out about Joe and her, he would be so disgusted he'd walk away and leave her with her heart damaged. Maybe beyond damaged.

He was nothing like Ross, he of the good looks and charm. She'd never worry about Ross finding out. There wasn't the depth of feeling there, she realized now. Back in the beginning, though, she'd been fooled into thinking between them was mutual respect. It took a relocation across the Atlantic for her to discover that because Ross's revered grandfather, the earl, thought she, the run-of-the-mill American, was so not of Ross's status, she couldn't possibly be part of his life.

On no day and in no way would Ross ever measure up to the man who was dogging her heels this morning. Charlie Camville was a real aristocrat—and man—instead of a pretend one.

She crossed the street ahead of him to where his gorgeous black car awaited them. Not for the first time did she wonder what a man whose family had lost all its money was doing with an expensive toy like a Jaguar. Yes, she knew he'd sold his business and surely had something to spend on himself now.

But treating himself to a Jaguar? The thing must have cost him a small fortune. Dressing himself in clothes that even she, who didn't shop until she had to, knew were made for him? Working in an office that just reeked of architectural design? This man owed something to the people of Bisby. He had lease holdings around the village. Why wasn't he improving them?

Charlie stepped around her to open the passenger-side door. She ducked in without letting him help her and sank back into the lush, welcoming seat. Breathing in the scent of the butter-soft, caramel-colored leather, she fastened the seatbelt and decided she didn't care whether he could afford this car or not. It was too comfortable and she was going to ride in it, at least as far as Prescott's.

He slid in on the driver's side and slammed the door. "Ready?" He buckled his seat belt and started the engine.

After that lapse in judgment back in her apartment, was she? She ran her fingers over the scar on her right palm. "Let's go buy some seeds."

Charlie brought the car to a stop in front of the cavernous building that was Prescott's Nursery just as Andy stepped out. Before Charlie could come around to open Annie's door, Andy had loped over and pushed Charlie aside. He reached down to help Annie out and gave her a kiss on the cheek, a kiss Charlie thought was a bit too close to her mouth.

Looking at his watch and then up at Charlie, Andy said, "It's a good thing I didn't have anywhere to go this morning." And then he smiled broadly at Annie.

Charlie cleared his voice in an obvious way. "It's been my observation that some of us can't manage to find tasks to occupy ourselves with when an opportunity arises."

As Andy guided her to a table just inside the building, Annie looked over her shoulder at Charlie and shot him a frown. Focusing instead on Annie, Andy said, "Sorry you had to put up with this tosser, but you're with me now, so no worries from here on out. I've got all the seeds I think you'll want this time, sweet."

Charlie's hackles rose. *Sweet?*

Annie picked up one of the small linen bags Andy had assembled and placed on an old wooden work table marked with nicks and gashes. She studied the label attached to the bag. Glancing up, she said, "I've read something about how lettuce used to taste before the big, multinational agricultural companies did all their genetic tinkering and we ended up with what tastes like paper." A smile lit her face. "Thank you, Andy. This lettuce is a wonderful find!"

"I got all these seeds from the Center for Organic Gardening in Wellingborough." Andy gave a half-shy shrug, which Charlie would have found amusing, if he didn't want to tell the arsehole to bugger off.

"How was Jane, this morning, Andy? When you left her. At home?"

Without bothering to look Charlie's way, Andy said, "She's fine." And went back to helping Annie look over the seeds he'd gotten for her.

Charlie huffed an annoyed breath. His so-called mate had forgotten who'd brought the woman to his damned place of business. Andy needed to back off, he needed to—

Charlie shoved his hands into his pockets. Was this jealousy? He'd already determined he was fascinated with the gypsy girl. She was an exotic—and yes, generous-hearted—creature. To be jealous because Andy was monopolizing her time over bags of seeds? That was too outlandish to be taken into serious consideration. He needed to put such nonsense out of mind.

"Let me know if I can be of any service to you lot," he managed. "When it comes to gathering together the results of all this shopping, I can act the convenient pack horse and carry whatever packages you find too heavy."

Brown eyes wide, Annie looked up from the damn seeds. "I'm pretty sure Andy has someone who can carry everything for me to your car. But thanks." She looked around at Andy, it would seem for affirmation. Andy, however, was looking not at her but at him, a strange, arrested expression on his face.

Charlie waved a hand at Andy. "Stay busy, fellow, if you will. I'm paying you for your time, and I expect excellent service."

One corner of Andy's mouth twitched with reproach.

After examining and approving each bag, Annie put the last of them back on the table. "Is there a ladies in the building somewhere?"

Andy pointed it out. She excused herself.

The smile that had been on Andy's face disappeared like the little canvas bags being packed up by one of Prescott Nursery's staff. "All right, Charlie. What are you doing with her?"

"Sorry, but have you got a reason for asking, old man?" Charlie kept his hands in his pockets.

"Yeah, I have a reason. Let's not forget I know you."

Charlie took a step back and easing his hands out of his pockets, folded them behind his back. "A statement of truth to what purpose in this conversation?"

"Bugger and blast! Don't be more of an arse than you can help. Weren't we talking about the women in your life, not two nights ago? Didn't I say you should find someone who'll be right for you, unlike some of those looneys you've been with? Annie isn't one of them."

"All I'm doing is helping Annie restore her garden to its original shape," he heard himself say and wondered why he wasn't struck dead for telling such a lie.

"It better be true, Charlie. You and I, we've always been best mates. But if you hurt that girl, I'm not so sure we will be."

Later, when he was driving them away from Prescott's, Annie sat in Charlie's fancy car, the precious bag of seeds clutched in her arms, and glanced now and then at him. He drove steadily, if on the fast side, one hand on the wheel, the other hand resting on his thigh. In her apartment, while they'd stood close to her bed, those strong, long-fingered hands had slid down her back. They'd pulled her against him and she'd felt the insistent hard shape of his arousal against her belly.

He wanted her. She'd have to be an idiot if she thought otherwise. But while she'd been busy selecting seeds with Andy, Charlie had looked at her with attention she could only describe as jealousy. Like he thought she could have a thing for sweet, sometimes silly Andy Prescott, who was so not her type. Even if he were, he was married, which made him off-limits. She was scrupulous about these things. Too bad Joe's wife, Cindy, hadn't thought so.

In a weird way she was flattered that the duke of Lindsey wanted her. She knew better than to be too flattered, though. She glanced at him again. The man was total catnip, with his gorgeous, black Italian eyes, his high cheekbones, strong nose and jaw, black curls a little disheveled this damp, English morning, and lips that could kiss better than any she'd ever kissed back.

Awesome as it was to be wanted by such a man, it was going to get her in trouble. She risked another glance. And no, not in that sexual way that she couldn't seem to stop thinking about.

"So," she asked, her voice altogether too perky, "how does a duke support his many serfs in this day and age?"

He glanced at her, one eyebrow raised before giving his attention back to the narrow, curving road. "Carefully, I suppose. Although it must be said, these days, we dukes don't refer to our people as serfs."

"Don't think I'm being nosy."

His mouth twitched. "Never."

She took in a breath and gripped the bag of seeds harder. "The thing is George."

He frowned. "What about him?"

"He thinks of us as serfs."

"Because he and my sister want you to agree to move the garden?" Jaw working, Charlie said, "I told you. I'll take care of it."

"Thank you, Sir Lancelot, riding in to save the day." She began to play with the end of her braid. "But before you go off on your charger, you might want to think about the position this puts me in."

He sped up. "What position would that be?"

"Where I had to tell you about what Viola said to me. It felt like I was snitching on her. Like I was stuck in the middle."

His hands flexed on the wheel. "That's not the case."

"All because of my concern for the garden."

He downshifted on the descent into Bisby. "I told you not to be concerned."

"I worry you won't be able to resist moving the garden like Viola told me so there'll be jobs."

"Jobs? You made mention of that before. According to what I've heard, I'm not sure any will materialize."

"Still, the money will be too good. I've read the entry about your family in Wikipedia, you know."

He snorted a laugh. "Ah, a reference source as detailed as the Encyclopedia Britannica."

She wondered what he knew that he wasn't telling her. "The consortium could give you a way to fix it and your family's balance sheet since your father, according to Wikipedia, screwed over your dukedom."

"Wikipedia has that one right."

Annie's gaze slewed up to his face. Those words had come out upper-class clipped. They were words spoken as the duke of Lindsey. "How right?"

"Right enough. He almost destroyed everything, including a reputation fought for over the centuries by my family." There was more flexing of his fingers on the wheel. "Were there any other details about my father?"

Asked with caution.

"Not really."

"Perhaps I should have one of my people take a look at that entry."

Into the uncomfortable silence that followed, Annie fidgeted in her seat. It was a wonder he'd said as much as he had about his father, British reserve and all. They'd known each other days. It wasn't as if they were close. Except there'd been the kiss. "Just to be curious…"

He slowed down and gave her a sideways glance. "Something you're massively good at." Now, Charlie—not the duke of Lindsey—was speaking.

"I make no excuses for curiosity."

"Nor should you."

"Considering what Wikipedia says he did, how do you pay for—" She paused. "I mean, how do you—" The words stuck in her throat.

"What? Stopping now, Annie? Why let a little thing like tact keep you from finishing that sentence?"

Sometimes she wondered how even *she* could be so tactless.

Charlie pulled up in front of the restaurant and shut off the engine. "What do you suppose I do in that office in London?"

"That fancy place? I assume you have to keep up appearances."

"I don't need to keep up appearances."

"Then, what?"

"That day when you burst in upon me didn't you look around? There were a dozen young persons tapping away on their laptops whilst ensconced on the sofas I've provided for them."

She'd noticed. "So?"

"They're my team of researchers. They're going back in history to discover all about the Camvilles, dukes, earls, barons."

"That's some undertaking. Why do you bother?"

"Because I'm proud of them. If my ancestress, Nicola de la Haye, hadn't persevered and held Lincoln Castle against an invading French army in 1216, we might now be speaking French."

"While I love French food, I'm terrible at the language." Annie did a little fist pump. "Hooray for Nicola, who I never heard of."

"If it was up to me—which it is—you will. That's why I've hired all those researchers. To find out about Nicola, her husband, Richard Camville, their children and grandchildren and all the men and women in my family who were part of the making of English history."

"It's nice, I guess, to be spending all that money on stuff that's going to go in a history book."

He leaned across the console and ran one gentle finger across her cheek to the tip of her nose. Like a stone thrown into a pond, his touch radiated outward and her skin began to bloom. "If you want to know how I can afford it, why don't you ask?"

It became hard for Annie to catch her breath. "Okay. How can you?"

He took her face in his hands and kissed her. By the time she'd blinked twice, he'd already dropped his hands back onto the wheel. Still looking at her, he smiled. "Sweet Annie, has no one told you I'm filthy rich?"

The impression of his lips lingering, her brain took a flyer and she weighed the meaning of the words, *filthy* and *rich*, as used together in the same sentence. "How filthy rich are you?"

"After I sold Rotherforde Group? Cybersecurity, in case you were wondering. Richer than most in this sceptered isle." He grinned, opened his car door, and came around to open hers. "Let me take that from you." He held out a hand for the bag of seeds.

For a second she studied his hand. If she touched it now, she was sure it would feel the same as it had thirty seconds ago when, with the other, he cupped her cheek. And yet now that hand was different. The tumblers in her brain began to twirl. That hand represented an opportunity that hadn't existed thirty seconds ago.

"I'm not sure I've ever met anyone who's filthy rich." She handed him the bag and scooted out of the car.

"We lot don't wear a sign on our heads identifying ourselves as such." With long strides he crossed the street. "That would be a bit pretentious, don't you think? However, knowing the reputation of The Ocular, I would be willing to bet you have met more than one filthy rich person. They, too, wouldn't have worn signs."

As she hurried to keep up with him, she only half-listened to what he was saying because the tumblers had clicked into place. "What do you think of Bisby?"

She glanced up and down High Street at all the shuttered storefronts. "Do you think it's quaint?" She followed behind him as he stepped across the sidewalk, weeds growing through the cracks, to her apartment's pink door. "If there was a way to make it into one of those restorations, Bisby would be cute, don't you think?"

Taking the key from her, he unlocked the door. "'Cute' is a word one uses to describe a baby. And then sparingly." He stepped aside for her to enter.

As she started up the steps, she looked over her shoulder at him coming up behind her. "If we restored it and replaced the current vacant stores with some cu—some historically accurate establishments, think of all the people in town who would have work because Bisby would become a tourist spot."

He reached around her to open the door to her apartment. His arm brushed against her breast and her nipples came to attention. She gritted her teeth. Think of Bisby, she told herself.

"Did you just use the pronoun 'we,' Annie?"

"Yes, I did." She ignored her nipples. "As in me with the ideas, and you—"

"Yes, me with the money." He deposited the bag with her precious seeds on her kitchen counter, the depository for all her mail, which she never opened. Except for the return receipt notice she got once a month from the US Postal Service letting her know Sheryl Quatrone had received her latest envelope.

With him in her apartment, how small it seemed. How hard it was to breathe with him towering over her, that seductive smile on his lips and in his eyes and the memory of the kiss and how her nipples were now pushing their way up against the fabric of her blouse.

"Yes, you with the money." He was mere feet from the bed she slept in. "It's fine that you spend money employing all those people sitting on those couches looking up stuff about your ancestors. But your ancestors are dead, and it won't make a lot of difference to them if you find out more about them than you already know. Or if you don't find out another thing."

"When put like that, yes. Dead is most certainly dead." His smiling mouth gone serious, he lifted one of his eyebrows and put his hands behind his back.

Not caring that she'd offended him—she knew she had—she began to stride around her apartment, at least as much as it was possible with him in its center. "Unlike your ancestors, the people of Bisby are alive, but not thriving. They're the people who couldn't see themselves moving away from the homes of their ancestors—and yes, Your Highness, people other than dukes and earls have ancestors. If you'd put your money to good use and help them out, you'd be accomplishing something worthwhile." She stopped striding as silence spooled out from the tail end of her tirade.

He brought his arms around to fold them across his chest. "This is a favorite subject of yours, isn't it? I've heard you speak on it before. When you came down to London for your visit, for example."

She risked a glanced up at him.

"Have you had a lot of experience spending and using someone else's money, or is this your first foray into the enterprise?"

Money. It always came back to money. If Charlie ever found out she'd been accused of stealing at Carne… The air in the room cooled. He would think she was an opportunist spending his money for her own benefit.

But he couldn't know anything. Not even Ross knew. She hadn't told him. Pushing the ugly memories of her old life aside, she said, "Don't you recognize that you have responsibilities in Bisby? They're your people, according to English law, or at least they were your people, because from the time of the serfs, they farmed your land and went to war for your Camville ancestors at all the battles you guys fought in and were part of the history you're so anxious to—"

He put a hand on her shoulder, giving it a gentle squeeze. "Annie, Annie, Annie." The smile returned to his eyes. The room grew warm again and she forgot about his ancestors and her paranoia. "Yes?"

"You're right. I do have responsibilities to the people who live in Bisby and every other part of my demesne. I call it a demesne, not a word you're familiar with, I imagine. I'll explain later. But now, I want you to notice I don't call the people who live on my demesne serfs. We dukes of Lindsey know that would be so twelfth century."

She untangled her fingers. "And the dukes of Lindsey always try to live in the correct century. Is that right?"

"So right. To answer your question—or your point, or whatever the well-meant jeremiad was you have just subjected me to—I've been trying to think of something I could do to reverse Bisby's fortunes. Truly. That was, in part, why I hired the people who sit on my sofas in my office in London. Yes, they're researching Camville history. But their main task these last months has been to come up with something that would improve Bisby's economy. To date, they've come up with nothing I favored."

A grin lit his gorgeous, sparkling eyes, and hands on his hips, he leaned down, bringing his face within inches of hers. "Had I consulted with you, I would have learned you had the solution all along."

"I did?" Her brain was working on only the most basic level. "The solution?" she managed and forced herself to breathe.

"Right. A destination location. Bisby as restored village. Now I'm trying to picture what would work better. An Elizabethan village spanning Bisby's High Street? Or perhaps a medieval one?"

Her mouth opened, which meant one part of her body was in working order. She wasn't so sure about other parts, since now her brain seemed to have closed up for directing any comment at all.

He ignored her stunned silence. "I, myself, would favor an Elizabethan village. Sir Walter Raleigh and cloaks and all that, although we'd have to dig a hole in High Street over which our Sir Walter would demonstrate his gallantry for the crowds every afternoon at three o'clock. But that doesn't make sense, does it? Digging a hole where one doesn't exist. So perhaps no cape, then. And no Sir Walter."

Charlie's humor was catching. Brain back in the thinking business, Annie caught up to it. "Boring, Your Highness, totally boring. Besides the hole, the clothing would be ridiculous. Can you picture women in those big, high collars, and those big skirts? Good Lord, can you picture George in a ruff and one of those short, puffy, tutu-like skirts around his rear end?" She snorted a laugh. "Not a look for him."

"Oh, but I think it would better suit old George than your medieval dress. The armor, you know. Quite uncomfortable, and there's all that clanking. But the real challenge would lie elsewhere. Or fit elsewhere, as it were. Do you know how hard it is to find a good codpiece these days?"

It took Annie a long time and a huge wad of tissue to wipe her streaming eyes before she could stop laughing.

At the end of their debate, which got sillier and sillier, they decided to go with the medieval theme. Annie suspected Charlie didn't care which of the two themes they chose. She suspected he might have known he was going to go along with the one she favored. To reward him for being so clear-sighted, she took him down to the restaurant and fed him lunch.

CHAPTER EIGHT

In the end, they decided they didn't need to visit the garden. They knew what needed to be done. The next morning Charlie went back to London for some meeting or other. Afterwards, his plan was to drive back up to the county. It wasn't just because he wanted to be there when the garden was re-plowed, but because he wanted them to talk further about Bisby as an historically-restored village, complete with half-timbered houses with daub and wattle and tile roofs. He wanted to talk about partnering with a group experienced in doing historical re-enactments, one that would bring medieval Bisby to life.

As Annie slipped into the restaurant earlier than usual—she was so excited she hadn't been able to sleep—she thought that maybe, just maybe, Bisby was about to catch a break. Charlie, it turned out, cared about Bisby as much as she did. That had her face fixed in a perma-grin. Except when she was laughing over last night's talk of clanking armor and codpieces. Though she was alone—with her pans and bowls and flour and sugar—she kept her snorts and guffaws to snickers. She wouldn't want anyone to walk in on her and think she'd lost her mind overnight.

She'd decided to bake. Most times, she left dessert to her pastry chef, Sally. But there were times when Annie had too much to think about that she reserved making dessert to herself. Sweet and flaky, sweet and crunchy, sweet and decadent, or sweet and tart, making dessert was her all-in-one aromatherapy, exercise, and legal upper.

Standing at her prep table, she pondered her choices. She reached for a knife to slice some cheddar cheese for a snack and stopped, mid-cut. She dropped the knife with a clatter to the board and flattened a hand over her heart, which had begun to thump hard enough she could hear it. Putting the bite of cheese down, taking a step away from the prep area, she sank down on a chair at the VIP table, bare now except for a folded-up tablecloth and napkins.

Last night she hadn't been thinking about Bisby. She'd been thinking about Charlie kissing her, about being in his arms. About being more than in his arms. Being with him. A lot. Making him dinner. Spending the night together. In bed. Could it be that *she*, like Bisby, was finally catching a break? Could what she'd thought of as impossible be possible? Did it not matter, after all, what happened in New York? Did it not matter, either, that there was a big difference in life experience and rank between Charlie Camville, who happened to be an aristocrat, a duke, and Annie Lukin, a commoner, who happened to be a chef?

Her cell rang. She looked. Viola. The smile faded. "Hello?"

"Annie, do you think you can come up to the Manor for a quick sec?"

Uh huh. No preamble, no *hello, how are you*, not even a *what's up*. No need for one when you were upper class. This upper-class woman was Charlie's sister.

In that so upper-class way, Viola said, "I want to show you where I think we should do the luncheon. I'm not quite sure it's right and I want your opinion."

"I'll be by in a half hour. Will that work?"

"Perfect."

Annie had a feeling it would be the furthest thing from perfect.

Annie had only been inside the Manor once. Just after the Swynfords had moved in, they'd held a lord-of-the-manor Christmas party for Bisby's villagers. Since then she'd heard it said that they'd updated the dining room but not much else. Annie didn't think there could be any place to have the luncheon other than the dining room. Viola had summoned her to talk about something else.

Like moving the garden.

She told herself to chill. Charlie had said worrying about the garden was his to do, not hers.

Only he hadn't said outright that he wasn't going to have the garden moved.

Annie trod the length of High Street, all five minutes of it, a seed of worry growing inside her head. She told herself not to think the worst, even though her whole life, except for the last three years in Bisby, she'd had lots of practice thinking the worst because the worst kept happening.

She walked past the destruction of the garden to the Manor's packed-earth path, worn by hundreds of years of feet tramping its length. If there'd been a real Lizzie Bennet, she might have walked this way as well.

Viola stood in the doorway, waiting. The overly focused look in her eyes didn't quite match the broad smile on her face. "Thank you for coming. Getting all this sorted is important to me."

She beckoned Annie in to the central hallway. As they walked past it, Annie peeked into the restored dining room. With its polished wood parquet floor and high ceilings, bas-relief figures of cherubs romping all around the perimeter, Annie had to admit it was beautiful. Viola had had the room painted an off-white with a tinge of pink. It gave the huge room warmth, despite its oversize furniture—a table that sat an easy two dozen, high-backed dark wooden chairs, and large sideboards with ornamental silver centerpieces filled with flowers in an 1800s kind of way.

But they weren't going into that room. Instead Viola led her back to the kitchen, which with its faded yellow-painted walls, linoleum-covered floor full of nicks, the ancient Aga with its six burners, boxy refrigerator, and single sink was pretty much in the same 1960s shape it had been before the Swynfords moved in. "What's up, Viola?"

Viola beckoned Annie to sit. "Can I get you something? A cup of tea or coffee?"

"I'm good."

"Thank you so much for coming."

"No problem." Annie could hope that was true.

Smoothing her hands across the surface of the table, Viola continued, "Actually, why I asked you here has nothing to do with the luncheon."

Big shock. "Okay."

"I want to talk to you about something that has come up." She kept smoothing. "But I don't want you to think badly of me or of my husband."

"I would never think badly of you." She would of him, however. If she knew anything, George had sent Viola in to pinch hit for him about the garden.

"You must know—" A hectic flush colored the pale skin of Viola's neck and jaw. "George was not blessed with support from those who should have provided it in his life. His father, for one."

George Swynford was a slimy bastard because he'd had a less than loving childhood? That story fell into the let-me-play-a-sad-song-on-my-tiny-violin category.

"My father, as was the case, made things more difficult for poor George because when we married, there was nothing left of my inheritance to bring to the marriage."

Why was Viola unburdening herself to her? They were less than acquaintances.

"We had been poised to come about, but now, well…" She bit her lip and cast her gaze up toward the kitchen's high ceiling. Taking a quick breath, she added, "My brother has decided to stick his oar in."

Now not only was Viola talking about her husband's poor-little-privileged-boy-upbring-ing, she was criticizing her brother? Annie couldn't decide whether to vault out of her seat and flee this total TMI situation, or come to Charlie's defense.

Viola went on smoothing her hands across the table. "For some odd reason, when he has kept away for so long, Lindsey has decided it's time to visit Bisby."

The odd reason was her. Annie knew not to mention that. "Perhaps it was to have dinner with you and your husband." Unable to resist a bit of snark, she added, "And his cute, blonde friend, who has a thing for storybook animals."

"Good Lord! Friend!" Viola tsked in a ladylike way. "Fiancée more like."

Annie's heart had a meeting with her stomach. "Well, I suppose then congratulations are in order."

"Not yet. Lindsey is not quite finished playing."

What did Viola mean by playing? Was the whole thing about medieval streets in Bisby him playing? Annie's heart sank further. Was he playing her?

"Now Lindsey has decided to put himself into the discussion with the consortium after it had all been decided."

Annie cleared her throat around the lump that had formed there. "But Melbury Manor is part of his—whatever that thing is called—a demesne. Why wouldn't he think he should be part of the discussion?"

"And have you two talked about that?" Viola tilted her head to the side, a sly cast in her eyes. "Perhaps you have. Everyone in the village knows yesterday you and my brother went off together."

Annie dropped her hands into her lap. She didn't bother to respond to the verbal fastball Viola just lobbed at her head.

"My brother told me you and he spoke about the garden." Viola wagged a finger at Annie. "How clever of you, getting him to listen to your opinion on its placement."

Annie clenched her hands into two hard fists, the better to keep from reaching across the table, taking that finger of Viola's, and turning it around and jabbing it in her eye. "Charlie is good at listening."

Viola's light blue eyes widened. "Oh my. I had no idea."

"No idea of what?" Annie realized she was sweating.

"That you call my brother by his first name. No one does."

"Maybe somebody should. Maybe then people would think he's just like everyone else. You know. Normal."

Viola laughed. "What a quaint American concept."

Annie couldn't decide if she should be insulted. "Um, Viola. You wanted to talk about the luncheon. Can we? I need to get back to the restaurant." And someplace quiet where she could repair the heart she didn't think could have been wounded finding out Charlie had a fiancée. Or an almost fiancée. And finding out she'd been wrong about a man one more time.

Viola came to her feet, leaned her hands on the table and looked down at Annie, that odd, overly focused look back in her eyes. "It seems that Lindsey has developed an interest in you. Quite a strong one, actually."

"It's just business between us." Annie leaned away, her spine hard against the back of her chair.

"If it is just business," Viola said, "then I'm sure you understand that the consortium getting what it wants to develop Melbury Manor is just business as well."

A spurt of temper took Annie. "You asked me up here to talk about the garden, and the need you and George have to make it go away. It was never about the luncheon, was it? Please just say so."

The skin on her cheeks now all mottled, Viola leaned across the table. "Well, then. Yes, I will say it straight out. I'd like you to speak to Lindsey and tell him you've changed your mind. You don't want it to be put back where it was and that if he wants to move the garden, it will be all right with you."

Annie's head was spinning. "I don't want to tell him that."

"You said you would think about it. The other night at the restaurant. When we spoke." She huffed a sharp breath.

That breath told Annie everything she needed to know. Viola had been drinking. "I know what I said. I did think about I and this is what I've decided."

Viola bit her lip. Again. "There's the other matter."

Annie couldn't spend one more moment sticking around to hear about *the other matter*. The legs of the chair she'd been sitting in made a harsh, scraping sound against the linoleum, as she shoved it with the backs of her knees and took a step toward the hallway. "I need to go."

Viola reached out and snagged Annie's wrist. "Don't you want to know what it is?"

Annie wrenched her wrist out of Viola's grasp. Her heart began to thud with growing anxiety. "No, I don't."

"My brother doesn't say so"—she came right behind Annie—"but he has never warmed to my husband."

And they were back to the matter of George. If what Viola said was true, for that, if for nothing else, Annie was going to have to give Charlie five gold stars. She swallowed a nervous laugh. "Oh?"

"George has nothing."

Annie stumbled on a raised corner of the linoleum flooring. Viola pulled on the back of her shirt. "He has not one acre remaining of the Swynford lands in Lincolnshire. The town-house in London has been gone since his father's time."

Annie yanked her shirt out of Viola's grasp. "Nothing I say to your brother will gain George a single one of those acres or do anything to get the family's townhouse back."

Viola shook her head. "Lindsey thinks letting us live in Melbury Manor will be enough. But it's not and it's why George has spent so much energy investigating what's to be done here. If Lindsey decides against the consortium, or worse, refuses to break the entail, we will be—"

"Don't tell me." Annie was at a movie. No, she was *in* a movie. Thriller or horror. Maybe both. The only thing missing was the popcorn.

"The Swynfords were once one of the first families of Lincolnshire. If Lindsey doesn't break the entail, we'll never be anything but beggars. George's pride will be destroyed."

Annie tried to open the door. Viola put her palm against it to keep it shut. "My brother was entirely caught up in his business until he sold it. He spent many years thinking only of himself. Now is the time for him to think beyond himself. To us."

Annie yanked on the doorknob. No avail.

"Lindsey is attracted to you. For the moment. You can help my family. You can help secure my future."

Finally Viola let go and stepped back. Annie jerked on the handle to swing the door open and took a grateful step outside. Turning around, her heart beating a fast tattoo, she stared at Viola, whose hands were clasped together at her chest.

"I can't do that."

"Yes, you can. It will show you to be a person of kindness and generosity. Don't you want to be thought of that way?" She gave Annie a little-girl smile. "And really, since you'll be doing our luncheon, how much more will it take?"

As Annie reached the safety of her kitchen and calmed down enough that the blood rushing through her brain didn't threaten to flood out her gray matter, she realized how desperate Viola must have been—as well as drunk—to ask that she go to bat for George so he could feel good about himself. If she'd disliked George before, she hated him now. And Viola scared her.

But Viola had done a lot more than bother her. She'd made Annie feel guilty. Viola was a silly, sad woman. Every once in a while when Annie had seen Viola with George, she got a vibe that Viola was uncomfortable with him, maybe even scared. Could it be that he was abusive? If Annie didn't agree to let the garden be moved, would George take it out on Viola?

She'd made her deal with George to locate the garden on Melbury Manor land to help the children of Bisby. She snorted a humorless laugh, thinking about Joe, Cindy, and Michael, the sous chef at Carne, who always needed to borrow money and how she gave it to him. Was she destined to be caught doing the right thing and then finding out she'd done it wrong? Once more was she going to be in trouble for trying to help out?

Annie didn't want to take on more guilt. Didn't she have enough? True, Viola's needs were not the same as Michael's had been. Carne was not Bisby. Joe and Cindy were in her past. Annie looked down at her right hand and the scar that ran from the heel of her palm to her index finger. It hurt more than usual today.

But still. Her foolish personal angst—and equally foolish guilt—were going to impact the children of Bisby. She was being used as an upper-class family football, all because of a community garden and the deal she made with George to have it in a place it had no business being in. She should have known. Talk about unintended consequences… Who knew a plot of land could have the makings of such a soap opera?

148

about unintended consequences… Who knew a plot of land could have the makings of such a soap opera?

CHAPTER NINE

She waited for Charlie on the path to the Manor. He was on his way back from London. He'd texted her.

I want to talk about the garden after all. Meet me in front.

And she was there, waiting. And imagining. She could see it, him driving up, getting out of his rich man's car and with deceptively kind eyes and a comforting hand on her shoulder telling her why—so sorry but he had to do it—he'd changed his mind. Really, darling—he'd call her *darling* in that so snobby upper-class way—*what will happen if your garden is somewhere else? You'll still be able to grow your wonderful vegetables.*

And then he'd tell her how much he loved the concept they'd come up with for Bisby. He'd put her in touch with some of his people, who would work on it with her, if she still wanted to do that. Then he'd pull out his cell phone and look at a text that he said he had to read. He'd laugh gently and say what a brilliant chef she was, and it had been such a pleasure. He was going to give Samantha a ring tonight. As he said it, his black eyes would sparkle with happiness.

She shivered. The damn cold today. She hadn't thought when she'd gotten his text that she'd need a sweater to walk a few hundred feet. She'd come out in one of her long skirts and skinny t-shirts, perfect for working in the kitchen, not so perfect for being outside in the late March weather. She looked up at the lowering sky. It was going to rain. She hoped Charlie would arrive before it did.

She was toeing a clump of dirt when she heard the serious grumble that signaled his arrival. The Jag coasted to a stop in the lane in front of her. The wind blew up and raised goose bumps on her exposed arms. She should have insisted they meet somewhere warmer.

He was already smiling. As he stepped out of the car and across the road, she took a step back and tripped on the clump of dirt she'd been playing with.

"Be careful!" He lunged to grab her before she could go over. The feel of his hand around her arm was almost too much to bear.

"I'm good," she said and backed away a step. Her feet sank into the loam. She tucked her hands into her armpits and hunched up in the cold.

Head cocked, his smile more watchful, Charlie said, "What's this look on your lovely face? I rather think I remember it from the first time we met."

"It's my resting bitch face."

"Oh?" Both eyebrows went up in tandem. "Am I about to be slapped?"

"I'll hold off on that."

He tramped into the dirt after her. "None of your usual jokes. What's wrong?"

"Nothing's wrong," she said and turned away.

He took her by the shoulders and gave her a gentle shake. "If I've learned nothing in this life, I've learned that when a woman says 'Nothing's wrong', there's something wrong. Out with it, please."

She wished she could feel the heat of his hands everywhere on her body, not just warming her through her flimsy shirt. But wishes were horses. All at once the angst of everything came boiling up. "Why won't you break the entail on Melbury Manor?"

He dropped those big hands from her shoulders. She felt their loss. "Why do you care about the ownership of a property that has been held by the dukes of Lindsey for the last many centuries?"

"Your sister called me up to the Manor for a little talk this morning. We spent quite the interesting few minutes, Your Grace." A hard breeze kicked up. "I got a lesson in how entails can make for some unhappy people."

His face closed up. "My name is Charlie. Did you forget?"

She looked down at the earth and toed a dead sprig of something that had been green and alive a few days before. When she picked her head up again, his back was to her. He stood, looking at the Manor, his hands on his hips.

"*Charlie*," she mouthed to savor the feel of his name on her lips and tongue, maybe for the last time because when he turned back to face her, that would be when he told her what the new plan was for the garden and the medieval village in Bisby. And then he'd walk away from her forever.

"Was George there when you were talking about the entail?" His tone was conversational.

"He wasn't. I met with Viola alone." Annie pretended an interest in dirt, which she kicked here and there as she walked away down one still-defined row.

"My sister never ceases to amaze me," Charlie said, coming up behind her. "She has not the first understanding of the family business. Yet she finds a need to discuss the entail."

Annie wanted to order him to back far away because she didn't know if she could take it, him being so near.

"I think it's time I told you something about myself."

Please don't she wanted to say. She remained mute.

"Viola and I grew up at Melbury Manor," he said. "My father was gone for great swaths of time, which was a good thing for my mother, Viola, and me. For the house, too. It saved a lot of bric-a-brac from being smashed against walls."

The wind gusted again, dirt swirling around, stinging Annie's legs. Annie looked down the path to where it curved to meet High Street's first buildings. She should start walking, get at least as far as the Strangling Duck before the skies opened up and before the torture of Charlie standing just behind her became too much to bear. But no. Her body seemed unable to do what her brain demanded, and she remained rooted in place.

"There was none of that silver-spoon business. After my grandfather died—my duke grandfather, not my sculptor grandfather—my father managed to gamble away all our very safe investments and the property that had been in the family for generations, sometimes centuries. If not for what was entailed, there would have been nothing left."

"Your sister told me enough," she said as the leaden skies let loose a steadier rain. Her feet sank farther into the garden's dirt. "You don't have to explain."

"Yes, I do."

She didn't want to know anything else personal about him. It would make it oh so much more painful when he launched into his so-long-farewells. She could withstand his presence if she didn't know about Charlie Camville growing up where his upper-class status didn't seem to have protected him—and his sister—in a sad, unstable home. She turned her back to the wind and the rain. Needle-like drops fell faster. She began to shiver in earnest. "I need to go. Can we talk some other time?"

As in never?

She could hear a zipper gliding down and the sound of his jacket slipping off his shoulders. Before she could say no, he'd come around to face her and draped the jacket around her shoulders. He fisted his hands over the zippered opening to draw it tighter around her.

It dwarfed her as only a jacket that belonged to a man who dwarfed her could. She closed her eyes against the retained heat of his body and the citrusy scent of him that rose from the silken lining. She never wanted to give his jacket back. She wanted to hate him for tempting her to think that way. "Charlie, I can't do this."

"Can't what? Hear about what comes next? Or is it something else you can't do?" Charlie slipped his arm around her.

"Dammit, Charlie!" She tried to pull away. He responded by dragging her closer.

"When I left home for school," he said in her ear as the rain came down harder, "Viola was alone with our mother. Suffice it to say my mother, the lovely Lady Jocelyn, was hardly a warm and loving parent.

She wanted her children to be raised by someone else."

"Well, hooray that you didn't have to put up with that. Too bad your sister did."

"Viola never got over that. I rather think she never will."

The rain began to come down in a torrent. Charlie's jacket was doing a fine job of keeping Annie's upper body from getting any wetter. But her hair was soaked through. Drips of water snaked down the back of her neck. And he, with nothing but his shirt and jeans, was drenched to the skin. She stuck a hand out of the jacket and grabbed his. She didn't want to want him. She didn't want him to get sick either. "Let's go."

The skies opened up. "Right then," he said. With the roar of the cloudburst all around them, Charlie dragged her the short way to the Jag and hauled open the door. She scrambled in her side as he rushed around the hood to the other. He started the engine and turned on the heater full blast. Annie shivered and her teeth clacked, cold as she didn't think she'd ever been in her life.

Charlie's slicked-back hair lay flat against his head. Rain drops stood out on his forehead. His t-shirt was so wet, he would have been better off not wearing one at all. The soaked cotton was plastered to his biceps and chest. His nipples stood out with the cold.

He reached into the back seat for a roll of paper towels and began to rip off sheet after sheet. "Here." He handed a sheaf of sheets to her. "Dry your face while I wipe down my upholstery."

There was something prosaic about a man having a roll of paper towels in the back of his fancy car so he could wipe down his upholstery when it rained. She smiled through her misery.

Shivering, he sopped up the wet, which had gone everywhere. She sighed and something gave. She reached for the paper towel roll and pressed a sheet of paper onto his face and over his hair. Rivulets of water zigzagged their way down his cheeks onto his sodden t-shirt. She tore off more toweling and, hesitating only a moment, leaned across the console and pressed the paper against his shirt and his chest and then the back of his neck. He stared at her, unblinking, his somber black eyes even blacker in the subdued light. "Thank you," he murmured.

They were too few inches apart. Abruptly she sat back and dropped the sodden paper in her hand to the floor where the rest lay in clumps. His jeans, up until moments ago a denim blue, had darkened to black. The waterlogged cloth glistened with the torrent that had soaked them through. "I think you're going to need way more than this paper to get everything dry," she said.

"Later." He engaged the gearshift and headed away from the Manor. The rain beat down on the windshield. "There's more to the story. We can't go on without my telling you."

She caught her breath. We? He was talking about going on? With what? "I don't understand."

"I find myself wanting you to understand."

And he pointed them north. The rain continued to fall, cold and lonely, on the windshield. The wipers pushed the downpour away. "I understand my sister's need to be safe and cared for. It's why she and George and the girls are here in Bisby."

He reached across the console and took Annie's hand in his and kept driving. "They'd been living in London." His other hand firm on the wheel, Charlie accelerated, leaving Bisby farther behind. "George had just lost his latest job. They found out their landlord was about to raise their rent. They couldn't afford it. My sister came to me, asking for help. I'd done it once before, having to come up with a few thousand to get them out of a hole George had dug himself into. This time I decided I didn't want to do that."

Charlie's one hand on the wheel was white at the knuckles. He accelerated. "My land manager here had just quit." He accelerated even more. "My sister and my nieces needed somewhere to live. I thought this would be a position my brother-in-law could fill."

Annie let the implication lay there.

"They moved in. I gave Viola the funds to restore the dining room." He glanced across at Annie again and pressed his lips together. "Then she asked me if I would break the entail." He slowed. "I knew where that question came from. I asked her how she thought George was going to pay the duchy for his purchase of Melbury Manor."

Annie tilted her head toward him. "Couldn't you have given it to them?"

"I could. I wanted to. And I would have. Until George came to me with this consortium nonsense. That put a different twist on things. My experience with George tells me he leaps before he thinks. If I didn't look at it closely myself, I was afraid he wouldn't read the fine print and, unknowing, give away control of Melbury Manor altogether."

The rain let up. Charlie slowed as they came into the town of Market Rasen, rolled across the cobblestoned town square, and up to the Aston Arms pub. He came to a halt in front and turned to Annie. "I cannot trust anymore that George who should, will keep my sister safe. I won't give up the entail to him."

Charlie turned the engine off. In the intimacy of the car, Annie imagined she could hear the drip, drip of water leaching out of Charlie's jeans and her skirt. But the heater had taken care of that.

No. The sound was not water but her heart.

How had she not seen it? The caring, the love for a sister who Annie had misread completely. She might be more than a little snobby upper-class. Or weak. She might be firmly under her husband's thumb. Or a daytime tippler. But she needed taking care of. And she, Annie, knew how important it was to take care of people who couldn't take care of themselves. Charlie was doing what he needed to keep his sister—and her children—safe.

What did that make him? That Annie also knew. He was more than the most desirable man she'd ever known. He was more than she'd thought him before, more that warmed her in ways the heater didn't. If she didn't know better, which she'd been telling herself all along she ought to, she thought she might have at last and irrevocably fallen in love. It made her want to cry.

"Are you cold?" Charlie asked, reaching for the heater knob to turn it up another notch. She'd gone pale. It was the story, of course. It would turn anyone pale. It did him every time he thought of Vi and the girls stuck with George, that bastard.

Annie's smile didn't quite reach her eyes. "No, I'm good."

He gave her a long look before turning them again toward Bisby. It was a wonder, what he'd just said. Shocking, really, when he never told anyone what it had been like growing up at Melbury Manor.

All the way back from London, he'd gone over every encounter between them and analyzed how he felt each time. He realized how much her face enchanted him, the way her emotions brightened her eyes, the way her lips quirked up in humor. Or down in disdain. Annie Lukin had no capacity to hide what she was thinking. She was so alive. She made him feel alive. When he'd kissed her, she'd molded her body to his. Her back arched, she'd pressed her voluptuous breasts against his chest. He wanted her.

She shifted in her seat. "What time is it?"

Tearing himself away from his side excursion into desire, he looked at his watch. "Oh, right. I need to get you back to Bisby to the restaurant."

She was silent as they swung onto East Wold Road. He glanced at her. Her face always told all, but now there was no hint. He didn't like it. He wasn't having it. "I wanted to meet at the garden to tell you what I've decided. I need to stay in the area for a few days." Which was the excuse he'd offer her.

"Oh yes?" She stirred. "Why?"

"It's been a long time since I've been out and about in the county. I'd intended to take a bit of a ride, perhaps tomorrow. I thought you might come along. Your presence, I feel quite sure, would ease the way for me."

"Me? Ease the way for a duke?" Eyes fixed on the road in front of him, he felt rather than saw the surprise on her face.

"Why not? You're the celebrity. You're the businessperson of note."

"Oh, please, Your Majesty," She made a dismissive sound. "You're the big kahuna around here."

It was true. In Lincolnshire his position was firmly established. Denying it to her was his way of teasing her out of the black mood she'd sunk into. He'd succeeded. The color had returned to her face. But there was still a look of distraction in her eyes. If he were any kind of judge of these things, Annie wouldn't be happy until she spoke about what was on her mind.

"Are you still thinking of the latest bit of business? With Viola?"

At first he thought she might withdraw again. But then, "Not really anymore." She sighed. "Your sister called me up to the Manor to discuss the luncheon she wanted me to do for her Wednesday afternoon."

"And your feelings about serving that luncheon are…?"

"Confused."

"I wouldn't be surprised after everything you've heard from me and everything she said about the garden, if you decided to back away."

She gave him that look he was becoming used to, a look he delighted in. "I said I was confused, not crazy. You think because I had a weird encounter with Viola that I'd walk away from a piece of business that would net me a nice chunk of change and give my people some extra money for the week? Good Lord, Your Majesty. If I did, I would legit be a fool."

"Weird encounter?"

"I thought it was, then." She paused and then rubbed a thumb against the palm of her other hand.

"But after what you've just told me? Not so much. I think it's important for me to support Viola."

"Even if there might not be a consortium to prepare a luncheon for?"

She sighed again. "I suppose."

"That's honorable of you," he said. And so like her. Changing her mind about Viola and deciding to treat her with kindness. There was no woman—no person—of his acquaintance who would do that.

"You're not telling me everything, are you, Annie? There's more you and Viola spoke of, isn't there?"

"She was upset. She said things."

"If it concerns something I've done to disturb you, I want to know what it is."

She kept still. Even her hands were still. She took a deep breath. "Are you and Samantha engaged?"

With a twinge of annoyance, he said, "Where did you hear that rot?"

She laughed, a short, brittle sound. "You just asked me to tell you what Viola said didn't you? So I'm telling you." She snapped the seat belt across her body. "She was warning me off. As in she was afraid I might not know you're taken."

"No, Annie. I am not taken, as you so quaintly put it. And to keep you from wondering, I don't plan to be taken. At least not by Samantha."

She squeezed her eyes shut as if she were in pain. "I guess that means I'm going to do it then."

"Do what?"

"Tell you what's on my mind." She took his left hand in hers and gripped it hard, startling him. "I want to have you, Charlie."

CHAPTER TEN

Annie could tell she'd shocked the hell out of him. Who said things like that? She blamed it on the windshield wipers that he'd set on intermittent. They'd spoken to her. *Have him.* Pause. *Have him.* Pause. *Have him.*

"Sorry. What did you say?" His right hand spasmed on the Jag's wheel.

There was no sorry about it. There was no sorry about him. His hair was all messy, the curls atop his head now dry. His t-shirt, though, was still wet and it stuck to his skin. There was no disguising the cut of the muscles beneath that shirt. Or his taut waist, or how narrow were his hips beneath his still-wet jeans. There was no disguising, either, what had become visible between his legs.

Eyes on that part of his anatomy, she said, "I want you."

"That's twice you've said it, proving I'm not hearing things."

"Your ears are working just fine."

"I certainly hope you didn't share this bit with my sister."

"Get real."

Charlie took his hand from hers and placed it with the other on the wheel. "Perhaps you could explain." He drove, paying minute attention to the road and its curves, making sure to keep them headed steady on while his thoughts were the furthest from steady. "We Brits can be a bit lacking in the direct-speech department."

"Charlie." She said his name like a caress. "Stop the aw-shucks modesty. You know you're a hottie."

He cracked a laugh. "Of all the names you've called me, I believe I may like this one better than the rest."

"I like it, too." She held up a staying hand. "But it's not so much how you look, so don't congratulate yourself just yet. Even if you're about as gorgeous as a man has a right to be, you should know that some hotties have turned out to be serial killers."

He wanted to howl. She made compliments into insults that were compliments. She was the best entertainment he believed he'd ever had, and her words, words no one had ever said to him, had him wanting to punch the gas pedal to the floor to feel power and exhilaration and euphoria. "Oho! Then I don't know that I like it at all."

"Do I really have to tell you everything about you is hot? Your eyes. I love the way they snap and smile and sometimes get all angry and arrogant. Or wanting."

"Good Lord. I don't think anyone has ever described my eyes in such detail. I believe I'll have to study them in a mirror the first moment I can."

"It's your hair, too. All those curls. I want to run my hands through them, keep them messed up like they are now."

"I'll throw away my brushes if that would make you happy." It was getting hard to speak.

"Before, in the garden, when you held me, I felt cocooned and safe. You're so strong. You have such muscles. I wished I could have run my hands over all of them. And you're hot, as in heat hot. Your skin is like a wonderful furnace."

He sat straighter. His jeans seemed to be shrinking.

"Back at my apartment—" now she was whispering— "when you kissed me, I wanted to run my tongue over your lips and even over your teeth."

He gritted his.

"And I wanted to do—well, I wasn't sure how you'd react if I reached down and put my hand on— you know, if it would be too nervy for me to—"

"My dear girl. You can call it by its name. And nothing should have stopped you, if that was your intention." He spoke much louder than necessary.

When she put her hand on his thigh, he heaved himself back against the door and the car swerved toward the center of the lane before coming back around straight. He muttered beneath his breath. He was within seconds of wasting a perfectly good ejaculation in his knickers.

"Whoa!" She snatched her hand away from his thigh. "Do you need to take a safe driving course?"

"Fancy you talking about safety after dropping all those bombshells about me and placing your lovely hand on my person in a way that gives me ideas of what you should do with that hand." He breathed deep to steady himself.

"Maybe you should pull over and let me drive. I'd like to get back to Bisby in one piece."

"Sod it, Annie. My zipper is threatening to rip itself apart and you're talking about taking this wheel? Not knowing—since you don't have a car—what kind of a driver you are, I will not let you take the wheel of this beast. In fact, it will be a cold day in the nether regions when someone besides yours truly will." When he knew he could speak in a normal tone, he added, "What brought this on?"

"That kiss in my apartment." She folded her hands in her lap. "And…"

"And what?"

She huffed a breath. "Just concentrate on the kiss."

"That kiss in your flat was a lifetime ago. If you wanted me then, you could have had me there on your bed. I wouldn't have minded that it was unmade or that it might have collapsed under us."

"I couldn't tell you then. I didn't know about you."

"A cryptic remark, that." The clouds in the sky made it seem like dusk was approaching. He slowed as they came upon a convenient hard shoulder. Easing onto it, he brought the Jag to a stop and threw the gear stick into park, letting the engine idle.

In the short time Charlie had been acquainted with Annie, he'd noticed she had a habit of rubbing the thumb of one hand against the palm of the other when she was nervous. She was doing it again. "I knew the moment you walked—rather, rushed—into my office."

Her head came up, and she stared at him, eyes narrowed. "Knew what?"

"At first it was what you were wearing." He cupped her chin, pressing his fingers against her cheekbone. Her eyelids flickered downward. "The skirt and how it flowed, allowing me a peek at your lovely legs. And your not-quite-so-lovely but in their way charming combat boots."

Her eyes snapped open. "I'd put them on to work in the garden. When I saw what had been done, I was so mad I forgot to change them before I got onto the train."

He dropped his hand to her breast and cupped it as he had her chin, pressing his thumb against her nipple. It grew to a hard point. She gasped.

"I most especially liked the blouse you wore that just covered the lovely black lacy bra that I wanted to see more of. And what was beneath."

He reached up to smooth his fingers over her tightly bound hair. Leaning toward her, he placed tiny kisses on her mouth. "But what I liked best was your face." He kissed her again, harder this time, his hand on her shoulder to steady her, the other at her breast, smoothing his hand over it, around it, lingering at her nipple. "I liked your eyes." Another kiss. "The way they spewed fire and brimstone at me." Another kiss. "And your mouth." Another kiss, just there. "How you called me Your Majesty and Your Highness and Your Holiness." He cupped her breast another moment. His mouth hovered a breath from hers. "Only your mouth wasn't meant for all that. It was meant for this." And he kissed her with a mouth that was open…wet…and hot.

Her breath, mingling with his, came in sharp puffs. He drew back an inch and dropped a kiss on the corner of her mouth. "What I liked was what was between us. Something of an understanding, which I thought odd since we were strangers. The Italian part of my family calls it simpatico. I call it something else. I—"

"Stop. You don't have to talk it to death." She drew back a fraction, breath increasingly uneven. "I said I wanted you. We can get to it tonight. Only it has to be after service."

"After service." He laughed. "So unromantic." He tried to find a comfortable way to sit. Knowing it wasn't going to happen, at least until *after service*, he flicked a glance at the road where a lorry was passing. "I've got a room at a charming hotel in Lincoln close to the Cathedral."

"What? You're not staying with your sister? And George?'

He tutted and touched his fingers to her mouth, just where it had turned up in one of her wicked half smiles. "Said with such innocence. No, indeed. I didn't stay there over the weekend. Nor will I, now. I like my privacy too much for that. And my comfort. Unlike Melbury Manor, my hotel has got an en-suite bath. And a king-size bed. Big enough for me. And you." He gave her a long, slow kiss. "After the last diners leave The Ocular this evening, sated from all your wonderful food, I'll pick you up and take you to my hotel. And we'll sate each other. Not with food, however."

She ran her tongue back and forth over her bottom lip. The short hairs on the back of his neck stood to attention. In spite of it being frustratingly awkward, he reached across the console, gear stick and all, and took her in his arms. Winding both around her shoulders, he twisted one hand in her braid, still wet, and wrapped it around his hand. He drew her face toward his and brought his mouth close to hers. "May I assume from your non-verbal signal that you have no objection to my hotel room?"

And then he kissed her again. It was a full-out melding of his mouth to hers, of their mouths open to each other, as if he needed her to understand that this kiss was not so much about a precursor to coitus—although it was that—but possession.

He straightened away from her and stared down into her eyes. He wanted to tell her how much being with her meant to him. He would have if she hadn't shut him up. *I call it something else.* Later, tonight, then. It would be time.

Her lips were wet and her eyes slumberous, as if they'd just made love. She reached up and laid her palm against his cheek. He took her fingers and repositioned them against his mouth and then into his mouth, and sucked.

In a thready voice she said, "You can make that assumption. And yes, I'll go with you. But remember. Not before midnight or twelve-thirty."

He began to smile and reach for her again. But she held him off. You don't need to come in to get me. I'll come out when I'm finished." She paused and added, her voice strengthening, "Drive on, Jeeves and while we're talking about it, another thing. Make sure you park your classy car somewhere other than in front of my restaurant. I don't need the people of Bisby thinking I've gone to the Dark Side."

That one startled him into laughing without restraint. As he knew his heart and lungs were keeping him alive, he knew he needed the gypsy girl in his life.

***

"Earth to Annie!"

Annie blinked and looked up from filleting the bass Arthur Horncastle had brought her straight from the Humber early this morning, to see Lynette, arms folded, a little smile on her face, both eyebrows raised.

"Oh, sorry. I didn't see you."

"Or hear me, either. I've said your name oh, I don't know, three or four times." Lynette stepped into the kitchen. "What far distant planet did you go to? And speaking of being away, I was looking for you before. Where were you?"

"Taking your advice."

"Oh? What advice is that?"

Annie rolled her eyes. "The other day you encouraged me to go out and have fun with the man with all the names. That's what I was doing."

Lynette clapped her hands. "Brilliant."

"And I'm going to have him. Tonight."

Eyebrows snapping together, Lynette said, "Sorry? Have him... As in shag the man?" Annie huffed a laugh. "He's this amazing male who's not just good to look at, but good to kiss. And other things beyond kissing. Why shouldn't I have some of what I can tell you he's more than willing to offer?"

Lynette whistled. "I'm proud of you. And I'm proud of me for offering you such excellent advice." She crowded closer. "Now, do tell. How long do you plan on having what he's willing to offer? By that I mean will it be something—shall we say—long-lasting?"

Annie leaned back against the table and folded her arms across her chest. "Excuse me, but weren't you the one who said I shouldn't think beyond a date or two?"

"Well, yes I did. But is there such a thing as too much shagging?"

Annie couldn't imagine there'd ever be too much shagging when it came to Charlie. "I'll be spending the night with him. At his hotel in Lincoln."

Lynette crowed a laugh. "Brilliant!"

Annie bent to the fish she was filleting so Lynette couldn't tell by the look on her face how merely talking about the man affected her.

"Wait." Lynette knocked a fist against the prep table. Annie looked up.

With a canny smile on her face, Lynette said, "I get the feeling whatever you say is between you and your Charlie, you really would like it to be a bit more than spending a night or two in a hotel room with him."

"Why not?" Annie kept her voice steady. "He's hot. He's rich. He has a great sense of humor. It would be nice."

"Just nice? Is there some hallucinatory substance in the food you've been eating here? A man who's hot, rich, and has a great sense of humor is hard to find. I know because I've been looking for years and haven't found one. Good Lord, Annie. That doesn't sound nice. It sounds like perfection."

Annie hoisted the board she was filleting the fish on and set it in front of Davey, whose earbuds were blasting music loud enough she could hear it. She yelled, "Can you finish this for me?"

With unusual patience, Davey had been showing James how to make an agrodolce sauce for the bass. He nodded and took the board from Annie. She walked to the front of the restaurant and sat down at table two. Lynette followed. "We're too different."

"That's insane. He speaks English. You speak English…well sort of… He stands upright. You do as well. Where's the problem?"

"He's upper-class and all that goes along with that. I'm not."

"You're making too much of this class business, Annie. This is the twenty-first century. We Brits don't care about it that much. If you have differences—and what couple doesn't—why wouldn't the two of you talk and get on with it? I don't see the problem."

Lynette wouldn't see it because while their class differences were part of it, it was Carne Annie was beginning to think more and more of. Annie forced a laugh. "You wouldn't because you're too busy matchmaking up a storm. You want to have a best friend who's a duchess."

"Pray tell what's wrong with my thinking about that? Just imagine the doors that would open for me. I might start getting invited to posh parties in London at exclusive clubs. Or picnics by the Thames. I might get my picture in *Tatler*, smiling and standing next to some super rich prince from some country in Europe no one's ever heard of. Can't you see it? Me holding a flute of bubbly, and wearing a long, flowing dress and a pair of those stilty high heels?"

"Well, don't get too caught up in that fantasy if you're planning on me making it possible. I've got too much going on in my life here in Bisby, what with the restaurant and my people.

"You are being totally illogical, Annie, and I am out of sorts with you." Lynette got to her feet. "Everyone in the village remembers the old duke, that rotter. Upper-class your Charlie might have been born, but other than that, he's had to struggle like the rest of us. Think about that, if you will. Then tell me about differences." And she was gone.

Dinner came and went. Annie managed on automatic. She smiled and laughed her way through service, shook the occasional hand, and took a few reservations for birthdays and other celebrations coming up in the months ahead.

After her diners were gone, after everything in the front of the house was clean, after every surface in the kitchen was scrubbed, after all her staff left, she stood in her empty restaurant and wondered if she did decide to tell Charlie about Joe Barra, when she would do it, and how. Maybe she'd tell it like it was a big joke, how funny it was being accused of sleeping with the boss and then stealing money from his till.

For a moment, when Lynette had been talking about Charlie's father being the loser he was, she'd thought, yes, she could do it. She and Charlie had a struggle in common not of their own making.

She flexed her right hand. Parts of the tendon that knife had sliced into would never be the same. There'd always be pain to remind her of that part of her life, and to remind her she was on her own.

She put her hand on the doorknob and took a deep, preparatory breath. She damn well wasn't going to tell him tonight. Tonight was for her. Tonight she'd touch him wherever she wanted, in any way she wanted. She was going to be intoxicated by the feel of his body next to hers, covering hers, inside hers. What she wasn't going to do was tell him about the greatest shame of her life.

Stepping outside and locking up, she glanced down to her left and there he was coming toward her. In the light cast by a bright moon, he looked so inviting in his black leather jacket—the one he'd wrapped around her that afternoon. Her hair follicles heated in anticipation of him reaching her, of seeing his mouth curve up in his deceptively reserved smile, that mouth that later would do more than smile at her in his hotel room in Lincoln.

But when he'd almost reached her and she looked up into his face, she could see, in the light of the bright moon, he wasn't smiling. He wasn't looking at her, either, but beyond her. She turned to see what he was looking at. There they were: Bisby's trio of nosy retirees. They were always around but never before, she thought, in the middle of the night. Certainly not loitering in front of the doorway that led up to her apartment and the shocking pink door that was leaning like a drunk against the side of the building.

CHAPTER ELEVEN

Her breath caught in her throat. She darted toward the stairwell. Charlie blocked her way.

"No, Annie."

She began to pant. "Let me by!"

"Annie, sweetheart. Please." Charlie dragged her flush against his body, her back to his chest, and wound his free arm around her shoulders. "Gentlemen," he said over her head. "Did any of you see what happened? Has anyone called the constable?"

Retired postal worker, John Goodwin—who hadn't bothered to throw pants on over his pajama bottoms—raised his hand. "Yes, s-sire," John stuttered. "Er…Your lordship."

A wholly ridiculous bubble of hysteria rose to Annie's throat. It was twenty-first century Bisby. And

John looked like he was about to take a knee to the duke like a fourteenth century serf.

Harry Braithwaite, suspenders sagging off his shoulders, made a strange hissing sound. "He's Your Grace."

John's eyes got big. He skittered a glance at Annie. "I called the constable. Neil."

"That's Neil Duffin," Pete Watts spoke up.

"We was sleepin', all of us," John said. "Then we heard. 'Twas the noise. A right loud sound."

Was that the sound of her flimsy furniture being smashed to bits? "Let me go, Charlie," she gritted, unable to get the image out of her mind.

He tightened his hold and what a joke that was. She'd wanted to be in his arms not seconds ago. Just not like this.

"Go on, gentlemen," Charlie said.

With a vigorous nod, John said, "We don't expect it here in Bisby. And we come out to see and—" He pointed at the un-moored door. "We was thinking it was the wind."

"Gor blimey, John," Harry said. "Have you lost the plot?"

John drew himself up to his not inconsiderable height. "I heard it. You heard it as well, Harry." He turned to the other man. "You, too, Pete."

Pete shrugged. Harry, with his pot belly and low-slung trousers, stared, incredulous, at John. "Are you so blinkered you can't see somebody's done it on purpose?"

Annie's stomach clenched. On purpose, yes. But for what purpose? She began to struggle harder.

Charlie ran his hand up and down her arm and murmured, "There's nothing you can do now that won't hold until Neil gets here."

Annie laid her head down on Charlie's hard, muscled forearm. She was getting nauseous.

"In clipped tones Charlie said, "All right. How long ago did you hear this sound?"

The men began to argue among themselves, while Annie imagined one awful scenario after another. And then she imagined one even worse. "What about the restaurant?"

Charlie turned her in his arms and put his hands on her shoulders. "Didn't you just lock up? You know no one's in the restaurant."

"But there's a back door. Suppose they got in that way? Suppose they were just waiting for me to leave?" She swallowed convulsively. "Suppose while we're waiting for Neil, they're in there wrecking everything? I need to see." She reached into her pocket and took out the key.

Charlie snagged it. "I've got this." Striding the few feet over to the restaurant, not letting her get in front of him, he unlocked the door and stepped inside.

Doing her best to regulate her breathing, Annie stumbled in behind him. Charlie threw the light switches. The eleven tables sat unclothed and ready for their dressing up tomorrow. The vases, empty now of herbs, stood in rows on a sideboard. In the kitchen, all her knives were in their sleeves, all her pots lined up, the workstations bare, the doors to cabinets shut. Charlie went downstairs to check on the cooler and the storage room, and the three stooges—they'd trooped in, despite Charlie telling them to stay put—stood in the doorway and muttered.

"If anyone has been in here, which I doubt, they're not now." Charlie came up from below. "Let's close up. While Annie and I wait for Neil—" he pointed to the three Bisby-ites—"you may go."

Only no one went. There ensued a discussion of what kind of time lapse there could have been between when someone might've heard a sound and when they all came outside to stare at Annie's pink door. She listened, not caring. No one had gotten in. The worst hadn't happened. And she was no longer nauseous.

The stooges continued prophesying—like the Witches of Endor—what horror they'd find when Neil arrived and they could go upstairs. Charlie slung his arm across Annie's shoulders. "Don't listen to them. No doubt this is the most exciting thing they've had to talk about since we Brits beat Argentina in the Falkland War. Let's not worry until and if there's a reason to."

Through gritted teeth, Annie said, "What's the big deal about waiting for Neil?"

"You know what the big deal is. We wait."

"You didn't hesitate to go into the restaurant."

"The likelihood that someone was in the restaurant immediately after you left it was next to nil." He held up a hand. "Yes, yes. The back door. I didn't think. But it's done and in any case, your flat has one entrance." He pointed to the stairwell. "Our three friends may have come on the scene before the perpetrator could make his escape. He could still be up there."

Charlie's slightly mint-scented breath warmed Annie's face. "Here's what I think. Someone took the door off its hinges because they couldn't open the lock. Then they dropped it. They panicked. And they never went upstairs."

Charlie's jaw was set. "We're staying down here."

"For sure Neil was asleep when you called. It'll take him an hour to get here."

As if the god of mischief was laughing his ass off, Neil took that moment to pull up. He eased out of his well-used and long-driven Ford Fiesta in his slow and deliberate way. Once, when Neil had come with his wife to dine at The Ocular, he'd eaten his food that way, too.

He looked at the door and then at Annie. "Looks like someone's a mite cheesed off with you, Annie." He shook his head, bemused, and turned to Charlie. "Been a while, Your Lordship."

Harry made that hissing sound again.

Ignoring Harry, Charlie said, "We didn't go up. We knew we had to wait."

Neil nodded. To Annie, he said, "It's a good thing to wait for the constable."

Said as if he were Wyatt Earp. With his stick straight, Saxon-blond hair flopping over his forehead, his Manchester United tee and jeans, Neil looked as much like a constable as the three Endors looked like a trio of parliamentarians. She stepped into the stairwell. "I'm going up."

Charlie took her arm. "The order of things is *I* go first, and you come behind."

Neil held up a staying hand. "The order of things is *I* go first. By myself." His mouth widened in a sleepy smile, which did nothing to offset the steel in his up-to-that-point lazy blue eyes.

Charlie took a step back. Rank, Annie noted with a seed of satisfaction, did not always have its privileges.

Neil was only a moment. "All right," he called from above. "Come ahead."

Annie started up the stairs, but once again Charlie stepped in front of her. A buzz of frustration skated up her spine.

"You're getting on my nerves," she muttered as the others came behind her.

"I heard that," said Charlie, his voice floating back to her as he stepped into her apartment.

Annie was prepared to see things strewn about, drawers open, their contents pouring out, all the mail she'd piled on her alleged kitchen counter torn open and thrown on the floor, her chair and partially broken table completely broken, her mattress slashed into shreds and lying, like the pink door downstairs, tipped on its side propped up next to the bed's frame. She wasn't prepared for—nothing.

The room looked the same as when she'd left it earlier. Yes, a wreck, but a wreck she'd made.

The others crowded in, murmurs of "sorry" and one "pardon" from Charlie as they jostled each other in the tiny space. She moved her chair to the other side of her table to make a bit more room for everyone. "My furniture's intact."

Charlie put his hands in his front pockets. "Too bad."

"Can you check to see if you're missing anything, Annie?" Neil pointed at the table, its surface cluttered with things she never bothered to put away. "Your electronics, a laptop or some such, any other kinds of valuables?"

"I keep my laptop at the restaurant, and I don't have any other valuables."

Neil eased over to where her mail lay in a pile on the kitchen counter. "Could there be something in here? Perhaps someone mailed you money, someone else knew about it, and they've gone and nicked it. Will you look?"

"Nobody sends me money."

"Your Grace," John Pajama Bottoms sketched a bow of sorts. "Best we leave now. We'll set the door straight, then."

His fellow Endors nodded in agreement and left.

While Annie poked around, wondering if she could have missed something after all, Charlie and Neil proceeded to talk. They decided the vandal or vandals had kept their vandalism to the door and never made it up to Annie's apartment.

She listened to them with half an ear. Until she remembered the box that contained her carefully annotated records. It was in the drawer next to her sink. Once a month she sent a check to Sheryl Quatrone at the Cooking Institute. Then she fed her savings account for Brandon's procedure and Molly's dental work. After, she put the black lacquered box with the Chinese figures dancing across the lid back where it belonged.

With a quick glance at the two men who, continuing to speak, now ignored her altogether, she opened the drawer. The box was there. With one finger, she lifted the lid a fraction and breathed a sigh of relief. Her papers were as she'd left them, all wrapped up in a rubber band. She eased the drawer shut. It squeaked.

Conversation stopped.

"Find something missing, did you?"

Annie glanced up at Charlie. He stood there, waiting for her answer. As did Neil.

"Nope."

"Well, I'll write a report before I go home," Neil said with a look that said he knew a lie when he heard one.

"It's just a box," she said, trying not to sound defensive. She opened the drawer again and lifted the black box out. "You asked me if I had any valuables. It's not valuable. Just pretty. I wanted to make sure it was still here."

The smile back on his lips but not in his eyes Neil shook her hand. "If you need me, ring me up and I'll be back." He paused by the door and turned. "And Annie, if you find something missing from that pretty box of yours, you'll call me."

Annie knew better than to think that was a request. While she assured him she would, she felt Charlie's eyes on her. Once Neil left, the interrogation would start.

"What's in the box?"

Annie rubbed a hand across her stomach. The pain, which had subsided when she knew no one had gone into the restaurant, was back. "Nothing of value except to me."

"Then it's valuable, isn't it? Unlike the rest of what my poor eyes have to look at in this sad excuse for a flat."

She reached into the drawer and pulled out the box. She flipped it open. "See? Papers. Who's interested in papers?"

Eyebrow raised—again—he said, "Exactly. Who would be?"

She was so tired of being alternately ignored and then interrogated by first two and now one managing male. She put the box on the table, hard enough it clunked. "It's no one's business but mine."

"Your usual lovely answer."

Charlie thought from the way Annie kept rubbing her belly, she was in pain. Then when they'd stepped into her flat, knowing the restaurant was safe, and no one had come up to her living quarters, she seemed to feel more the thing and be back to her old self. Until she'd taken that box out. He didn't think it was *just* a pretty box.

She snorted. "Like I said."

He ignored her snappishness. "I'll let it go this time because at the moment I'm only interested in—and after this, doubly so—securing this room." He pointed toward the counter next to her fridge. "I notice you have a lock. As it's laying there amongst your papers, I assume you haven't made use of it, certainly not this evening. We'll make use of the lock now, as we're leaving. I'm taking you with me, as planned, to Lincoln."

She stiffened. "Is that an order, Your Lordship, Your Highness, Your Grace?"

For once Charlie was not entertained by her calling him pet names. "I prefer to think of it not as an order, but as an intelligent next step."

"Really? You've been giving so many orders, you'd have to pardon me for not recognizing it as"—she made air quotes—"an intelligent next step."

"What are you going on about, pray tell?"

"You and Neil. Even the Endors."

"Who are the Endors?" He ran a hand through his hair. What was this inexplicable fit of temper?

"The Endors, the three stooges. John and Harry and Pete." She whirled around and stepped up to him. Dark brown eyes flashed. The color was back in her face, too much of it in fact. "You think because you're who you are, you can just take over, don't you? Be the guy, the big man, Charles in Charge, the duke riding to the rescue of the poor little female, right? Well, I've got news for you, mister—Oh, sorry. Your Grace. The break-in was in *my* apartment. If there was damage, it would have been done to *my* things. Neil should have been talking to me! Not you!" She poked him in the chest.

"Ah, so that's it," he said, annoyed. "We're indulging in a bit of militant feminism, are we? This once couldn't we say that expediency is what's important? And just as a point of being altogether fair, if you wanted to be part of the conversation, you could have spoken up at any time."

"You think I was going to be able to horn in on the bromance between you and Neil?"

"Easily, my dear." A pulse of real temper washed over him. He kept a hard grip on it. She was in a fragile state in spite of her angry words. "From the first moment we met, there was never any question in my mind that you were able to take or wrest control of any situation or any conversation."

Into the silence that followed his sharp words, Annie's color went scarlet red. He closed his eyes and took a deep breath. "This is insane. What are we doing?" He laid his hands on her shoulders and gave her a gentle squeeze. "I shouldn't have said that. I'm sorry. I truly am. Will you forgive me?"

For a moment the look on her face made Charlie think the apocalypse had arrived and hell had come to earth. But then her shoulders slumped and she leaned her forehead against his chest. "There's nothing to forgive," she said, her voice muffled. "I'm the one who should be asking you to forgive me. I went off like a—I don't know—a rocket to the moon?" She turned her head, pressed her cheek against him, and wound her arms around his waist.

He took a deep breath to get his rioting pulse under control, and sleeked one hand across her scalp. Beneath her thick hair, her skin was hot.

"What is wrong with me?" she asked with a plaintive cry.

"You're in shock, darling."

She gazed up at him, a lost look in her eyes. "I don't like feeling like this. Not in control."

"It's okay," he murmured. "From time to time, even you must let someone else be strong for you. Me, for example. Which is why we're leaving. When we get to the hotel, you'll take a shower, get into a nightie, and we'll crawl into bed together. I'll hold you in my arms. The only thing you'll need to do is sleep and get strong again."

Annie's lashes fluttered and she gave way, a tiny smile lighting her eyes. "Going to your hotel; that was the plan, wasn't it? I don't need to bring much. Just let me grab my—" She reached down to pick up the nightgown that was tangled in the blanket on her bed. She flipped it back and gasped. There on her sheet in big, red, wavy letters was written *FORGET THE GARDEN BICH.*

CHAPTER TWELVE

She dropped the nightgown on the floor, stumbled backward, and began to laugh. "Boy, does the school system here suck. There's a T in bitch."

Charlie reached for her. She was bent over, caught in a fit of hysterical laughter. Laying his hand on her back, he stared at the monstrous message on her sheets and knew whoever had broken into her flat hadn't been after things. The goal had been to scare Annie. It succeeded. He would ring Neil to let him know. After he got her away.

Charlie urged her upright. There was a fine tremor running through her body. "Your garden has certainly gotten a lot of attention. Someone is willing to threaten violence to keep it from being restored."

"I know." She panted and swallowed. "All this is about a simple community garden. Don't you think it's a little over-the-top?"

What he thought was whoever had done this was going to pay. Whatever assets he had at his disposal—and that was a lot—would be Neil's without him having to ask. They would find the degenerate who did this. Whoever it was would be punished.

She continued to laugh. "Darling, let's go."

She didn't budge. "You have to give it to them. It's creative." She pointed at the sheets with one trembling finger. "They could have painted their charming message on the wall. But no. They looked around and thought, let's make this more interesting, although, now that I think of it, Charlie, maybe you did this? A ploy to make sure I'd come with you to Lincoln." Her voice had gone high and thin. The color had so leached from her face, her lips were dead white.

"Ah, Annie, that's daft." He reached for her, to hold her, to give her all the strength and comfort he could offer.

"I know, I know." She kept taking shallow sips of air. "I'm just being silly."

She seemed stuck to the floor. "Darling, we really need to leave. Come with me, please."

She pressed her face against his chest and muttered something.

"What are you saying?" He nudged her.

She lifted her face, now splotchy, one tear snaking its way down her cheek. "I don't have much luck with sheets. This is the second set I'm going to have to throw out."

He didn't ask what she meant. Rather, he stared into the depths and luminosity of her lush, dark brown eyes, dilated and black with shock. Hair that had come loose from her braid framed her face in wayward straggles. A new tear forged a crooked path down the other cheek. He patted it away.

She sniffed. "Who did this?"

Well she should wonder. "We don't know that yet, do we? We will."

Sighing, she stepped out of his arms, and began to move around in this place that was a mere step or two up from a hovel. She bent to pick up her nightgown and held it up to study it—he supposed it was to see if it, too, was marked with paint.

"I wonder if George did this," she said and stared down at her bed.

"Little as I think of the man, I'm quite sure George knows how to spell 'bitch.' And I don't think he would know how to remove the hinges from a door."

"But he could have hired someone."

"He could have, indeed. I still don't think it was George." George could be cunning, but he wasn't creative.

She made a sound he took as agreement, but otherwise remained silent.

He stared at her lacquered box and wondered what was in it. "Had you given any thought to purchasing a bigger table, perhaps even a better one? You know, so you would have room for more things?"

"This table works just fine." She continued to stare at the bed.

That response, if no other, told Charlie how out of it she was. She'd missed the irony in his voice.

"That's it," he said. "We're going now." He took her by the hand and pulled her back into his arms. He slid a hand underneath her braid to cup the back of her neck. He could feel the pulse there rioting as if it were Guy Fawkes Day. He swayed with her, hoping the motion would help her regain a measure of calm.

"Maybe I shouldn't. Maybe I should stay here."

"Now, that is truly daft. No."

She stirred in his arms. "I'd be okay with it."

"You would be? Have you changed your mind, then, about wanting me?"

She stiffened in his arms. "No, Your Majesty. I did not."

"That's good, then. There are six condoms all lined up, like little soldiers, on my night table, awaiting you with great impatience."

"Seriously I should stay here because of the break-in. I'm responsible for my things. I need to make sure nothing else happens and I can't do that if I'm gone."

"Oh, right. What was I thinking? Taken taekwando, have you? Your plan is to garb yourself in one of those pajama-looking outfits, set up a perimeter here, and defend it for the next twenty-four hours or so. Have I got that right? I'm assuming you've laid in a good supply of amphetamines. Annie, if you think I'm going to let you get away with that—"

She jerked her head back and looked up at him. Her eyebrows came together in the middle of her forehead. "There you go again, thinking you're Duke Charles in Charge." She planted one palm on his chest and pushed. "When are you going to figure out that I determine what I'm going to do with my time, not you?"

"Since right now, actually."

Annie should have been annoyed when Charlie got all high-handed and duke-ish with her but she was too wiped to challenge him further. She knew she couldn't stay in her apartment. Not with the door downstairs off its hinges. Even if she fastened the lock on the upstairs door—the lock she never used that was lying with her unopened mail on the counter—she'd feel the furthest thing from safe.

She'd never admit, especially to Charlie, that the stillness wouldn't comfort her as it usually did. The air would be ominous with the threat of what else might happen. Who might return.

And so she waited for him in his fancy car while he checked the restaurant, just to give her peace of mind, he said. He didn't bother to ask. He'd just taken the key from her.

He was back. Slamming the lid of the trunk shut, where he'd just stowed her bag—the one he'd packed for her. He came around to open his door and slide in next to her. "All ready?" He was way too chipper an Englishman at four a.m. and a fast-approaching dawn.

"I'm pretty sure you know I am." She locked her jaws to keep from yawning.

"Good point." He pressed the ignition button and eased off down High Street.

Breathing in the comforting smell of leather, Annie let herself be lulled by the hypnotic motion and comforting purr of Charlie's powerful beast of a car.

He was silent, and she was grateful to him for it. She knew without looking that he turned toward her every so often to make sure the slap of that message on her sheets hadn't gotten her totally unhinged. She tried to stay awake, but failed. When she opened her eyes, they were pulling up to his hotel, a block from Lincoln's majestic cathedral.

Once in the hotel room he was just as efficient unpacking as he had been packing. She watched him tuck the clothes she would wear tomorrow into the dresser and lay her nightgown on the bed.

Standing in the middle of the room, Annie swayed in place. Her eyes kept closing. It felt like all the salt in the North Sea had lodged inside them and was burning away whatever moisture there might be cushioning her tired corneas.   Glancing, through slitted eyes at the king-size bed, she felt as if it was calling her name.

"Why don't you have a wash, and I'll turn down the blankets," Charlie said. He gave her a gentle push toward the bathroom.

"There you are giving orders again." She trudged toward the bathroom.

"Things must be at a point nonplus if you're not calling me one of your pet names whilst sounding like an eight-year-old."

She would have called him one of those names, but not so much when what she wanted was to wash her face and her hands, and brush her teeth, as if doing that would wash away the memory of the message in red. When she was done, she shuffled toward the bed. Her knees met its edge, and she began to fall down into all its warmth.

"There you go again," he said and snagged her arm, pulling her around to stand in front of him before she could get prone. "Perhaps you'll sleep in that excuse of a bed in your flat, and in your clothing, but you're not doing that in my bed."

That brought her marginally awake. In a voice that sounded slurred, even in her own ears, she said, "Did you know I read a novel that took place right here in Lincoln during the Regency in a hotel room like this one. Or…maybe it was an inn?"

"No, I didn't know."

"You know what the Regency is, right? When it took place? Prinny. The early 1800s."

"Lovely history lesson, darling. Thank you." He pulled at the hem of her shirt. "Now, raise up."

"Why?" Her eyes were closed. She kept them that way.

"I'm going to take you out of your clothes, and no, not because I plan on having my way with you, as they said during the Regency. You need to be comfortable. Sleeping in your clothing won't do."

"Okay." She leaned forward and kissed what she could of him, which happened to be his chest. His t-shirt smelled all citrusy and of his Charlie maleness. Eyes barely open, she pointed at the armchair with its wide seat and thickly upholstered back. "You know, if you were like dukes in those Regency novels, you'd offer to sleep over there. Or maybe even the floor."

"Not bloody likely." He pulled the shirt over her head, her braid snagging in the label inside the collar.

As he freed her braid, her head started to spin. "I love those stories."

"Happy for you." He began to unravel her braid until the mass of her hair fell around her shoulders and down her back.

"Everyone thinks I came to Bisby for Ross."

"Didn't you?" He paused and then unsnapped her jeans. "May I?" He laid his hands on her jean's waistband.

Did she care that he was about to unclothe her lower body? She didn't think so, since she was wearing her one pair of very nice, very lacy white panties and she'd put them on for him. "No, it was because I loved the England of those books. It sounded so beautiful and peaceful. I loved the idea of peaceful. I really needed peaceful."

He eased the zipper down but then stopped. "And then you discovered the reality of life in England and how it's not the States."

"No, then I discovered it was better than I thought it would be. And I fell in love with Bisby." She kissed his chest again, settled her hands on his hips, and drew him closer. She peeped up at him beneath lids that were now almost too heavy to lift. "Can you tell me why they're always ladies?"

"Who?"

"In the books. I like that they're ladies. I try to imagine what it would have been like being a lady in 1820 in England."

"I think you can manage by yourself." He flattened his hand against her spine, his fingers pressing against her bra.

He didn't mean she could manage 1820. He meant she could unsnap the bra without help from him. "Charlie. Your Grace." She craned her head back and looked up at him but made no move to take off her bra. Her jeans hung open at her hips.

She didn't care what state her clothing was in. All she wanted to do was feast her eyes on his so beautiful face, his high cheekbones, his to-die-for black eyes, his half-smiling mouth. "You are such a gentleman, despite being a duke." She reached up to smooth her fingers across the back of his neck. "Just like in those books." She pulled his face down for a kiss. "And because you're a gentleman, and would have been a gentleman, do you know what the next thing would be you'd say?"

His smile faded, his so-serious black eyes bore into hers, all unblinking. "Why don't you tell me?"

"You'd say, I want you to be pure of body for your husband, who I would spoil you forever for should I have a lapse of judgment and give in to my baser instincts. Which is why, dear Lady Annie, I can't take a chance being in this bed with you for fear I'll do my worst in spite of my saintly intentions and end up taking your virginity."

"Are you a virgin?" He began to smile again, and one eyebrow cocked up, he crouched in front of her, at last sliding her jeans down her legs.

She stared down at his busy hands. "What are you smoking, Charlie? You know I'm not."

"All the more reason—" He grunted with the effort of getting her to lift her feet so he could slide her out of the jeans. "For me not to sleep on the floor. Or the chair."

On some dim level she realized how ridiculous she must sound, talking about an imaginary scene taking place in a time long past. It was like in the aftermath of the break-in, the door, and the writing on her sheets, whatever apparatus inside her that normally guarded her tongue from saying crazy things freed her to say whatever she wanted. Later she wouldn't be so bone-tired exhausted. Then, when she felt strong enough, when she didn't want more than anything in the world to be comforted by a pair of strong arms—Charlie's strong arms—she had a feeling she was going to blush recalling her unfiltered blabbering.

"Well, then." He stood.

"You're still supposed to be kneeling."

"I am?" A crooked smile played across his lips. "Why is that?" His gaze traveled from her face down to linger on her lace-covered bra and then at a leisurely pace down the rest of her body.

There was only the suggestion of a smile on his face now. The atmosphere in the room grew charged. His black-as-night eyes began to heat. He hesitated and then put a hand on her shoulder. Drawing her toward him, he placed a kiss on her forehead.

She closed her eyes at the feel of his lips against her skin, at the feel of his clothed body and hers, unclothed—except for her lacy white bra and lacy white panties. She pressed her lips against his t-shirt-covered chest. "What's with the mixed signals? First you give me that sexy look like you're about to jump me. And then you kiss me on the forehead."

He stepped back and pulled his shirt up and over his head, and she got an eyeful of hard, muscled perfection, a pelt of soft, springy black hair, and dark, erect nipples.

Throwing his shirt on the floor, he said, "My body and my brain are at odds. My body would very much like to have you. Standing, sitting, lying down in my bed. But my brain, whose counsel I try to favor whenever possible, tells me what you need is comfort, not me poking at you with my friend, John Thomas. That's why I'm going to visit the loo whilst you get into bed and pull the covers up to your chin." He kissed her, this time on the lips, this time with heat. But then he disappeared into the bathroom, closing the door behind him, denying her a chance with his nipples.

"Yowza," she mumbled. "That is some amazing washboard you've got there, Your Grace." It was just as amazing as his chest, all muscled pectorals. And those nipples. And that mat of soft black hair. For a man who'd made his gazillions sitting in front of a computer coming up with all kinds of e-tricks to prevent baddies from hacking into company servers and wreaking havoc with personal records, he looked more like he made a living running up and down a soccer field or a pitch or whatever they called the damn things.

Slipping off her bra she let it fall to the floor. Then, not bothering with her nightgown, she stumbled into the bed, and pulled the blankets up over her shoulders. She closed her eyes and snuggled deep into the covers. And was asleep.

***

Charlie was gone no longer than two minutes. Just long enough to strip out of all his clothes but his briefs, and then to brush his teeth. When he came out of the loo, there she was; sound asleep, on her back, in the middle of the bed. He watched her for a moment, watched the rise and fall of her beautiful breasts beneath the blanket.

It had been almost more than he could bear, undressing her. He'd had to recite Antony's speech to the Roman Senate from *Julius Caesar* to maintain even a shred of control. To touch her as he undressed her without giving in to what his raging body wanted him to do—bury himself in her so deep that he would be a continuation of her and she would be a continuation of him—proved he had incredible willpower. For which, if life were fair, he would have earned free entry to heaven.

For one moment, he weakened and thought about waking her. But that would have been cruel. She was exhausted, both physically and emotionally. He didn't believe in torture. More than he needed to be inside her—and that was a lot—she needed to sleep. He could wait.

CHAPTER THIRTEEN

Later, something woke him. He picked up his head. Eyes opened to mere slits, he studied the light coming in through the gap in the drapes. He snaked one hand out from under the covers and picked up his mobile. 8:30. He deposited it back on the table with a *snick* and turned on his side toward the woman in his bed.

She was faced away, knees drawn up, the riot of her hair pouring onto the pillow and down her back. He eased across the bed to close the gap between them. Gently, not wanting to wake her—at least not yet—he hesitated only a fraction of a moment before he did what he'd been wanting to do: touch her hair, feel, let himself be lost in its texture and glory. He wound one curl around a finger, then unwound it. Did it again. He sighed. His fantasy fulfilled.

The blanket and sheets had slipped halfway down her back. He feasted on the sight of her, of how her skin beneath her hair glowed pale in the morning light. He lifted his arm over her slight body, over her seemingly fragile—because fragile was the last word he would use to describe Annie Lukin—ribcage and flattened his palm across her belly underneath her generous breasts. His groin tightened. He reminded himself that she needed this sleep. Never would she admit she'd gone through trauma last night, but she had. Which was why *he* should wait. Which was the message he sent downstairs, where the message was not well received.

He spread his fingers so they spanned her middle from beneath her breasts to her navel where just beneath her silky, smooth skin, her life's blood coursed through veins and arteries and warmed the palm of his hand. He pulled her back toward him, his chest and belly hugging the march of her spine from her shoulders to her bum, and buried his nose in her hair, which smelled faintly of nutmeg and chocolate. He closed his eyes. If he hadn't known it before, he knew it now. She was a woman one savored. She made a little sound. He froze, held his breath, only letting it go when she sank back into sleep.

He risked moving his hand upward a fraction, to lodge under the slope of her left breast, where the skin was hot and damp. He flexed his knuckles against its soft weight. He breathed quietly, absorbing the feel of her. Beneath the blanket, his briefs grew tight. He inched backward. This was not how he'd imagined their first time together. With one of them awake, the other sleeping. He could wait.

That was what he told himself again.

Until she pushed her bum, with the sheer panties just covering it, back into his groin. Like it had been called to action, his cock sprang to full attention. He told himself to ignore the creature, to treat it like the insensate animal it was. But he couldn't. Not when he couldn't keep reasoning with himself over what was beyond reason. He was a sodding ass; that's what he was. She was in his arms, and he wanted her. He gave up.

He turned her, and she came around onto her side. She slipped her arms around his waist and pressed herself against him, breast to belly. She pushed a leg in between his, her thigh up against his now fully aroused privates. Her nipples made little indentations in his chest. She rubbed her nose against the hollow of his throat. The heat of her breath sent rolling waves of lust to all the extremities of his body.

He ran his hand down her slender back to her lovely round cheeks and cupped first one and then the other. Touching her, the tips of his fingers pressing into her warm flesh sent even more shock waves through him. He shifted her onto her back; once more, he buried his nose in her riotous curls.

Into the silence of the dark room—broken by the occasional street sound, a lorry shifting gears, a muffled loudspeaker announcement, a tour group leader calling her foreign-born chicks to her, perhaps—Charlie lifted his head. Listening to the sound of his own harsh breathing, he reached under the sumptuous fall of her hair and cupped the smooth slope of her shoulder.

It was a gradual thing, realizing she was now fully awakened. It was, perhaps, the way she seemed no longer boneless. Or the fact that now, in addition to the sound of his own breathing, he could hear hers.

"I never thought I would do something like this, even as much as I wanted to," she said in a voice husky with sleep.

He lengthened his caress, his hand sweeping from her shoulder, down across her arm to her hip, lingering there, and then back up again. "What do you mean, darling?"

"Be in bed with a man I've known less than a week. What does that say about me?"

"How discerning you are?"

She shifted and stared up at him, eyes luminous in the semi-dark. "I so enjoy looking at you."

He smoothed his hand across her scalp and tangled his fingers in her hair. "We're shortly to be joined in the most intimate of ways. I hope you're going to want to do more than look at me."

She didn't smile at his poor attempt at levity. "There's something about you that draws me to you. You're at the center of a whirlpool, and I'm caught in your current." She pressed her mouth to the side of his throat, and against his skin she whispered,

"Nothing seems to be able to stop me from drowning in you."

His heart surged. It was as true for him as it was for her. From the beginning he'd been in over his head. "Well, then," he said and reached for a condom to place it on the pillow between them. "I think one of us should wear diving equipment. So I can save you, that will be me."

Annie could feel his penis, ramrod hard, digging into her belly. "I'm tired of resisting you, Your Majesty."

He hovered over her, his black hair mussed with sleep and all over his forehead, his mouth in a strained smile, his eyes shining with heat. "Now I understand. You've been calling me Your Majesty because it's code. You really want to call me your lord and master."

She lifted one hand to the nape of his neck and pulled him down so his mouth barely touched hers. Against his lips she said, "If that's what you want to think, buster, knock yourself out." She lifted her head a fraction to run her tongue over his bottom lip. "Just make sure you satisfy me first."

His gaze flickered from her eyes to her nose to her mouth. He angled his head to the side and brought his lips to hers in a scalding kiss. She met him tongue to tongue. Winding her arms around his shoulders, she drew him over her so they touched everywhere. The heated weight, the tensile strength of his muscles, of him, held her in the welcoming cage of his arms.

She shifted her legs to bring his body closer to where it mattered most. She lifted one leg over his hip to pull him in. He stared down at her. "I'd like us to take our time about this, at least for now. But that's not what you want, right?"

The back of her hand against his cheek, she ran her fingers from the crest of his high cheekbone to his firm jaw. "In addition to being to-die-for gorgeous, you're perceptive."

He grimaced through heightened breathing. "Shall we save it for next round?"

"I can go along with that." She rubbed herself against him. Hearing him gasp, she knew he was as affected as she. She pulsed in her belly and her breasts, in the hollowness of her, knowing the only way to make the hollowness go away was for him to fill it, the sooner so much the better.

She captured his mouth with hers. Fumbling for one of his hands she pressed it to her breast. The feel of his palm against her nipple, circling and circling, the exquisite pain of it shot directly to where she was wet and beyond wanting. "Oh, Charlie," she squeaked. "You said we wouldn't take our time."

"I did say that." He breathed the words against her skin, tangling a hand in her hair. "I changed my mind."

She panted and took hold of his hand, sliding it down her body.

"Darling, do you mind?" He squeezed her fingers and eased out of her grip. "I know you like to take charge, but really, I promise. I know what to do."

To prove his point, he slid his hand beneath her silky, sheer panties, all the while kissing her with plunging tongue and open mouth. She arched against him. "Oh, that's so, so good," she groaned. "Don't stop. Keep going." She widened her legs farther.

"Right." He pressed against her cleft, and then eased first one finger and then two into her most private passage. She shuddered on deep intakes of breath. She lashed both arms around his shoulders. Palms flat, she caressed his back, the skin there grown hot and sweaty over flexing muscles. With his fingers working their magic and his palm just where she needed it to be, shock waves sped out from her center. His fingers kept up their relentless rhythm. Until he shifted their bodies so they lay side to side.

"No," she moaned, as he took his hand out of her panties.

He breathed a chuckle. "Patience is a virtue. Don't they teach that to you in the States?"

"What they teach you in the States is the early bird gets the worm." She reached down and wound her fingers around his penis. "Although this is way more than a worm."

"Thank you for that compliment," he said, seeming to have trouble forming the words.

Through breaths that were coming fast and faster, she said, "Get back to what you were doing, please. With your hand." She arched up her pelvis.

"I would, but apparently you weren't taught the proper way to get undressed." He got busy skimming her now entirely wet panties down her legs. He disposed of them and of his briefs, throwing the blankets back as he did. "Now we can take care of matters."

She heard the rip of the condom packet and him sheathing himself. One part of her wanted to help. The other part cared not at all about helping, only what was going to happen once he was suited up.

Unrestrained by the hindrance of her panties, he once more slid his hand between her legs. He ran his fingers up and down her slick, plumped-up flesh. She moaned.

"Now, Annie. Now." And he sprang above her. She felt the head of his penis at her opening. Her breath caught as he began to ease his way inside. First, just entering. And then withdrawing. And then again, entering more. And then withdrawing again. She wound her legs around his waist, trying to force him to stop playing with her.

"I want to make you come, Annie," he said through gritted teeth, "Like you've never come before and like you'll only come for me." Slowly he slid in, filling her until all her spaces were tight with him and she was whole.

She felt his heart thud against her breast bone. Hers beat in time with his. He wound an arm around her shoulders and clamped his hand around her upper arm. He began to move as if on the slow ascent of a roller coaster. All his focus seemed fixed on getting to that crest, on rising and rising as he breathed in rhythm with the push of his hips against her. He insinuated a hand between their bodies to slide his fingers over where they were joined, to press hard and pulse them against her, and her heart thudded harder and beat harder with his. "I…I…I'm…"

"Y-y-yes!" His voice was a husky whisper and he began to come.

A sunburst, an explosion that spread out in waves from her center. She lost track of everything, even existence.

It was a slow slide back into consciousness. Awareness of herself, her body and his. Cooling skin, breaths grown steadier. The pulsing inside her fading; his penis softening and slipping out. He made a sound and shifted from her body and to the side. He took her with him and brushed the corner of her mouth with a kiss and then her closed eyelids, then behind an ear, and then back to the corner of her mouth. She didn't have the strength to turn her face so the kiss landed on the center of her mouth, which tingled for the feel of his.

She stayed within the haven of his arms and pressed her face against the notch at the base of his throat. She felt him remove the condom. "For missionary sex that was pretty spectacular, Your Majesty."

He snorted a laugh. "We can try something else you like better. Just say the word." He eased his thigh between her legs again and pressed against her core.

A surge of passion that was almost too painful flowed through her. She closed her eyes and moaned. "No, please. Too much."

"Is that a no I hear?" He relented and subsided back into a resting position. As time snapped back into place and reality set in, she remembered how cautious she had to be with him.

She drew away, just able to resist the tightening of his hands on her shoulders. "What time is it now?"

He picked up his head and fumbled with his phone on the night table. "Almost ten."

She lifted the covers and scooted out. "Time for a shower in your perfectly appointed bathroom. Sorry, but I can't call it a loo. It always makes me think of a huge hole that goes all the way down to China."

He swung his feet over the edge of the bed. "Do you want some company?"

She looked for her various items of clothing, strewn across the floor. "Better not. We'll be right back in this bed if we do that, and the bedclothes will get incredibly wet."

There was a pause. "You've a point there." He stood. "Besides I have business in Bisby that I must attend to this morning."

"You do?"

"How soon they forget." He came around the bed, switched on the bedside lamp, took her crumpled-up shirt in his hand, and tossed it on the bed. He was all muscle, that pelt of black hair on his chest arrowing down to his now somnolent penis. Everywhere else on his glorious body he was supple, glowing skin. She felt her mind and body melt.

"What am I forgetting?" She didn't try to stop what must be a ridiculously sappy smile stretching from one side of her face to the other. It was a wonder she wasn't drooling.

"You're forgetting the break-in."

Of a sudden, the smile was gone. She wrinkled up her nose. "I'd like to forget it if I could." She bent to pick up her panties. Placing them on the bed, she colored, remembering how he'd taken them off. "Besides which, it's my responsibility isn't it? Not yours."

He looked away and his lips tightened. "I'm not ever going to forget what some sick sod did to you. No, what I meant was while you attend to business at the restaurant, I'll talk to Neil about the warning on your sheets."

He took her hand in his. "I'm going to take care of it for you. True, you know Neil, but you've never been involved with anything to do with our system of policing in the UK. The legalities. Obviously I have."

Policing. The legalities. Her heart rate sped up. "What do you suppose they'll look for in my background?"

He stared down, eyebrows knitted. "What does your background have to do with the break-in?"

Yes, what did it? She hadn't done anything illegal three years ago in New York. Only shameful. "I agree with you. How different can it be from the States?" She let go of his hand.

He nodded. "No doubt he'll want to ask you questions. But only to talk about who you think might have done it." He smoothed his fingers across her forehead and grinned. "Why the worry lines, darling? Do you think I'll take over in my most duke-like fashion?"

For once that wasn't what she'd been thinking.

"I can promise I will act in an advisory capacity only until I speak with you. There will be none of the lord-and-master business on my part. I will only play that part in bed."

She gave him a bright laugh. "Oh, well, I would legit be a fool to turn you down then, wouldn't I?"

"And you're not a fool."

She sat back down on the bed. He sat too. Taking her hand in his, he turned it over. Laying his fingers over the scar, he said, "Won't you let me make things right for you?"

How it soothed her to sit with the man she loved on the bed they'd made love in. Because yes, this was love. His thigh, his hip and arm and shoulder pressed to hers. This was the way couples sat together when passion was satisfied. This was how they would be to each other in intimacy. It was more dangerous than sex.

Annie reached up and cupped his cheek. She kissed him, a touch of her lips to his. "Of course I will," she whispered. If only they could be a real couple, that would be what she'd want to do for him. Always make it right. Always make everything right, he for her, and she for him.

"My dearest Annie, thank you," he murmured and put both his arms around her. "In my entire life…" He breathed a laugh. "Including my ducal life, I've never wanted anything more."

Pain lanced through her head. She hopped up. "I need to take that shower. Get ready for tonight."

He came to his feet as well, his smile replaced by confusion, but then it was gone and she hoped he hadn't sensed her dread. "Then there's that other piece of business that needs my ducal direction. The garden. Setting it to rights. I took your point, you know," he went on. "Bisby's children will get something wonderful out of it. I daresay the adults will, too. And you, my dear, need to be there to supervise its planting."

"Do you mean to go forward with it anyway? Not move it like Viola suggested?"

The good-humored cast to his features disappeared into hard, cut lines. "That garden will be in the precise place it was before because I say it will.

There will be no moving it. If it's up to me—and it is—you're going to end up with a garden that is better and bigger than the one you had before."

Her lungs felt heavy as she took in a breath. "I'll be there."

He patted her on the ass and steered her toward the bathroom. "In you go."

Charlie didn't know how to explain it, but there'd been something off the way they left things, after they'd made love so gloriously. Perhaps it was the way he felt her withdraw. And then there was the chatter on their drive back to Bisby. Annie was not a chatterer. He let her go on without interrupting until he couldn't stand it.

"Annie, darling."

She stopped talking.

He raised an eyebrow, the cessation of sound almost as unsettling as her run-on comments about this and that, nothing of any importance. "When you were in the shower, I heard from John Peele. He can come out this afternoon as I'd hoped. He thinks we'll have the garden ready to plant by three o'clock this afternoon. Will you have time to come by the Manor to watch? Oh, and supervise, as well?"

"Absolutely." She began to rub her thumb over her palm.

"Why do you do that?"

She stopped. "You mean this?" And she repeated what he'd seen her do so many times.

"One day, back in New York, when I was working two jobs and too tired to think straight, I did what I knew I shouldn't but did it anyway. Rather than taking a chisel, I used one of the larger knives I had nearby to cut into a frozen piece of meat. I had the point of the knife firmly in place in the meat and a hammer at the top of the handle. I had my hand above the blade. Only my hand was slippery and slid right down across the blade. I cut my palm open from my pinky to the fleshy part of my thumb. Injured a couple of tendons. It took twenty-six stitches."

He took her hand in his, squeezing gently. "You're continuing to heal it as it were."

"It reminds me that I need to be more careful."

"That must affect your ability to work."

"Only sometimes. When it's humid. Or very cold." She eased her hand out of his. She withdrew from him at the same time in a way he couldn't like.

He pulled over to the side of the road and brought the car to a halt. He left it in idle. "What's the matter?"

"It hasn't even been a week that we know each other. Don't you think it's an issue that we haven't taken the time to learn about who each of us are much more than where we come from?"

Welcome to the minefield, he thought with resignation. "I know you come from the colonies."

She gave him a sharp glance. "Funny. Ha-ha."

"Give over. What's on your mind?"

"Nothing."

And for a moment he thought it was nothing. That she'd abandoned that conversational gambit. Until she took a deep breath and pasted on a broad smile.

She tossed her braid—she'd wound it tight to her head back in his hotel room—over her shoulder. In a bright voice, she said, "This morning was good between us. Fantastic."

He flexed his hands on the wheel and looked away. "Don't, please."

"Don't what?"

"Don't diminish what's happening between us."

"I'm not. It truly was fabulous. But it was nothing more than the two of us scratching a really annoying itch."

He dropped his hands into his lap and sat back, stunned. "Are you telling me it was nothing more than a good fuck?"

"Charlie, we need to think about the gorilla." Two spots of color burst onto her pale cheeks. "I don't have to curtsy when I walk into a room you're in. But the differences between us exist. The whole title thing. You have one. I don't."

"And you don't have to say it because I know. I use it to my advantage when needs be. Just as anyone would use whatever weapons they had at their disposal when needed. But Annie." He leaned an arm on the console between them. "My title is nothing more than an anachronism."

She straightened. Her nostrils flared with the breath she took. She wouldn't look at him. "If you're using it to your advantage, it isn't an anachronism."

"My title doesn't matter between us."

"Says the man whose forebears ruled Britannia."

"Says the woman who should have more self-esteem than to be so focused on what and who I was born."

"Maybe who I was born doesn't matter now." She'd lowered her voice, but each word she spoke was said with intensity. "In any relationship we have, eventually it will."

Irritation pulsed at his temple.

"Since I've been in your country, I haven't had many run-ins with the upper classes and the moneyed people," she continued. "When I have, it's been a good lesson. I'm reminded of my place, which is just a rung or two above the kitchen help." She huffed a humorless laugh. "As if there's something wrong being the kitchen help."

"I have never reminded you of your place, except for the one I want you in. With me." He reached for her hand again and brought it to his mouth for a kiss.

She sighed. After a moment she drew her hand back and placed it over the other in her lap. "We're into each other right now. The sex for starters. It might have been only that once—"

"The first," he interrupted her.

"Okay, the first. But…"

There was something about that *but*. Charlie braced himself.

"Right after I got on the *Times* list, I got a phone call from a woman named Emily Torquil."

Charlie ran through his internal address book in an attempt to place the name.

"She works at an event management firm in London, one with a high-net-worth clientele. Could she come to Bisby, she asked me, to arrange a party at the restaurant for some very important people. We'd have to close it for the evening, but she would pay top dollar—or pound—for the inconvenience."

Charlie remembered, then, who Emily Torquil was. The daughter of the Lord Lieutenant of Cumbria and a fixture in photo montages in *Tatler*.

"She came up to Bisby at least a half-dozen times to plan each detail of the dinner. We had such a great time together, I began to think she and I were going to become friends."

"And?"

"And one weekend she invited me to her house up north. I took a train to Carlisle and Emily sent a car to pick me up. My first view of the house—pardon me, the palace—blew me away. It's set at the top of a series of beautifully landscaped rolling hills. It's all white stone, with two huge wings and a huge half-circle driveway set in the middle.

"Later while Emily was waiting for the rest of her guests to arrive—although some had already—I went for a walk. There was a gazebo down the hill in the middle of a pretty little island. There was ornamental shrubbery everywhere, sculpted in the shape of animals. After a while I returned to the house.

"Set off to the side on the back terrace, there was a stone bench that called my name. There I was, kicked back, enjoying the peace of the afternoon, when two of Emily's friends came out. They didn't see me."

The silence in the car was broken only by the sound of their breathing.

Annie tapped her hands against her knees and took a breath. "I don't remember the exact way their conversation started because I wasn't listening at first, but it went from them talking about people they knew and things they were doing to what was the matter with Emily, inviting someone like me to spend the weekend. Good Lord, that thing I was wearing—one of my long skirts is what they were passing judgment on—quite ridiculous. Plus, what could I talk about that they might be interested in? What it's like to sweat in a hot kitchen—eew. They laughed. As if they would ever step foot in a kitchen. Could they compare notes with me on where to shop? Debenhams perhaps? My low-class New Yawk—and yes, they said it like that—accent gave them shudders. Then they disappeared into the house."

Annie sat straighter. "I didn't take that sitting down."

He cast a sideways glance at her. "As you shouldn't have."

"I ran after them. Camilla Heatherington with the big blue eyes, wearing the leather skirt and over-the-knee boots she no doubt bought on Sloane Street, and Ewan McGovern, with his straight, dirty blond hair, creased linen jacket, and shirt unbuttoned halfway down his skinny, milk-pale chest, startled looks on their silly faces.

"I didn't give them a chance to blurt out an apology, not that I thought there'd be one. I thanked them for their pointers. If ever I was invited to a weekend party at one of *their* houses, I would be sure to get some training so I wouldn't embarrass them. Then I left."

"Left the house, I hope."

"I went up to my room, packed, and then came down to say goodbye to Emily. She had tears in her eyes and said she was so sorry. She was furious with Camilla and Ewan. I said no worries. I knew she wasn't like her friends. We could get together another time."

Charlie had a feeling he knew what was coming.

"Over the next week or so I left Emily a couple of texts, which she didn't return. She might not have seen the texts, I told myself. I called her. By the fourth time I called, I knew she was ignoring me. It hurts, you know. Rejection."

"Bloody hell." He took both her hands in his. "You don't need Emily Torquil to be your friend, she or any of the rest."

"You're right. I don't. I have friends. I don't have to look to the so-called upper classes for more."

Charlie didn't live in a bubble. He knew about the kind of people who went to Emily Torquil's weekend parties. He'd known them his whole life. He'd gone to school with them, gone to birthday parties and weddings with them. He'd socialized with them. "I hope you don't mean to include me in that group."

"I could."

Said so softly. She might have shouted those two words loud enough to be heard in Bisby, miles away. "Oh no, you're not going to do that. You're going to spell out how you think I could be like those silly twits at Emily Torquil's party."

She was back to stroking her palm. "It's your world."

She was right. It was the one he was born into.

"It's your position, from birth and all those centuries back."

His heart sank. How could he deny the truth?

"It's the people in your life, who no matter how many times they're forced to be in the same room with me, they won't ever see my value as a human being. At Emily's; that wasn't the only time it happened."

He began to tap his fingers against the steering wheel. "What, with that wanker, Stoughton?"

"Yes, him, and his grandfather the earl, and his mother the earl's daughter. They were always so polite to me, but cold. They froze me out."

"A lucky thing," Charlie muttered, wanting her to get it all out, all the indignities she'd suffered from people whose type he knew too well, but wanting to stop her so he could protest that he wasn't like that.

"But it's your money, too, you know. I can't curl my brain around how much of it there is. There are things you assume just come to you because of it that would never enter my mind. That money separates us as much, if not more, than your title."

Charlie wanted to bellow. No matter that everything she said was true. "You're wrong," he said, making sure to keep the tension from his voice. "You don't know as much about me as you think you do."

"Charlie, you don't have to—"

"This is not the year 1066," he said, overriding her. "Times have changed. My best mate, growing up was Andy Prescott. He looked up to me on the football pitch, not as if I were on a warhorse in full armor leading the way into battle. It wasn't because I was the son of a duke he had to bow down to, but because I was fast and I could score."

She snorted. He prayed it was a snort of laughter aimed at him for his adolescent bravado. "My business partner was born in Pakistan. He and I met by happenstance at what you Yanks would call a networking event. We knew we were right for each other, our business strengths complementary. Together we built the Rotherforde Group and then sold it for a whopping sum, and yes, we're *both* among the richest men in England. Sami is welcomed most everywhere in England he wants to be welcomed."

"Not by Emily's set," Annie said.

"He doesn't care. That's my point. Andy and I meet for dinner three or four times a year and speak more often. The subject of my money never comes up, unless he's skewering me about it. He treats me the same way he's always treated me." He allowed himself a small grin. "Rudely."

She began to speak. He held up a hand to stop her. "I'm not done. Sami and I, as much money as we've both made, we talk about things everyone else talks about. Whether Arsenal is better than Manchester United, whether he's ever going to find a bird he loves who's going to be good enough for his mum, and how many times Simon Cowell will be rude to the contestants on his next hit show."

Annie made a scornful sound. "Oh, right. You never talk about your money."

He opened his mouth to deny it and couldn't. They did talk about money. All the time. "It's only money."

"Says the man who has so much of it, he doesn't have to think about it." She wagged a finger at him. "And you're still a duke."

Frustrated, he snapped, "We hereditary peers do not control the country. It doesn't matter that I'm a duke."

"And yet, everyone expects you to act like a duke. As a member of the aristocracy, people expect you to hang with others just like you. And maybe you're not going to marry Samantha, but they expect you to marry someone like her."

CHAPTER FOURTEEN

Was that what all this was about? Samantha, again? She'd gone back to stroking the scar. He captured her hand in his. "Do you want to know why I broke it off with Samantha?"

"You don't have to tell me."

"It was because she never disagreed with me on any subject, not even once."

Annie's lip curled. "You should have liked that, Your Majesty."

"It bored me."

Her eyes widened.

"I prefer a little spice in my life," he said, raising both hands, now clenched into fists, and kissed her whitened knuckles. "Having found it in you, why would I look for someone in the world I was born into on the off chance I'd find her there?"

He pulled her toward him across the damned console and slid one hand up her arm to the nape of her neck. With his fingers on her braid, he murmured, "I don't want some silly cow in my life who lives to please me. I want a woman who doesn't give a damn if I'm pleased or not if I'm doing something she thinks is wrong. I want a woman who does something with her life. I want a woman who's made it her goal to help those who need her help, help children whose lives she's trying to improve, whether it inconveniences me or not."

She folded her arms across her chest.

"I told Samantha it wasn't working between us the other night at dinner at your restaurant." He could tell the way Annie wouldn't look at him she was trying to keep him from knowing how he was putting paid to her arguments. "That's fitting, don't you think? *Your* restaurant?"

She brought her gaze to his.

For once his gypsy girl was all but silenced. It was a novelty he would savor because if he knew anything, it wouldn't last long. "When she insisted on joining me at The Ocular—I hadn't invited her—I knew why. I'd known it was over between the two of us the moment you stormed into my office."

"You did?" She took a deep breath and closed her eyes. "I don't see it. These things still stand in the way. How can we get past them?"

He leaned farther across the console. Hands on her shoulders, he drew her around to face him again.

"Well then, darling. I may have to purchase a pair of glasses for you because it's clear to me how it can—and will." He brushed a kiss across her lips.

She laughed, as he wanted her to with that bit of whimsy. He was determined to clear all her objections out of the way. He wouldn't say the words now. It wasn't the right time. She wouldn't believe him on top of all he'd just said about Samantha. But it would be soon.

After they were back on the road, he said, "Once I've spoken to Neil for you, after you've had a chance to see things are set for tonight at the restaurant, and before the garden is set to be re-plowed, let's go off, you and I, for an hour. Perhaps we'll sit in the car, perhaps we'll pull off the road, perhaps—"

"Perhaps you're letting your imagination run away with you, Your Highness," she said. "I have a restaurant to run. You need to get a grip."

"A grip you say? That's what I had in mind."

But that wasn't all he had in mind. He might think he'd dealt with all her objections. But something else was bothering Annie. It was something she wouldn't talk about yet. While he couldn't imagine what it could be, whatever it was, they would get past it. He knew who she was, and he wanted her for who she was. His job, as he saw it, was to convince her to want him for who *he* was.

***

After Charlie dropped Annie at The Ocular, and after she'd walked over to thank Hal Bullen for replacing the hardware on her pink door, Annie slipped into the restaurant to be greeted by her staff's curious stares. Molly was the first to ask her about the break-in.

"I don't know anything more than when Neil drove away in the middle of the night, so there's not much to tell," Annie said to Molly's questions.

What Molly might have said if Annie had told her about the message on her sheets was a whole other kettle of fish. There would probably be raised voices and more discussion than Annie could have withstood. She sensed James watching her with big, anxious eyes.

After the questions petered out, she set everyone about their tasks and opened the door to the basement. As she ran down the steps, her breath began to come fast. She prayed she could hold it together until she was inside the cooler. Yanking the heavy door open, she rushed inside and pulled it closed behind her.

The cold enveloped her immediately. She could see her breath in the air as she began to pant. The tears that trickled onto her cheeks felt hot on her chilled skin. She was ass over teakettle, out of her mind in love with Charlie Camville. He was her Mt. Etna Cake, and she wanted to delight in him. She wanted his body, she wanted his heart, and she wanted his soul. Because of her rotten past, the likelihood of her having any of him was less likely by the moment.

She thought he loved her, too. He'd done everything but said it. She dropped her face into her hands.

It had happened between them so fast. That frantic trip down to London…how crazy had it been, the only thing on her mind to get the hated duke of Lindsey to understand what a terrible thing he'd done and force him to fix it. She'd gotten way more than she'd bargained for.

He'd been the duke of Lindsey to her for less than the time it took to scramble an egg. He'd become Charlie the moment he began to tease her, even before she realized he was teasing her. She fell in love with him even before she knew it was love.

Talking about the class differences between them, back in his car, had been a desperate attempt at diversion. Even as she spoke about Emily and Ross's family, she'd known her protests were nothing more than a smoke screen she was throwing up to keep from having to tell him her ugly truth.

How had she ever thought she could escape her past? How could she have ever thought she wouldn't have to tell him? How would she be able to stand it when she did?

She wiped the trace of tears from her cheeks and looked for what she'd told her people she was coming down to the cooler for: the cod Arthur Hanstead had promised to deliver this morning. It was there, just to the right. She lifted the fish from the shelf and, after closing the cooler door with her hip, tramped up the steps to the kitchen, where she found her staff running every which way to Sunday. Amazed, she looked around at the unusual disorder. "Did the world just end while I was downstairs?"

Eyes shining with a mixture of excitement and anxiety, Molly said, "Remember that reservation for the VIP table that I took last month for tonight, where they said it was for someone in the government and they'd let us know? Well, we just found out. It's for the bleedin' prime minister. And he's bringing the Italian prime minister with him."

Annie slapped the package of cod down onto her prep table, and her mind went into overdrive. "Do I need to cancel everyone else's reservation for security reasons, comp them all, and make reservations for all of them for another night?"

"They said carry on as if the PMs are normal people." Molly began dancing in place with excitement.

"Then, that's what we'll do." Annie laid one hand atop the package of fish, grateful for the emergency, which would keep her from thinking too much. "Let's focus on doing everything we can to give them the best Ocular experience possible."

"Suppose they don't like our food?" Molly asked. "Suppose they don't think it's Italian?"

"It's not Italian. It's my Italian, just like it's always mine." She ripped the paper wrapping. "I think I'll make fish and chips."

Molly's eyes got big. "Gawd, Annie! Fish and chips is English."

"Yes, and we're in England. But it's going to be fish and chips Italian style."

Molly sidled up to the table to watch as Annie kept unwrapping the fish. "How are you going to make English fish and chips into Italian fish and chips?"

Annie tapped her top lip. "Well, that's the challenge." She turned in a circle, admired her pots, especially the stock pot she'd just bought, watched Davy prepping the greens she'd serve as salad tonight, and then at last turned and grinned at Molly. "We know it'll be fried."

Molly rolled her eyes. "Will the chips be fried, too?"

"Of course. But it's the rest that will make it Italian, not English."

Unsure only for another moment, Molly's face cleared. "Since you're making it, it'll be ace."

"Thanks for your faith in me." Annie pulled open the doors on the refrigerated cabinet beneath her prep table and took out eggs and milk. "Why don't you let me surprise you?"

"Okay. It'll be better than this morning's surprise."

Still concentrating on fish and chips, she said, "What surprise, Moll?" Molly's surprises could be anything from a house up in Horncastle had burned to the ground to they were out of Marmite at Tesco's.

"I happened to be walking by the Manor, and Lady Vi was standing on the steps as a fancy car drove up and a lady got out."

"Oh?" Annie took out a pen and grabbed some paper to make herself a list for what she needed to do before the prime ministers arrived tonight.

"It was the duchess."

Pen poised over paper, Annie looked up. "What duchess?"

"The Dowager Duchess. Your duke's mum."

As Charlie drove away from his meeting with Neil—there wasn't anything more to report than there had been last night, other than Herbert Thornborrow, Neil's assistant, was completing a talk with the Endors—he grinned to himself. It was humorous, wasn't it? Here he was, ready for the next stage of his life, restoring his land holdings and figuring out how to improve the lot of people living in and around Bisby—and just saying that made him want to groan at the affectation of it—and this came along. *This,* of course, was not the best way to describe Annie, an American woman who had a history of thinking aristocrats took up too much space on earth. Still, *this* was the woman who was going to be the next duchess of Lindsey.

What was most humorous, was, he, who lately hadn't had to work hard for anything he wanted, was going to have to work quite hard to convince his American gypsy girl he was worth it, despite the title and the money that came with him. His money and his title worked against him. Well, except when she imagined how she could spend it for other people.

She didn't yet know that being his duchess, she was going to have his great, whacking bank account at her disposal. She'd be able to help every person on her staff and every other person she might want to hire, and send them off to school somewhere to retrain them for the new century. She'd be able to plant a garden for children in every town and village in Lincolnshire if she wanted.

He pulled to a stop in front of the Manor, close to where later today Annie's garden would be put to rights. He looked up at the leaden skies. Or perhaps not. The weather, as it always did, would dictate whether today would be the day.

He didn't stop smiling until he reached the Manor's front door and Viola opened it to welcome him in. Although welcome might have been the wrong term if the look in her eyes told him anything. Relieved was more the thing.

As he stepped inside, his mother, always well-coifed and today no different, came around Viola and leaned up to give him her surgically-modified cheek.

"Dearest." Although that word didn't inspire him to think he was dear to her. He supposed she might have regarded him as dear when he'd bought her the pied-à-terre in Belgravia after his business began to take off. Even then, there'd been barely a thank-you.

"I thought I'd come to see how Viola and George are getting on in this old place. They've done wonders, don't you think?" She waved a hand in a limp way. His mother had been vocal about how much she'd always hated the Manor and Bisby. If she could have, she wouldn't have spent a single moment in the village, choosing London instead. But there wasn't the money to do that at the time, so she'd been stuck. Now she was back. Why?

"Good to see you too, Mother."

She raised an eyebrow at him. "Really, Lindsey. Good to see me? We know what a falsehood that is, don't we?"

Viola made a sound of distress. "Excuse, me, Mama?" Viola gave her mother an anxious look. "I must make a phone call." She turned and fled down the long hallway to the kitchen.

Their mother glared at Viola and then, with a half-shrug, turned back to Charlie. "You've received the loveliest invitation. I decided it was important enough that I give it to you myself." She glided into the dining room, and over to her purse on one of two Queen Anne chairs flanking the sideboard on the far wall. "It was delivered to your flat, and I had Bowers pop over to retrieve it." She picked up the black, hammered-leather purse—he remembered her telling him she'd paid £4,000 for the thing in a Mount Street shop—and pulled out a cream-colored envelope. From across the room Charlie could see the calligraphic type on its face. She glided back across the room, the way she'd been taught at the boarding school she'd gone to in Switzerland and perfected at countless cotillions during her youth.

Taking the envelope from her, Charlie knew. This invitation was the reason she'd come to Bisby. He flipped it over and saw where the invitation had come from. Buckingham Palace. "I would imagine you know all about this."

"Why, Lindsey, you attribute more powers to me than I have. But as it happens, I had a cozy little visit with Lady Minton and–"

"Ah yes. Your good friend, Lady Susan. A friendship you've cultivated assiduously over the years, especially after the queen asked her to be one of her personal assistants."

"Really, Lindsey. This habit you have developed of late, interrupting me. I don't like it at all. And Lady Susan is a lady-in-waiting. I don't know where you find this personal assistant nonsense."

"I'm calling it what it is."

She pressed her perfectly painted pink lips together. Only for an instant, though. She was nothing if not careful about how she arranged her features after that last bout with her cosmetic surgeon. "The queen is having a tea in June. Included in the number of those invited are all the dukes of England, Scotland, and Ireland. You, my dear Lindsey, are naturally included in that very select group."

"I have no desire to attend." Not after this morning. Not after this past week.

"But you must. It's expected of you."

"Who expects it, Mother? You?" He began to rip open the envelope.

"Do be careful, darling." She fingered the black pearl necklace she'd bought for herself last year. "You don't want to rip it to shreds. It is, after all, from the queen."

Charlie took the envelope in his two hands and ripped it down the center.

"Lindsey!" Horror reshaped her eyebrows.

For Charlie, that look was worth his childish fit of pique. "I don't need to read it to know what it says. It will start as they always start: 'The Master of the Household has received Her Majesty's command to invite…' And then it will have my name and title engraved in the finest, most exquisite calligraphic hand." He slipped the two pieces of the invitation from the envelope and aligning them, read. It was, in fact, as he'd said. He folded it in fours, not an easy thing to do considering the heaviness of the vellum, and stuck it in the back pocket of his jeans.

"This invitation couldn't have come at a better time," his mother continued as if nothing untoward had happened. "With the work that has already begun at the Manor, and soon at Rotherforde, it is the perfect opportunity to further restore the family's reputation."

"You think there's a way to do that in the short term?" For emphasis he added, "After what father did?"

"Yes, I do. You are not your father. You're doing all the right things, even if you've done it with business."

"Yes, all that filthy lucre. How it tarnishes things. How are you enjoying your flat, Mother?"

She ignored that last. "I told Lady Susan you were anxious to set our house in order and she was quite sympathetic. I am sure the queen will be, as well."

"Then I'm right. I have you to thank for this invitation, if thanks it is."

A careful but crafty smile twitched at the corners of her lips. "Thank you for recognizing what I do for the family. You know I've made it my life's work to help you restore the family's reputation."

Charlie had no idea why his mother thought anything she did would help, but whatever it was, he wished she'd stop, now that he was on the cusp of his life changing so much for the better.

"May I tell Lady Susan she will see you there, that you are planning on accepting the invitation?"

"I need to see if it will fit into my schedule."

"Lindsey! What could possibly take precedence over an invitation from the queen?"

That was easy. The peace he'd just made with his gypsy girl. Charlie moved down the hallway toward the kitchen. Over his shoulder, he said, "You do know how boring these things tend to be."

"Lindsey!"

He stopped in place and wheeled around. "Please stop barking my name."

She came to her full height, which was considerable. She folded her hands at her waist. He remembered the signs too well from a childhood fraught with upheaval, how she made a show of acting the proper gentlewoman when her hackles were up.

Even though he knew, he wondered why he couldn't stop himself from saying things that were wholly unproductive when in his mother's presence. No doubt their long history. "I do beg your pardon. Thank you, Mother, for trying to improve a situation that will take many more years to improve before our world forgets. People still remember that Papa, at age fifty-five decided to run away with Maria, a woman half his age and leave the properties and reputation of the Camvilles, honed over centuries, in shambles. An invitation to visit with Her Majesty is not going to do it. I promise you, though, if I can go, I will."

"Charlie, please try."

His blood sang a startled song. She'd called him by his first name. He couldn't remember the last time that had happened. Perhaps she had never done so. He looked down at the woman who had borne him.

On her face was a look of determination with the suggestion of a plea, and he realized how important it was that he accept the invitation she'd worked so hard to get for him. He found himself softening toward her. Even if she'd done a piss-poor job of raising him, she was his parent. Everything he was came either from her or his father.

At thoughts of his paternal parent, he remembered another reason why going to the queen's do was going to be so unpleasant. "Do you know if Nigel Anstruther will be there?"

His mother's porcelain skin whitened further. "I don't know." Her gaze slid away from his.

"As I said. Nigel hasn't forgiven the family for Papa drawing his father into that scheme that destroyed them both. I had a rather unpleasant moment with him outside the River Cafe only last month."

As it always did when Charlie thought about what his father had done to entice the senior Anstruther—a lovely man with a too trusting attitude and no knowledge of the perils of money—he barely held down the contents of his stomach.

"He cannot blame you for what your father did to his."

"Can he not? I wish you'd tell him, next you're in London should you see him." He continued down the hall toward the kitchen. He hadn't taken two steps when he stopped and spun on his heels.

"If I accept the invitation, it will be because the queen is a lovely old lady, rather like the granny I never had." He began to walk again. "I need a moment with Viola about some personal business." Over his shoulder, he said, "Allow us some privacy."

Viola was not in the kitchen. This was a good thing. He needed time to regroup before he went looking for her. Because after spending those few, corrosive minutes with his mother, he understood a bit more how Annie could worry about their class differences. But really... *He* was not his mother. Or any of Emily Torquil's friends. Or that wanker, Stoughton. Where was the problem?

He grimaced. He'd introduce Annie to his mother because he had to. His parent couldn't possibly understand Annie, a woman who worked with her hands, even if she was a rock star on the English culinary scene. But he did. And that was enough.

He found Viola down the slope behind the kitchen garden, sitting on the edge of the wall, her feet dangling down. She stared out into the midday mist. There was a chill in the air, typical of late March.

Viola shivered as he sat next to her. Whatever irritation he'd felt for his sister's meddling in the business of the garden melted away in the face of the despair he saw in her eyes. She leaned against him. He snaked an arm around her shoulders and held her as he had when they were children. "Charlie, there are so few things I've wanted in my life, and yet somehow I don't seem to be able to get any of them. Is it that I've done something terrible? Is it something I'm being punished for?"

"That's crap, Viola."

She was silent. He could feel her heart beating against his arm.

He wondered which of the two people in Viola's life was likely causing her such misery. He was ready to take either of them apart. With his mother, it would be figurative. With George, it would be wonderful, if unlikely, if he could make it physical. "Is it Mother driving you wild?" he asked by way of elimination.

Viola gave him a watery laugh and swiped at her face. "Mama has done her part. She criticizes everything. How I'm raising the girls, what they wear, what they eat, their lack of manners at table. And then there's what she has to say about George. It's—" She went silent.

Charlie nudged her. "It's what, Viola."

"George has been rather awful to me lately."

Charlie readied himself to hear how awful.

"It's really only been lately, she said with some haste. "It's because he's been under a lot of pressure. The consortium, you know. He wants everything to work to our benefit. He says it will be to your benefit too." Her smile disappeared. "But I know otherwise. It's because he's tired of being a…"

A failure, she was poised to say. In Charlie's mind that was not all George Swynford was tired of. It was not being treated with the respect he imagined was due him.

Charlie put one finger under Viola's chin and turned her face toward his. "Any business relating to the consortium should be between him and me, and yet it seems it's washed over onto you."

"You know he's never been much of a provider." Viola wouldn't look at Charlie. "I used to think that was all right. After all, in the vows it says for better or worse." She gave him a weak laugh. "I suppose one would say I got worse. Certainly, Mama continues to say that."

"You'll be happy to know Mama is focused on me now, not you."

"Mama has a great capacity to multitask. She'll find a way to focus on both of us." Viola made a face. "When you arranged for us to move here to Melbury, I thought it would be a good thing. I thought it would be safe here in Bisby. It's not anymore. You asked me what George has done. He shouts at me all the time, even at the girls. He's destroyed what sense of safety I have here in Bisby."

A buzzing filled Charlie's head. "Is that it, then? Has George—?"

"You mean has he hit me?" Viola's chin trembled.

The buzzing began to build. "Is that a yes?"

She slumped forward. In a dull voice she said, "It hasn't been more than once or twice since we've been here."

The buzzing in Charlie's head was replaced by a roaring. "Why didn't you tell me?" He could barely hear his own words.

"I couldn't." She straightened. "But now I've decided. I want to leave George. I want to move back to London and find a job. I want you to help me find a flat to live in for the short term. It doesn't have to be in the best part of London, like Mama wanted, just somewhere where there's a park for the girls to play in and until I can find something I can afford. I'll pay you back as soon as I can."

Charlie wound both arms around Viola, and hoped she didn't recognize the rage that filled him, that he looked forward to letting loose on George. "Consider it done. However, you'll have to put up with me buying you a flat. All you need to do is tell me where. And there'll be no paying me back. There should be something a filthy rich brother can do for a beloved sister and not have to deal with the messy business of her sending him checks monthly."

"Charlie…"

"No, no. It's nonnegotiable. Allow me my newly-wealthy-man idiosyncrasies."

Viola sighed. "I'm ashamed of myself."

Charlie patted her back. "Don't be daft. You have no reason to be ashamed of yourself. George does."

"Not that." She sat up and wiped her eyes with the back of her hand. Like a child. "I'm ashamed of myself for what I told Annie."

Ah, he remembered. This was what he'd come to find out. Charlie dropped his arm from Viola's shoulders and shifted in his seat on the wall to look straight at her. "What did you say?"

"I let her think you were going to marry Samantha."

"Why would you do that?"

"Because I was jealous. I wanted to hurt her. Annie is everything I'm not. Strong. Able. She would never put up with George the way I have."

A little part of him wanted to be angry with Viola. But the jealousy she felt for Annie was a compliment of sorts. And he had straightened out that bit about Samantha with Annie. Charlie took Viola's hand and squeezed it. His heart was heavy for his sister. "You will become strong and able. You're taking the first step."

"Annie would, wouldn't she?" Viola touched the back of his hand. "I believe you're in love with her."

He raised an eyebrow. "Is it that apparent?"

A trace of tears still on her cheeks, she gave him a radiant smile. "I saw the way you looked at her that night at The Ocular. Yes, very apparent."

"It was? I'll have to admit it then. Yes, I'm in love with her."

"How is that possible? You haven't known each other a terribly long time."

Grinning, he rubbed his chest. "I met her in my offices in London less than a week ago."

"In other words, a whirlwind romance."

Whirlwind was a good way to describe what Charlie had with Annie.

The smile that had spread across her face, even to her eyes, faded. "Be careful, Charlie."

His smile faded, too. "Careful of what?"

"Mama knows. I think she's here because George called to tell her about Annie. And you. She doesn't like it. She may have something planned you won't like."

CHAPTER FIFTEEN

He left Viola in the Manor's kitchen with a reminder that if George made any threats she was to call him immediately. He added, "Don't worry about Mama's intentions. If Annie's not afraid of George, she's certainly not afraid of our mother."

The thought of how his dear mother might try some of her tricks on Annie and how Annie would respond made him chuckle. It would be a treat to watch his gypsy girl make short shrift of his parent.

His lips tightened, thinking of George, who now he'd truly like to make short shrift of, albeit in a different way. Short of arranging for his murder—which as an idea had merit, absent the sticky business of murder being against the law—all he could do was make sure George adhered to the restraining order Charlie would insist Viola get once she announced she was seeking a divorce.

He felt the stiff vellum of the queen's invitation stuck in the back pocket of his jeans. This had been his mother's stated reason for making the trip to Bisby. Now he knew she had plans to put him off Annie.

He wasn't going to the queen's do, no matter what was on his schedule. If he hadn't met Annie, he might have accepted and shown his face, even if Nigel Anstruther, the Duke of Brompton, showed up, as he might well. He ran his fingers over the raised type… *has received Her Majesty's command*…and smiled. He considered ripping it in smaller pieces in front of Annie just as he'd ripped it in half for effect in front of his mother. It might actually put paid to that argument about class differences between them.

A smattering of drops blew into his face as he started toward High Street and The Ocular. No point in taking the Jag to visit his gypsy girl. It was a short walk, rain notwithstanding. Turning the corner, he saw Neil coming toward him.

Charlie raised a hand in greeting. "I don't suppose you've caught the miscreants."

Neil shook his head. "I'd like to say it was what we've discussed, a couple of kids wanting to do mischief. But that message left for Annie was too specific. Someone has it in for her. I'm taking that seriously. You should too, Charlie. Keep your eye on our girl."

"Until we find out who's the guilty party, there'll be somebody with her at all times. Day and night." He didn't mention who would be with her at night.

"That's good then." Neil looked up at the sky. "Seems like you'll get the plowing in after all."

Like Neil, Charlie studied the gray, cloud-thick sky. He had to admit clear was the last thing it was. "I expect Peele will ring me in a bit to say he'll be coming by with his equipment to plow."

"There'll be a crowd watching once he starts to work." Neil stuck his hands in the pockets of his uniform. "I'll be there watching, in case our fellow who can't spell shows up."

"Perhaps after everything settles down, you and I can grab a pint at the Strangling Duck. Annie and I have talked over some ideas about how to make Bisby a destination location. I'd like your opinion on those parts that would have an impact on public safety."

Neil raised his sandy eyebrows. "It'll be a pleasure." He gave Charlie a look of appraisal. "My mum is right. You're back home." And he ambled away.

The idea of Bisby being home as it once was didn't seem as unattractive as it had a mere week ago. That was because if he decided to make Bisby home once again, it would be a very different home than the one he'd lived in as a kid. That change would be due to one person.

That person was one he'd rung up, twice now. He frowned. She hadn't answered either time. Annie's single-mindedness—no question in his mind she was deep in concentration preparing for tonight's diners—was one of the many things he admired about her. Just not now when he was anxious to tell her about the invitation from the queen, show her how he was turning it down, and warn her about his mother. And perhaps have himself a snog or two at the same time.

"Damn," Annie whispered and took a step away from her cutting board. She looked down at the butcher job she'd just done on the cod for her Italian version of fish and chips. She'd sliced it too thick, a rookie mistake. That's what she got for thinking about Charlie, as much as she told herself not to think about him, and about what she was going to say to this man she loved.

Not that that wasn't complicated enough. There was also his mother. Why did this have to be the day the woman decided to make a trip to Bisby? From what little Annie knew, the duchess's presence could and probably would complicate things.

Her phone rang. Charlie, for the third time. The first two times he'd called, she hadn't picked up because she was too busy. No, wrong. She needed to be honest with herself. She'd been too filled with anxiety.

"Aren't you going to answer, Annie?"

Annie opened her eyes to stare at James. "What are you doing here? Isn't it early to be out of school?"

"It's a teachers' holiday still."

Didn't that say a lot about where her head was that she didn't remember why James was at the restaurant in the middle of the day? The phone stopped ringing. James glanced at it and then up at her, his eyes brightening. "Can I help, Annie? Is there a sauce I can make?"

Annie put a hand on his shoulder. Now that he'd made one sauce—with help—he was all over wanting to make another. She loved his enthusiasm. It warmed her knowing she'd nurtured it. Wasn't this what she lived for? She rallied. "I have a feeling Davey will have something for you to do, maybe even make a sauce. Right now you can check on the herbs out back and bring me a bunch of sage. I need some for tonight." She ruffled his too-long hair.

He nodded with enthusiasm and headed out the back door to the restaurant's hothouse just as she heard the murmur of voices out front and then a laugh. A deep laugh. She braced herself on the table as he came around the screen, all well-set-up muscled body, broad shoulders and chest, black curls disordered from the wind and curling on his forehead. Laugh lines radiated from around his deep black eyes, mocking eyebrows in the up position—of course— and knowing lips smiling at her, lips she knew were superlative in the kissing department. Drops of rain beaded on his black leather jacket. His worn jeans clung to his legs and outlined in loving detail every muscle, every bone, and suddenly when it made no sense and every sense, she wanted him.

"What happened to your mobile? Is it broken?"

Annie glanced around. Her staff, so busy up to that point, seemed to have nothing to do. She frowned at them. To Charlie, she said, "Sorry. I was busy. What's up?"

"I saw Neil. I thought you might like to know what he had to say." Charlie spoke in a low voice only she could hear. The concentrated look of intention in his eyes told her what she could expect from this visit and wasn't it a good thing that it was what she wanted?

Her mouth watered. "Shall we go somewhere private?"

Was that a snicker from Brandon of all people? She shot a warning glance at her allegedly shy server.

Charlie's eyes widened with deceptive innocence. "I think that would be wise."

She motioned him to follow her downstairs. "C'mon."

If there'd been snickers before, there were outright chuckles now. Annie ignored them and led Charlie down the stairs to the supply closet. She could feel the heat of him at her back. Her pulse, which had already been put through more of a workout than she thought she could stand, jumped like popcorn gone wild. For a reason she was too much of a coward to think about, she was starved for the "discussion" they were about to have.

As she reached for the handle, he placed one hand on the back of her neck, and reached around her to pull the door open. "Darling, is there a reason why you're moving so slowly?" He pushed her into the closet and pulled the door shut behind them. "We have too much to talk about and not very much time to do it in."

The rate of her breathing surged. "Is that what we're doing? Talking?" She wheeled around, rose up on her tiptoes, and reached up to link her hands behind his neck. "Is that it?"

"I have two things on my mind," he said, holding her close to him, running one hand down her back to her bottom, and then back up to her braid. "First, a message from Neil. He wants you to be careful. He thinks the break-in at your flat and the love letter on your sheets was done by someone who's trying to frighten you."

"Okay." She didn't give a damn about the break-in, what Neil said, or being frightened, not while her body was on fire. Her toes curled inside her clogs. Her muscles tensed. Her nipples hardened. Liquid pooled between her legs.

Charlie fingered the end of her braid, and pushed her against the closet's back wall. "The second? Quite simple, really. *I* want you to be careful." He ran his tongue over her lower lip. "Except with me."

Annie's heartbeat surged. The guilt that wouldn't go away intruded into her mind. She pushed it away with ferocity and wiggled one foot out of a clog. She arched her back and wound her leg around his thigh.

He pushed his between hers and pressed up against her mound and rubbed. She caught her breath. "This is not talking." Perfection. Talking was dangerous.

He dropped his head lower to tease her neck with his tongue and lips. "Perceptive." He began to wind her braid in one direction and then the other.

Eyes shut, her head beginning to spin, she murmured, "Why are you so fascinated with my braid?"

"I like imagining what it's like when I undo it and spread your lovely hair across my pillows." He gave the braid a gentle yank.

A pillow she might never share with him again. She squeezed her eyes shut and knocked her head against his chest. She wanted the forgetfulness of having him. "Imagine away," she whimpered. "Like now. I have two prime ministers coming for dinner tonight."

He tilted away from her, his mouth, which had been performing magic tricks on her neck now wreathed in a big grin. "Two? Brilliant, my darling. Even if you weren't before, you're most assuredly on the map now." He ran his hands over her shoulders and down her arms. "I feel tension, here. All these high-powered people coming to you because The

Ocular is such an extraordinary restaurant. It's worrying you."

Though she'd used having two prime ministers dining at The Ocular as an excuse, their presence wasn't what was knotting up the muscles in her shoulders.

"Perhaps I can relax you. In a therapeutic way, you know." He took a step back, but kept her in place, with one big hand on her shoulder. The wall was cool enough to give her chills. The heat and hardness of that hand gave her a different kind of chills. She grabbed his sweater and yanked him toward her. "Wait—"

"No comments please," he ground out.

She shook her head. Then she lurched against him. Slipping her hands around his waist, she laid her cheek against his chest. "Will you hold me first?"

Because if she held him and he held her she could put everything else off. At least for a few moments. And she could be silly and foolish and think of it as if it would be forever.

"I can. But first why don't I do this?"

He went down on his knees and unsnapped her jeans. "Let's see. We can start by checking to see if you're wet."

Her breath catching, she stared down at his bent head and at his hands and fingers, busy tugging her jeans down below her knees. "What are you doing?"

"I said no comments. And no questions either." He looked up, his black eyes blazing. "Besides which, if you don't know, darling, there'll have to be a tutorial." And then he looped his fingers under the edges of her panties, sending them downward in the direction her jeans had just taken. "Let me demonstrate."

She banged her head against the wall. "This is a bad idea. Everyone is upstairs. Somebody might decide to come down."

"I don't know about the somebody part or the down part. About the rest? That's what I rather hope will happen." He pressed her thighs apart, as far as he could with her jeans and panties hung just below her knees. He kept a hand on one thigh and, with the other, cupped her mound, his fingers burrowing into her.

She gasped and pushed against the constriction of her clothing. Forgetting every other thought she'd ever had, she could focus on one thing only: how she wanted her jeans and her panties gone.

But he had other ideas. He brought his face to her and inhaled. "Extraordinary," he whispered and began to wield his tongue like the unchaste weapon it was. He licked her as his fingers entered her and retreated, entered and retreated. And again. She thrust her fingers into his silky hair and dug them into his scalp. He wasn't stopping. He tongued her hard, burning her up. She felt herself spiral skyward as the ravishing agony built. She raised one hand to press against her mouth and muffle the scream that would blow the doors off the closet.

At the end, as the pulsing diminished, she came back from the place he'd taken her to. "What was that?"

He came to his feet and took her in his arms. She stood on tiptoes and pressed her face into the hollow between his shoulder and the base of his neck. She could feel his pulse thumping.

"A change of pace?"

She tried to regulate her breathing. "X-rated sex?"

"Not in my mind." Annie felt his gusting breaths against her scalp.

She cupped a hand over the bulge in his jeans. "You didn't get anything out of it." She ran her fingers up and down, wanting nothing more than to unzip him.

"I'll keep until later," he said, taking her hand away. He edged back and ran an index finger down the center of her forehead. "When I saw you, darling, I knew this worry line was too deep. I wanted to smooth it out."

"If we're talking about sexual healing, Botox couldn't have done a better job," she joked, her laugh a little too sharp. "That was wonderful, but now…sorry. I have to get upstairs."

"Before you do, I have something to show you." From his back pocket, he pulled out a wad of torn-up paper.

With one inquisitive look at him, she took it, adjusted the pieces, and read. "Well. Your boss—she is your boss, isn't she? —demands your appearance. I guess you better pencil—no, not pencil—pen that date in. In indelible ink."

"No pen, indelible or otherwise. I'm sending my regrets."

"Why?"

"Because these things are suffocatingly dull. Because I don't want to go. Because I have better things to do."

He bent closer, his mouth a breath from hers. She scented herself on his lips.

"And because I want to spend as much time as I possibly can with you."

Annie wound her arms around his waist and stared up into his beautiful eyes. "Won't she miss you?" Annie asked when what she wanted to do was tell him how much she loved him. Except the words were stuck. "The queen, that is."

"Perhaps she'll note my absence or perhaps not."

Annie slipped her hands beneath his sweater's hem. She grabbed handfuls of his t-shirt as a lever to anchor him to her. "I thought about something you said." At least *this* she could confess.

"Which something would that be?" He was back to playing with her braid.

"Maybe I should stop lumping all you peers and peeresses and people with hyphenated names together and thinking all of you are useless. Maybe some people with hyphenated names are nice."

"Maybe you should, certainly with the latter. They were given those hyphenated names at birth. That makes them innocent of intent."

"I'm going to try to be less judgy," she murmured.

He held her away from him. Gaze traveling from her forehead to her nose to her mouth, he smiled and bent to kiss her. "Don't try too hard. What you see in people when they're being obnoxious—like Emily Torquil's friends—is refreshing and honest. Poking holes in pretension…you do that so well."

She raised up again and placed a quick kiss on his lips and sank back down on her heels. "I suppose now I'm going to have to look for some titled people, maybe even another duke or two, and make myself like them as well as I like you."

"You can look for all of them or none of them, my darling. As long as you don't like any of them as well as you like me."

CHAPTER SIXTEEN

I t was a struggle for Annie to focus.

As long as you don't like any of them as well as you like me. His words, softly spoken, haunted her. Charlie Camville could be sure she would never like anyone as well as she liked him.

Did he like her as well as she liked him? She was sure he liked her when she poked holes in his pretension. He liked trading words with her. She knew he liked teasing her. He liked her food. No, wrong. He loved it. And he liked the sex.

Like was such a pallid word. She wanted him to love her. If he loved her half as much as she loved him… She couldn't finish that thought. On a soft exhale she closed her eyes.

"Have you decided what you're going to make for afters?"

Annie blinked and turned. Molly was staring at her, a quizzical look on her face.

"I'm toying with the idea of creating a bread pudding," Annie said, making herself concentrate.

Molly nodded. "It's English. You could make that."

"I could. But the problem is it's going to be too rich an ending for a dinner whose star is fried fish, whether it's English or my Italian version."

"You know you've got rhubarb down in the cooler. Henry brought some in before and it's beautiful, a really pretty deep red."

"I'm saving the rhubarb for a compote."

"Well, then. Why not make your Mt. Etna Cake? Most everyone who eats it doesn't mind that it's not English."

Annie snorted a laugh. "It's probably French in origin."

Molly nodded. "All right, then. I suppose the PMs won't mind that their dessert comes from that lot of surrender monkeys."

Annie laughed her first outright laugh of the day.

But when Molly headed down to the storage room for almonds, she was back to twisting her gray matter around that thing Charlie would be sure *not* to like about her when she told him her secret. And then it wouldn't be a case of him loving her half as much as she loved him. He wouldn't even like her.

She whimpered and made quick work of the genoise base of her Mt. Etna Cake. Davey fixed the cod fillets she'd rendered almost useless, and everyone else kept busy doing what she'd trained them to do. It left her way too much time to think. It was getting sickening to think. She was grateful, then, for her BFF's interruption. "You've got to see this," Lynette called out, coming around the screen into the kitchen.

Annie brightened. "What exactly would that be?"

Lynette grabbed her arm. "John Peele has just driven up on his tractor. He's going to re-plow the garden. And it looks like there's some kind of quarrel going on between your duke and George Swynford."

Standing at the bottom of the path that led up to the Manor, and with the roar of John Peele's equipment in his ears, it took a moment for Charlie to realize his name was being called. He turned just as George came tramping up. "Lindsey," George called. "A word with you. Now."

It was a struggle of superhuman proportions to let the man come toward him and do what Charlie expected he would do, what he *wanted* him to do: hang himself with his own words. And then he would deal with George in a most satisfying way.

Charlie came to his full height and folded his hands behind his back to look down at the much shorter man. "Swynford."

Chin lifted at a combative angle, George said, "What is Mr. Peele doing?"

"It's apparent, don't you think? He's restoring the community garden."

The color rose in George's face. "To take this step without consulting me—"

"Is my right," Charlie snapped.

Charlie saw in George's eyes the moment he realized he'd overstepped. "Yes, of course, Lindsey. It's only that I think—"

"I don't care what you think, Swynford. It's more than time for Mr. Peele to repair the damage caused when you had the garden plowed up."

George faced turned purple and he sputtered. "When I—"

"I didn't pay full attention when we spoke last week. I'm to blame, in part, for the result."

Lips thinned in displeasure, George said, "Yes, you are. And if you'd truly listened to me, you would have understood. Not that any of it matters. I'm not blind, you know. I can see you're doing this for Annie."

"Nice of you to assume you know why I do anything."

The roar of Peele's equipment grew louder as he swung back toward Charlie and George.

"She's got you sympathizing with the children," George yelled. "As if you ever cared before this. You'll do anything to please her."

George had no idea to what lengths Charlie would go to please Annie.

"But really, Lindsey, we've talked about it." A carping tone crept into George's voice. "Making Melbury Manor over into a hunting lodge, creating a shoot out of what is really a lot of useless land is an excellent idea and I'm proud that I thought of it. If Viola and I are to attract the right sort of people, we cannot have the poor of Bisby and their offspring tramping about. That was the reason we got rid of the garden. Annie doesn't understand that, does she? Being burdened with that misplaced American sentimentality."

"She understands," Charlie said, biting off each word.

George made a dismissive sound and lowered his voice as Peele slowed at the other end of the garden. "She's got her hooks into you as she does with every man." He patted his chest. "Not I. I'm smart enough to have resisted her from the start."

A muscle in Charlie's right forearm spasmed. "I'm curious. If you were smart enough to resist her, how did you let her convince you to locate the garden here?"

A scheming smile lifted the corners of George's mouth, and he leaned toward Charlie in a conspiratorial manner. "Quite simple, old man."

"How simple?"

"I had something she wanted. And I gave it to her."

"What exactly was that?" Charlie could feel heat blooming at the back of his neck.

"That did sound like a bit of a double entendre, what? Apologies," George said. "I could never think that way about Annie. A lovely face, I'll grant you. But that abrasive pushiness, that sarcastic tone. One has quite a lot of difficulty with it, doesn't one?"

George paused for a moment. "It was the land, of course. I had the land."

It was getting harder for Charlie to maintain his composure. His hands were linked together so tight behind his back he imagined he'd be left with marks on his wrists.

"If you want a reservation at the VIP table at The Ocular, you need to reserve at least a month in advance, and even then you might not get it. I wanted to be able to get a reservation when I wanted, perhaps even knock some toff back to a regular table."

The smug look on his brother-in-law's face told Charlie George had no idea how thin the ice was under his feet.

"When Annie asked me if she could use this particular plot of land for the community's garden, I extricated a promise from her that with only a day's notice, I could have use of the VIP table. Even you, a duke, can't get that. Quite the coup, wouldn't you say?"

As Peele came back around, Charlie held up a staying hand. Peele brought the tractor to a halt. With a loud clatter the engine dropped to an idle. Keeping the tone of his voice uninflected, Charlie said, "Yet you went ahead and destroyed the space for the garden you'd promised her in exchange for the use of the VIP table just when the garden was about to bloom."

"I didn't need it anymore, did I? I'd shown the fellows from the consortium my influence, so to speak, not once mind you, but the number of times they came up to Bisby to survey the land. There they were dining at the most important table at one of the best restaurants in all of England at a moment's notice and all because I have the ability to take charge."

"Take charge, George? Really?"

"Yes. Of course."

"I wonder. Were you the one to take charge, as it were, of the mischief at Annie's flat?"

George looked at him so blank-faced Charlie knew it wasn't George who was responsible for the vandalism, which was too bad. He'd have preferred it be his brother-in-law, especially with the hole George continued to dig himself into with his snide comments about Annie.

"None," George said. "Perhaps kids?"

"It was about the garden, you know."

With a glance sideways, Charlie saw his mother coming down the path, Viola trailing behind. Off to the side, a crowd had begun to gather at the head of High Street. Charlie could pick out some people he knew: Lynette Leslie, who had been in his class at Bisby Primary School before his parents packed him off to Eton; Molly, the server from The Ocular, and the three men Annie called the Endors. Neil stood off to the side, his arms folded across his chest.

"Ah, there's my wife." George eyed Viola and, as if gathering steam, said, "That's another bone I must pick with you. You speaking to her about our personal affairs."

Charlie narrowed his eyes at the shorter man. "I'm not accustomed to asking your permission to speak to my sister about what troubles her."

George stuck his chin out, the red flush on his skin journeying its way up his neck to leave bright blotches in formation on his cheeks. "If something troubles her, it's partially your fault. If you let go of the strings you've attached to our ownership of Melbury Manor, if you'd broken the entail when I first asked, things would already have returned to a normal state between us."

"Normal? May I then assume that the ownership of the Manor, and the business with the consortium aside, you and Viola are quite content with each other?"

"Just so." The look on George's face altered from one of self-righteous fury into wariness. "We're like any other couple. We have our days. But Viola and I are in complete agreement on how to go on with our home life."

"Ah." Charlie took a step and crowded George backward. "If that's so, perhaps you can tell me why, this morning, I found Viola crying. I haven't seen her cry since she was ten years old and our father destroyed her favorite doll as a way of punishment."

All the blotches on George's face filled in, leaving his skin all over mottled red. Arms held ramrod straight at his sides, he clenched and unclenched his fists.

In a voice he forced himself to keep steady, Charlie said, "I've often wondered how you could speak to her with such cutting words. But if it bothered my sister, she never said. And I wouldn't either. Meddling is not done. I agree with you there."

George regarded him watchfully. "And?"

"I listened to you, you know, and I believe you're right. I need to let go of the entail."

George's face registered surprise. "Lovely, Lindsey. Just lovely."

"You realize Viola's name will be on the deed for the property."

"Of course." Greedy pleasure lit George's face like high-voltage light. "As Viola is your sister—and daughter of your late father, the fifteenth duke—you'd want her name to be on the deed, as well."

"Only her name will be on the deed."

George's features stilled. "Sorry?"

"Your name will not be on the deed."

Into the silence that followed, Charlie wondered why he hadn't heard the prophetic sound of a crow's caw. No doubt the roar of Peele's equipment had covered it up.

"What could you possibly mean, leaving off my name?"

"It's quite simple. After what Viola told me today about the abuse, both physical and emotional you've subjected her to, I've encouraged my sister to do what she's said she wants to do. Kick you out of her life."

George's skin went from red to white.

"And that brings us back to my point. You will never have any legal interest in Melbury Manor. I don't trust you to do the right thing with a property that has been in my family for hundreds of years. I will make sure that when the deed is written up— properly, I might add—there will be provision made for the girls and a life interest for Viola, should she somehow decide to stay in Bisby—until such time that the property reverts back to the dukes of Lindsey." With that, he turned to Peele. "Mr. Peele, anytime you're ready, please continue."

Peele tipped his New York Yankee hat at Charlie and then hopped up onto his tractor. With a roar of the engine, he began again to plow.

"You bastard," George hissed, his face beginning to glisten with sweat.

"Sorry, old man. That name will not do. As disgraceful as my father was, he was married to my mother at the time of my conception."

"You can't treat me in this shabby way," George snarled. "I have given so much to the family, beginning with propping up your sniveling sister." He threw up his hands. "If I have to hear her whinge one more time about how I wasn't justified when I..." His voice trailed off.

Charlie's head began to pound.

"If she had such a problem living on the income I've provided her, then she should have gotten a job. I certainly wasn't stopping her. The woman is a dead loss as a human being."

A red haze descended over Charlie's line of sight.

"You're a fool, Lindsey. You let women lead you around with their tears and their managing, man-killing behavior. First, your fool of a sister and then that American bitch who—"

It was only when George, eyes wide, was looking up, his arse on the ground and a fierce red blotch on the side of his face where Charlie had landed his punch, that Charlie heard the sounds around him again.

"Thank you, Swynford," he said, voice calm, though inside he continued to churn. "You've afforded me the opportunity to make a dream of many years come true."

As George stumbled to his feet, Peele, a grin on his face, watched while he plowed. Only then did Charlie sense that everyone in the crowd was watching, including Neil, his arms still in place over his chest.

"It seems I've been away from Bisby too long," Charlie said. "Had I known you were so universally disliked, George, I would have come back sooner."

"Damn you, Lindsey."

"Not Lindsey, my dear baron. Your Grace. Call me Your Grace, you useless cretin."

Breathing fast, George brushed off his suit and turned to stalk over to his wife, who stood, stiff and white-faced, just behind her mother's shoulder. "You! Come with me now. We're leaving."

"George…" Viola's voice trembled. "I'm taking the girls…"

"Damn the girls. They can stay here with their uncle. Let's see how he feels taking care of a pair of useless females."

By this time Neil had picked his way across the road. "I say, George. Why don't we take a walk over to the side and talk things out?"

The expression on George's face grew indignant. He rubbed the spot on his cheek where Charlie's punch had landed. "He hit me. Why aren't you taking him away?"

Neil seized George by his bicep. "You don't worry about him," he said and gave Charlie a warning glare.

For a moment Charlie thought George was about to cry. But then, like a lamb, he went with Neil.

Flexing his fist—the damn thing throbbed—Charlie stepped over to where Viola was standing. "Did I do the wrong thing?"

She gave him a half smile. "I would say you were acting the big brother. But I meant what I said before. I'm going to learn how to take care of myself and the girls." She looked down at the ground. Charlie thought he heard a sniff, but Peele had wheeled around close to them again.

But then she said, "Much as I love you for thinking I want to stay in Bisby, which I don't, if you break the entail, don't break it for me." She turned and hurried toward the front door of the Manor. He didn't go after her.

His mother, of course, didn't either. "Really, Lindsey. Should you have? Such an unfortunate scene."

"And you would have done what, Mother?"

"You didn't give me a chance, did you? Although Viola should have had a bit more backbone, don't you think? How I raised that young woman to be such a ninny, I don't know."

"I don't know either. How you raised her."

His mother bristled.

"Mr. Peele is almost finished. In just a bit there'll be nothing more to see. Why not go back inside?"

His mother raised an eyebrow. "Trying to get rid of me, are you? As you're the head of the family, I suppose I must listen to you, even in a situation like this one."

"I, the head of the family?" Charlie snorted. "How quaint of you to think of me that way. Besides, when have I ever been able to stop you from doing what you want?"

"It's an excellent thing that you recognize I don't take orders from you, Lindsey because I was being facetious. And now that we've sorted that out, I believe I will reacquaint myself with the people of Bisby."

"As if you ever cared about the people of Bisby," he growled at her retreating figure.

She skirted around the ground Peele continued to plow and stepped into the crowd watching Peele work.

Charlie narrowed his eyes. "Bollocks," he muttered and knew. She was headed for the last person he wanted her to have anything to do with. Annie.

CHAPTER SEVENTEEN

Annie arrived with Lynette just as Charlie flattened George. Not caring if anyone in the crowd saw, she indulged herself in a triumphant fist pump. What George could have said, though, to get that reaction from the normally calm Charlie, would have to take a back seat to what was coming her way. Or rather who. Annie's antennae stood up as the tall woman she'd seen with Viola made her way toward where she was standing with Lynette.

"Good Lord. I do believe the duchess of Lindsey is coming for a visit." Lynette squeezed her hand. "I just remembered I have to clean out my kitty's litter box." She stepped back. "Ta."

Annie would have objected if it hadn't already been too late. Charlie's mother's dark eyes—Charlie's eyes—stared straight at her.

"Are you Annie?" she asked in her sharply cut upper-class tones. Tall, thin, dressed in a slim skirt and a collared, bright white blouse, the duchess was in an outfit even Annie, who didn't pay attention to this stuff, knew was something that came from a classy shop in Mayfair or somewhere just as exclusive. Her black hair—not a white strand anywhere—was up in an intricate knot, and on her unsmiling face was a haughtiness Annie had only ever seen in a 1940s-era movie on TV.

Annie straightened and folded her hands together, her thumb pressing hard against the scar on her palm. "And you are?"

The woman raised one eyebrow. It was a family tick, it seemed. "I believe you know who I am."

Out of the corner of her eye, Annie saw Charlie start toward them. She gave him a warning look. He stayed put. Turning back to his mother, she said, "As I believe you know who I am."

The duchess pursed her lips, that one eyebrow still raised. "I suppose congratulations are in order."

Annie gave the woman her own raised eyebrow. "Thank you."

"The Ocular, your quite famous restaurant. I've heard from some of my friends who have driven up to Bisby for dinner. You are to be commended for bringing culinary brilliance to the East Midlands. One doesn't quite know how you do it."

An insult implied. The duchess of Lindsey could give Cruella de Vil a run for her money. "No mystery."

With her dark, unblinking eyes, Charlie's mother said, "My daughter tells me she asked you to prepare a luncheon for her. I think we may both assume, considering the scene my son and daughter made themselves part of just now, there will be no luncheon."

"Did they send you over here to tell me?"

The silence stretched into a prolonged, charged moment. In a softened voice saturated with hauteur, Charlie's mother said, "I don't do errands."

"There's no question about that, is there?" Annie said, keeping her voice even. It took a lot of effort as fast as her heart was beating.

"I would imagine you won't care if my daughter cancels. It would of course be the right thing to do to allow you to make your plans accordingly."

Annie pretended a smile. "So kind of you."

"I understand that in quite a short period of time some sort of relationship has grown up between you and my son."

Annie's heart skipped a beat.

"It could have quite serious ramifications. If it were to last." Tapping a foot, the duchess said, "What do you know about my son? Or said another way, what do you think you know about him?"

"As in what he's like, or who he is?"

"Both, if you please."

"I know he's smart enough to have built something huge—his business—out of nothing."

"Yes, Lindsey's accomplishments in business have been quite extraordinary. It enabled him to restore the visible aspects of his patrimony. The rehabilitation of the Manor. The restoration of Rotherforde Castle, our seat. Now that he has ascended to the title, the restoration of the family's reputation will take more doing on his part."

Annie held her breath.

"I believe this rather unusual—and I must say even if you think it rude—unfortunate relationship he has with you may prevent him from doing his duty. I believe it would be best for all concerned if you were to convince my son it should not continue."

Shades of Emily Torquil and company. She glanced once at Charlie who remained on the other side of the road. She could see, from the way his eyebrows met in the middle of his forehead, he wasn't happy.

She pivoted around to face his mother. "I'm pretty sure Charlie doesn't know you've decided to run interference for him. And here's something else I know about him. He doesn't send anyone to do his heavy lifting."

"A mother has to do many things for her children. Some of them are not pleasant." She raked Annie from head to toe with a frigid glare. "This is something that falls into that category."

"Consider your job done, then," Annie snapped, done with hiding her temper. "I am duly warned."

The dowager tightened her lips. Her malevolent black eyes shifted from icy cold to burning hot. "Then you take my point, I assume."

"You can assume anything you want." Annie tossed her braid over her shoulder. "I'll stay away from Charlie if I choose to. If I don't, I won't. I hope you take *my* point."

The duchess's face hardened into implacable lines. "I don't think you are fully aware of how tenuous is your position should you continue on with that attitude."

A sick feeling invaded Annie's stomach.

"When my son-in-law, George, phoned to tell me about you, he used two words to describe my son's regard for you. One of them was regrettable. The other was fascination."

"Oh?" Annie hoped that one syllable sounded like indifference.

"I thought, unusual as a relationship between you and my son might be, I would let my disapproval go unspoken. After all, the queen's granddaughter is married to a rugby player. However, there is one thing about you that I found insupportable."

A bead of perspiration snaked down the back of Annie's neck.

"I asked a young man I know to look into your background, and it seems, Miss Lukin, you've done some bad things."

Annie's head began to pound.

"You're a thief and an opportunist."

"I am not," Annie said in a fierce undertone, a tremor at the back of her neck.

"I can assure you, given what his father did, my son must know about that part of your history."

"I don't know what his father did. And don't care." The tremor was taking over her voice.

"My late husband was quite bad with investments. He had little regard for money except to spend it. Some years ago, he had to declare bankruptcy. It put the family in a parlous state."

A zinging sound filled Annie's head.

"Because of that bankruptcy, from the moment he learned of it, my son began to hate his father."

With venom in her eyes, the duchess said, "My son cannot tolerate the sound of the word. Don't you think he will hate you when he finds out about your bankruptcy?"

But I'm paying it all back, Annie wanted to scream. *Every last penny owed to anyone*. But the bias of Charlie's toward the word... Bile rose in her throat. How could she explain what she'd done was different? "Do you intend to tell him?"

"Never doubt me. I will."

A wild hysteria sang through Annie's veins. If she hadn't known it before, she knew now it would be impossibly bad, if she herself didn't own up. "Let me save you the trouble. I'll tell him myself."

A superior smile curved the duchess's mouth. "That would be excellent, my dear. Because you know when you do, that will be the end."

"Damn you," Annie breathed, her throat closing up.

"In case you change your mind, I do have in hand a trump card, so-to-speak, that will encourage you to break if off with Lindsey," she continued in that conversational tone. "I've asked my private secretary to contact the editor at the *Daily Prime*—a person she knows well—and tell her all about you. Being who they are, they will jump at the chance to write something about a woman with an unsavory background, who has attracted the attention of a member of the peerage. She will write it in such a way that my son will appear the victim of a grasping, greedy American female who is after his riches and title."

"Your son will hate that."

"Yes, he will, and even if it will put him in a bad light for a short time, it will be better than if he continues his relationship with you."

Annie was aware of nothing but the sound of the hateful woman's voice, low and modulated, drowning out the cacophonous drumming of her heart.

"They'll capitalize on the rumor that you slept with your employer and that you then stole his money."

"That didn't happen," Annie whispered.

"A suggestion is all that's needed." A twitch of her lip, a sly smile in her eyes, the duchess didn't attempt to disguise her triumph. "After that, your tarnished reputation might even affect your charming restaurant. One wonders if the smart people would be the first to stop coming up to Bisby. Who knows? Eventually your business might fail."

The duchess placed one finger over her lips and tapped. "No, I think you understand why your relationship with my son must become a thing of the past. After all, you wouldn't want to lose your livelihood over something like a relationship that cannot possibly last."

Annie wanted to be strong and angry and together. It was impossible in the face of the duchess's pitiless attack. "You'd want to destroy the restaurant, too and the people who work for me?"

"Do you think I care about the restaurant or any of those people?" The duchess began to back away. "I assume now you understand."

Later, when she allowed herself to think about it, Annie wished she could have made a world-class cutting remark to the duchess and then turn to stride away, head held high. Instead, with a catch in her voice she couldn't prevent, she said, "Wow." She pretended to look at her watch, although her ability to see the numbers was compromised by tears she damn well wouldn't let the duchess see. "I have to get back to the restaurant and finish up my preparation for tonight. I'm making dinner for two prime ministers. Not everyone can say they've done that. Have you?"

"When I entertained the former Prime Minister at my home in London, someone, much like you did the work."

Annie was just able to stop herself from lifting one shaking hand to the middle of her forehead where a pulse beat a mad tattoo. She took one step back and then turned away, knowing in the view of this stunningly beautiful, savagely hateful woman— the mother of the man she loved—she was a serf to be dismissed at will because she stood in the way of what the woman wanted.

As she pushed through the growing crowd, ignoring the glances of the curious, words of calamity and karma bounced around inside Annie's head. Defeat, too. In her smug upper-class way, the duchess had reinforced what Annie should never have thought could be otherwise. For the duchess of Lindsey, class difference finessed everything. But the cudgel with which the woman used to beat her off was the bankruptcy she should have told Charlie about when it wasn't a matter of her defending herself against disaster.

Don't you think he will hate you when he finds out about your bankruptcy?

The duchess held all the winning cards. The only card Annie held was the one where she deprived the woman the pleasure of telling Charlie herself.

Annie stepped up her pace, slowing only as she passed High Street's first closed-up storefronts. She needed to gather herself. It wouldn't do for her staff to see her so shaken. Nor would it do for Charlie to see her this way. She couldn't face him, yet. She had to prepare. Depending upon how fast he came after her, he might be only minutes, perhaps seconds behind.

"Annie, wait."

Or perhaps no time at all.

"You wanted to tell me your mother was in town and I might have to meet her, right?" She turned and gave him the biggest smile she could manage while her heart was trying to stuff itself into her throat. "She is some piece of work."

Black eyes—so like his mother's but not—were dark with worry. "I can think of other ways to describe her but won't. She is my mother, after all." He reached out for her hand. "What asinine thing did she say to you?"

Annie laughed, a sharp burst of heartache. "She wanted to compliment me on the food at The Ocular."

"Give over, Annie."

"I promise you she did." Annie couldn't help a hiccup of sound from escaping.

He ran a hand through his hair. "That's crap. Even from where I was standing, I could see she wasn't paying you any compliments."

"Really, Your Majesty," she managed. "You need to let me get back to the restaurant. I have to finish my prep for tonight." And wasn't that a ridiculous thing for her to say? He could catch her out if he walked into the restaurant and saw how everything was running as smooth as ever because she, Annie Lukin, was never unprepared.

Except she hadn't been prepared for his mother.

She whirled away from him and started up the street again. Hearing his steps mimicking hers, she said, "Charlie, please." She swallowed the sob that rose up whole. But it was too late and the tears came. He pulled her into his arms and breathed her name.

She pressed her face against his breastbone and inhaled the scent that was his and his alone. He felt like refuge. The scratchy, comforting texture of his sweater. The strength of muscle and sinew and bone, all of him, his arms a bulwark against a world of misery and loss.

Sliding her hands beneath his sweater, she stood in his arms, permitting herself this one thing. Then she made herself let go. She stepped away and lifted her face to his. Into his luminous, kind eyes, she said, "I can't talk right now. Remember? I have two prime ministers coming to dinner in a little more than three hours."

"Later tonight, then?" With his thumb, he wiped away the newest tear snaking down her cheek. "After you close the restaurant."

"Meet me in my apartment around twelve-thirty. I promise I'll tell you then."

He bent to give her one fleeting kiss on her lips. "You'd better," he whispered. "Because something besides my mother has upset you dreadfully, and I refuse to let anything upset you at all. Whether it's my mother or that something else, I won't let it come between us."

CHAPTER EIGHTEEN

Annie wore her best chef outfit for the two prime ministers, a lightly-starched, black double-breasted jacket over brightly-patterned, loose-fitting trousers, and black clogs. Throughout the evening, Annie was charm personified. She grinned when both prime ministers greeted her. She grinned when they complimented her on having thought up the idea of a VIP table. She grinned when they told her how jealous their staffers were that they hadn't been asked to make the trip so they too, could say they'd eaten at The Ocular. She grinned until she thought her jaws would crack.

Her fish and chips were perfect. Both men raved over the crunchiness, the sauces she served with the fish, even the presentation. Halfway through the meal, they indulged in a mock battle on the subject of the dish's national origins. Their laughter spread out like a wave over the guests at the other tables. At the end of the evening servers and guests alike were smiling. Even the stiff-legged security men stationed at various spots in her dining room, broke protocol and smiled. Annie comped everyone their dessert, and the servers got out-size tips.

When everyone, guests and staff said their goodnights, Annie turned off all the lights, locked the sturdy door, and headed upstairs to her apartment to wait.

The first thing she did was change out of her limp, sweaty clothes into something more comfortable, a black tee with the multi-colored skirt she'd worn down to London—had it been less than a week since then? She pressed her fingers against the beat of the pulse at her temple and sat down at the foot of the bed, the box with the dancing girls on its lid in her lap. She'd stripped off and thrown away the sheets with the offensive message scrawled across them, folded her excuse of a blanket and placed it up against the headboard underneath her equally awful pillow.

Downstairs, the hinges on the pink door squeaked—its new hardware would take a while to get broken in—and she heard Charlie pace up the steps. He strode into the apartment and stopped to look around, his gaze lingering on her rickety table and chair.

She jumped to her feet, hands clutching the box.

"Why is the door downstairs unlocked?"

"Oh." She blinked. "I forgot."

Eyebrow raised, he said, "Since we don't know who vandalized your flat, didn't we say you'd keep it locked from now on?"

She angled her chin in the direction of the table, a smidgen of spirit returning. "Whatever a vandal wants to take from this place, they can have it. They'll be doing me a favor. You said that yourself."

His eyebrows twitched into a frown. "That's a bit of a flippant remark."

The moment of spirit disappeared and she swallowed a lump in her throat the size of a baseball. "I don't mean to make light of the situation. I'm …" And she took a deep breath. "I know I need to be careful."

His face cleared. "From now on we'll be careful together."

She nodded even as her heart began to break into pieces.

Taking a step farther into the apartment, Charlie lifted his hand and then let it drop to his side. "What's bothering you? Was it truly my mother?"

Annie knew she was an easy read. She couldn't help wearing her thoughts on her face, which made it nearly impossible for her to tell the smallest fib. She came to her feet. "Not entirely."

His gaze tracked to the black lacquer box and then up again. "I almost asked her to tell me. But I've heard enough of what my mother has had to say today. I had no desire to hear more." In a softened voice, he said, "Especially about you."

Annie clutched the box to her chest. "She threatened me."

His eyes darkened with anger. Before he could speak, Annie said, "She thinks she knows something about me when I was living in New York."

She turned and put the box on the bed, removed the envelope, the one that was like all the others she readied and kept in the box until she mailed it. She clutched it in her hand and took a deep breath. "Right out of school I got a job as a pastry chef at Carne, in New York. It's a high-profile restaurant run by a celebrity chef named Joe Barra."

Her mouth was so dry. "I was the best he'd ever met, he said, in spite of how young I was, and he wanted to make sure he kept me so he paid me a big salary. Even after I paid my few bills, it was so much money I didn't know what I was going to do with it all."

With a faint smile, Charlie said, "Save it, perhaps?"

She ignored that. Flexing her right fist, she opened it and stared at the scar. "Joe's wife, Cindy, was the restaurant's business manager. She didn't like me. It was only later, after Joe fired me, that I found out why. She thought I was sleeping with him."

"But you weren't." Charlie's smile kicked down a notch.

"No! You know I wouldn't." Even in her own ears that sounded too vehement.

He folded his arms across his chest. "I can't imagine what a fool the man was to fire you."

"But he did." Her heart began a slow descent into her stomach. "See, there was this sous chef at Carne. Michael. He was always short of money. I'd loan him some when he asked. It didn't bother me that he didn't always pay me back."

A flex of tension hardened Charlie's jaw. "Lending money to a man like that… Not a terribly good idea."

With raised voice she said, "I know. And that's how it all started."

One of Charlie's eyebrows went up.

"I made the mistake of thinking Michael would give back the money when he could. He had a wife and a kid, and his little boy was always sick and they had big doctor bills. It made me feel good to be able to help someone out when there was a kid involved."

Annie clasped her hands together. "Then, one day he asked me for four-thousand dollars. He begged me. His wife was divorcing him. He needed to find an apartment and pay a couple of months' rent ahead."

Charlie shook his head once. "The man sounds bent as a nine bob note."

"There was something weird about how he asked me and at first I said no. But then he cried, and I felt terrible I'd doubted him. Even so I decided I'd only give him half because four-thousand dollars seemed like a lot. I made an excuse, said I didn't have it. He said he understood and thanked me."

Charlie's eyes softened. "Even half seems like it was foolishly generous."

"It was. Definitely the foolish part." She swallowed hard. "A couple of days later Joe and Cindy cornered me in the kitchen, just after lunch service. All the servers were there, the line chefs, the runners, the expediters, everyone. It seemed Michael had accused me of taking two-thousand dollars from the receipts from the night before. He saw me do it, he said."

Both of Charlie's eyebrows came down. "Bastard."

"They believed him." Annie clutched her arms around her torso. "Joe looked on while Cindy screamed at me. It didn't matter how much I told Cindy it wasn't me. I was mortified and petrified. The next thing I knew, I was out on the street, the back door to the restaurant slammed in my face. It opened again and Cindy was in the doorway, her neck and face all red, and a vein standing out on her forehead. 'Be glad I don't have you arrested,' she yelled. And then she threw my coat at me. Which was good because I was shivering. It was winter." With a laugh that held no humor, Annie said, "I wasn't sure I was shivering with cold or shock."

Voice soft, Charlie shook his head. "I know you didn't take the money."

"Thank you." Annie's knees began to tremble. "It was Michael who took it," she whispered. "He was making up the difference. He needed four-thousand to pay off his bookie."

Charlie's sighed. "Go on."

Licking her tinder-dry lips, Annie kept her eyes on Charlie's face. "I would never steal. You know me well enough by now, don't you?"

"I do." Charlie pointed to the envelope clutched in her hand. "What's that?"

Annie's heart stopped. She handed him the paper.

He looked down at it and turned it over to look at the note on the other side, the one with all the numbers. "Who is Sheryl Quatrone?"

Annie fixed her gaze on what he held in his hand. "She's a woman in the business office at the Cooking Institute, the school I went to for my training."

He handed back the envelope. "Annie, sweet. Are you paying someone's tuition?"

She lifted her eyes and held his gaze for a beat. "No. I'm paying off my own."

He blinked. And frowned.

With a deep, preparatory breath she said, "Every month I send a check to her. Right after I mail it, I address another envelope and put it in the box until it's time to send the next check."

"That's *what* you're doing." His direct, suddenly suspicious gaze bore into hers. "It's not why. Tell me why."

It was becoming difficult for Annie to regulate her breathing. "I owed them a lot of money."

One eyebrow went up. "Okay."

Her chin began to quiver. "The school doesn't send me an invoice. Legally they can't. I'm paying them anyway."

A tic appeared at the corner of his mouth. "This is not a wonderful story, Annie. I'm beginning to have a hard time hearing it."

"You're having a hard time?" She hated how her voice rose, how it sounded even more defensive than it had before. But then that's what she was doing. Defending herself. "How about the hard time I had with it? How about when Cindy spread her rumors, and I couldn't get a job at any fine dining restaurant in the city? I had to take two jobs, one at an all-you-can-eat buffet and a diner on the Upper West Side. Those two salaries didn't come to half of what I'd been making at Carne, even working seventy to eighty hours a week. But I managed."

"Go on." His voice continued in that soft way— in a way a mimic of his mother's—that was the furthest thing from soft. And becoming clearly less supportive.

"Then I cut myself." She turned up her right palm.

He took her hand in his and looked at the scar as if he'd never seen it. She closed her eyes, only realizing as the warmth of his hand flowed into hers that hers had been ice-cold.

"I didn't tell you, did I, how I couldn't work while it was healing. I lost both jobs. A friend, a server at Carne—I actually did have one who believed I wasn't the thief—insisted I live with her until I could get back on my feet."

He let her hand go. The growing distant look in his eyes told her she was losing his sympathy. "It was the way I cut my hand that did me in. I damaged the tendons. I couldn't close my hand for the longest time, let alone use it to hold a knife or a whisk, or roll out dough."

"Go on," he said, his voice no longer soft.

Dropping her hand to her side, she went on doggedly. "During that time, the school turned me over to a collection agency. I'd get phone calls from them at all hours of the day and night. I stopped being able to sleep. Which didn't help the healing process."

He folded his arms across his chest. "Did you try to make an arrangement with that agency?"

"With what was I supposed to make an arrangement? I'd gone through all my savings. I had nothing, not even health insurance, which meant I owed the physical therapist, too."

"You have a grandfather." Now his voice was relentless. "Why didn't you go to him for help?"

"I called him," she went on. "Not that I wanted to. Because I knew he would say he'd done enough for me, taking me in after my parents died. He lived on a fixed income and couldn't give me anything more than a couple of hundred dollars." She looked down at her hands. She began to rub them together. "So he did. I gave the money to the collection agency."

"And then you gave up?"

"I didn't want to. But what other choices did I have? I couldn't go to a bank and ask for a loan, or accept one of those endless credit card offers that came in the mail every day, complete with their exorbitant interest rates. Even if they'd accept my application, I'd just have one more debt I couldn't pay."

She pressed her hands to her hot face. "I got a job at another diner and then lost it because someone from the collection agency showed up to harass me. I didn't know what to do anymore. That's when my friend's father, who's an attorney, suggested bankruptcy."

He took a step back. He exhaled a sharp breath. "You—?"

She stared up at him, words of explanation stuck in her throat as that terrible word had stuck in his. "Your mother told me about your father's."

His eyes black as onyx, his jaw hardened to granite. "Did she? It seems discretion is something I need to discuss with her. My father's bankruptcy is not information I bandy about with just anyone."

Just anyone. She flinched as if he'd hit her. "I'm not making an excuse for what I did," she said, her voice breaking. "I would never have walked away, if I could have helped it, I—"

"But that's what bankruptcy is, isn't it?" His voice held a hard-edged iciness. "It's walking away from your obligations. What about Ross Stoughton?"

Her mind blanked at the sudden switch of topic. "What about him?"

"Was meeting him a mere serendipitous coincidence for you to escape your responsibilities?"

Annie's knees almost gave. "Do you think that's why I came here with him? To escape my responsibilities? Because I showed you that I'm not. I'm paying the school. You see that I—"

He turned away.

She gasped, caught in a storm of words stuck inside her head. She stared, unblinking, at his strong back, wanting to pull him around to face her, ask him to please understand. She would have offended a total stranger less had she followed through. "Charlie, please…"

He did turn back then. "That's enough," he said in a steely voice, his eyes an impenetrable black, his skin a dead white.

"If I could have done something—anything—to avoid it, I would have," she went on in suffocating tones, not willing to give up, not yet.

"I suppose it's commendable how you send a check to the Quatrone woman, but when I put all of this together: the accusation that you slept with your boss, the one about you stealing that I didn't believe until—"

"I didn't! I swear, Charlie. I—"

He held up a hand. "Even coming to England with Stoughton when it might seem you were using him to run from what you couldn't face."

Her thoughts curled in on themselves, gyrating in slow, cyclonic motion. She cupped a hand over her mouth.

"This is all too much for me." He looked away from her. "I have questions I don't know how to ask, questions I had no idea I should ask. And it makes me wonder if I didn't fall in love with you when I truly didn't know you."

Her head began to pound with bitter joy. To find out, *this* way, that he was in love with her…*had* been… Each one of his words was a knife in her heart, a knife sharper than the one that had sliced her hand open.

He stared in a fixed way at her table and, with one finger, reached out to touch her hooped earrings, still in the dish. Then he took a step away and leaned one hand on the back of the chair, which took that moment to give up the ghost and crack, sending it, in pieces, to the floor.

He gave her one hard look and bent to pick up one of the legs. He kicked the rest to the side. Staring at the leg, he said, "Put a few things together. Some night things, some clothes for tomorrow. I'll take you to Lincoln. I'm driving back to London so you'll have the room to yourself."

"You don't need to do that for me. I'll stay here tonight."

"There's no need. There's a bed there that has sheets, pillows, and a real blanket, unlike your bed." Through his teeth he added, "And you won't have to wonder whether the damn thing will collapse under you."

She would ignore his biting remark. "I'll stay here. I'll be fine. I'll lock the door downstairs behind you and bolt the door up here. I'll be safe. And the bed will not drop me on the floor."

When he looked squarely at her, his always mobile, smiling mouth a straight, uncompromising line, she dared, "Will you call me tomorrow? Could we talk then?"

His nostrils flared. "I don't know. My mind is elsewhere."

"Okay," she whispered. There was nothing okay.

He threw the chair leg he'd been holding into the corner by the sink, where he'd kicked the rest, opened the door, and stepped onto the landing. "Come with me downstairs. Lock the door behind me."

"You go." With trembling fingers, she linked her hands together. "I'll be down in a moment."

She risked a glance up into his distant eyes, eyes that told her there was no more to be said. "I promise, Charlie, I will." Pressing her knuckles against her forehead, she shut her eyes and whispered, "Please. You need to go. Now."

She didn't open her eyes until she heard the door downstairs open and then close behind him. He was gone.

It would be an amazing thing if she ever saw him again.

CHAPTER NINETEEN

Charlie took the curves in the road that led to Lincoln entirely too fast, the control he'd kept on his emotions shredded to pieces. The smallest part of him wanted to regain that control, because losing it meant making bad decisions. The other part didn't give a damn.

He'd allowed himself to be fascinated by the gypsy girl.

She'd enchanted him and he'd let her. Oh, he knew she was doing the right thing, paying off the debt to her school. But hearing her say the word, *bankrupt*, had broken something loose in him. He'd spent years pushing the memory of that one, terrible day—the day his father left—as far down in his subconscious as he could. Now it came back to him in full force, the memory of that day outside Melbury Manor.

Viola had come into his room. She'd made herself small, sitting in a corner next to his closet, humming nonstop, and folding endless pieces of paper into origami designs. He could hear his mother and father, arguing, his father throwing things. And then hearing his father say the word. Charlie thinking, *No, no. It can't be.* And then hearing a horn sound. He ran outside to find his father pacing next to a cab while the driver loaded his luggage into the boot.

"What did you do, Father?"

Hazel eyes bloodshot from too much drink, his bulbous nose red with broken capillaries, his father had looked up. *"It wasn't my choice to declare bankruptcy, but when I did, I got the monkey off my back, didn't I?"*

They'd lost everything, except for the entail on Rotherforde Castle, Melbury Manor, and a small property in Devon. They'd lost the Camville name and reputation. How proud he'd been, growing up and reading about his family—*his* family—in schoolbooks. There were a few boys with him at Eton, who had, as he did, an ancestor who'd crossed the Channel with the Conqueror. Fewer still who could say they had an ancestor who fought with Henry at Agincourt. Or like Roger Camville, Earl of Thorne, who stood for the king against Cromwell and was made duke of Lindsey. Charlie's father had, without thought or care, reversed centuries of courage, honor, and reputation. And Charlie felt the shame.

To think the woman, he'd fallen in love with, whom he'd decided to marry, had done so many things beneath dignity… Charlie gripped the wheel hard, taking the next turn too fast. His lane warning device beeped as he strayed over the line. He righted himself.

Perhaps she hadn't. Only there was so much she'd told him all at once. Could it all be as she'd said? That she was a victim, not a crook?

He'd been prepared to ask Annie to be his duchess and make his home in Melbury Manor once more…until just now.

He wanted to admire her for paying her debt to the school. He'd cringed when she'd related how it felt, that shameful moment in front of all those people in the restaurant. How she'd been accused of stealing. Her voice breaking, he could see it. It rang hollow and yet it didn't. The thought that she might have a different kind of morality was scouring him raw.

But why, the voice of his nineteen-year-old self cried. Why had she caught him so unaware? If only she hadn't waited to tell him until after that chance meeting with his mother. If only she hadn't waited until then to be honest with him, leaving him to wonder if Annie would have ever told him about the blot on her name? Where was her honor? Where was courage? Where was her honesty? Without honor and courage and honesty, how long would it be before he stopped sleeping with her in the same bed, stopped loving her?

Because he loved her more than he thought he would ever love anyone.

They'd known each other a mere week. She should have told him everything. Trusted in his love. He would have accepted her explanation without a doubt. And now he wondered if he would ever be able to forgive her.

By the time he pulled up to the hotel, he had a raging headache. He stepped into the lobby, quiet except for one young woman, the clerk on duty, behind the front desk. He was exhausted, the adrenalin that had buoyed him on the trip from Bisby gone.

"Pardon me," he said to the clerk.

She stopped whatever it was she'd been doing. "May I help you?"

"I'm going up to my room to retrieve my things. I'll be down in a moment to check out. Please have my statement ready." Without waiting for her response, he made his way to the elevator and up to his room.

The first thing he did was take a couple of ibuprofen. Then he began to pack up. Looking at the bed, pillows plumped, sheet folded back with precision over the duvet that had not one crease in it, he remembered with too much detail what it had been like being in that bed with Annie. How he'd touched her. How she'd touched him. How she'd writhed beneath him. How it felt to be inside her. How, in the subdued light of early morning, they had done things to each other that had gone beyond coupling.

Before he let heartache give way, he snatched up his bag and hurried down to the lobby, letting the door of the room where they'd loved slam behind him.

The clerk must have been new. His statement wasn't ready. She dithered and fretted over his record, looking up at him now and then with anxiety as she tried to make her computer spit out the correct information. Charlie drummed his fingers on the desk. Why hadn't she told him? She could have found a way or a time, couldn't she? She—

A chorus of laughs kept him from getting further enmeshed in that circular argument. He glanced across the lobby, which had been empty until a group of keffiyeh-and thobe-clad men came in from the outside. Amongst them was a single man in Western garb. Ross Stoughton.

Every muscle in Charlie's body tensed up. He planted one clenched fist on the desk. The hapless clerk lifted her head to stare, openmouthed.

"Do your best to hurry this along, please."

Out of his peripheral vision, he saw Stoughton leave the group and make his way over to him. Charlie huffed a sharp breath.

"I say, Lindsey."

It would have been a lovely thing to cut the man. The last thing he wanted to do, though, was make a scene, and so Charlie took the hand Annie's former lover offered. "Stoughton. What brings you to Lincoln?" He looked at his watch. It was two o'clock in the morning. "At this hour."

"A business dinner, don't you know." An unctuous smile spread across Stoughton's face. Lowering his voice and angling his head in the direction of the group of men across the lobby, he added, "My clients do like to linger over their food. And the occasional glass of forbidden fruit."

"Ah." Charlie eyed the clerk, who was getting nothing accomplished fast.

"One of them, the short one in the middle, is the client I spoke about the other day. He's a Saudi prince. Oil. Pots of it. Millions, perhaps billions of pounds, more than he can spend. I'd like him to spend some of it with me, heh, heh." With a hand clasped on Charlie's arm just above the elbow, Stoughton steered him away from the desk.

Charlie looked down and then back up.

Stoughton hastily removed his hand. Clearing his throat, he went on. "He is set on purchasing Melbury Manor."

"I believe I told you only the other day that Melbury Manor is not for sale."

Stoughton grimaced. "But I thought with the garden gone, it meant…"

Charlie's patience was at low ebb. He resolved never to check out of a hotel at two o'clock in the morning. "Meant what?"

"I thought you'd come to your senses when you had it plowed up. That garden should never have been located there in the first place. Horrid thing, what?"

Charlie stopped thinking about checking out and turned his full attention on Stoughton. "You and George Swynford have quite an interest in that garden."

"Yes, well. It's an oddity. Not an attractive one, either." His gaze began to seesaw from side to side, lighting and then skipping off, a moth flitting around a lightbulb.

Charlie folded his arms across his chest. "However, it's good for the children of Bisby. Rather, it was. Until it was plowed up."

Stoughton's upper lip lifted in a sneer. "Everything would have been so much easier had Annie considered establishing the garden elsewhere. One wonders, doesn't one, considering the garden was such a short distance from The Ocular, if she cared more for the convenience of having it close by for access to its produce than for the poor of Bisby and their children."

Even when he'd had that idea the first day they'd met, Charlie knew Annie would never do that. More, he knew she cared for the children of Bisby. As a man who had slept in the same bed with her, how tone-deaf could Stoughton be?

"One would think she would agree to move the garden, considering," Stoughton went on, seemingly oblivious to the antagonism Charlie was sure was radiating out of his pores. "You do know, don't you, that I'm due the success of her little restaurant because I brought her here. We were lovers, don't you know."

Charlie flexed his sore fist.

One corner of Stoughton's mouth turned up in disdain. "I realized she was not the type of woman one wanted to bring into the family. Not really our sort. There are class differences for a reason, Lindsey. I was a fool to think it could be otherwise. My point was proven, wasn't it, when, with her straggly garden, she spoiled the pristine beauty of a lovely old property, owned and lived in by those who were born better. She needed to know that, what?"

Did Charlie want to deck another man because the imbecile had not just had Annie before he had, thought it all right to say so, and was willing to malign her as well? Why, he—

Suspicion coalesced into realization. "It was you. You vandalized Annie's flat."

Ruddiness bloomed high on Stoughton's cheekbones. "No, no, never me." He held up both hands in protest. "I would never do that kind of thing."

"Then who did you pay to do it for you?"

Stoughton took a step back. "Please, Lindsey. Not now."

"Who, Stoughton?" Charlie demanded, his voice whip sharp. "Tell me now or your client will see something that will have him spending all those billions of pounds with another estate agent."

Stoughton cast a furtive look over his shoulder at the client and his entourage. "It was Tom Hewitt."

The hulking, silent man who'd sat in the Strangling Duck the night he and Andy had gone for a pint. "Neil Duffin will know about this conversation."

"You can tell him what you want." Stoughton lifted his chin…his wobbling chin. "I only told Tom to leave a note on her bed."

"He took you quite literally." He clasped Stoughton by the shoulder. Hard. Stoughton flinched. "Let this be a warning. Stay away from Annie. I better not hear that she's been harmed further. Because then, I will forget that I was raised a gentleman. Do we understand each other?"

Stoughton adopted a look of affront. "No need to threaten, Lindsey. We're both gentlemen."

"That's questionable." Charlie let go and turned his back on the bastard. Two minutes later he was in his car. Twenty minutes after that he was downshifting into Bisby.

CHAPTER TWENTY

After tossing and turning and crying so hard that her sinuses were filled to overflowing, Annie forced herself stop to keep from choking to death. Taking out her second box of tissues, she lay down on the floor, her pillow and blanket and a puffy coat she hardly wore all that stood between her and unforgiving wood. As hard and uncomfortable as it was, it was better than her bed. Even with the destroyed sheets gone, she'd never be able to sleep on it again. Eyes closing, she fell into a stupor.

It wasn't enough of a stupor to get Charlie out her mind. At some point—she must have dozed off—Annie opened her eyes, this time fully. Pushing aside her blanket and coat, she stood and padded across to the apartment's one window. She looked out on High Street, all broken pavement, deserted and forlorn. The worm of an idea slithered into her mind.

She should fight for him. Not give up. She'd done it before. Fought for what she wanted.

Three years back, she'd first stepped foot in this place with Ross. Everything about Bisby had been foreign to her. She'd had no idea how she'd put her life back together. But she had. Because she hadn't given in. She fought.

But this was different. This was not making friends. This was not proving herself as a restaurateur. This was getting the man she loved to believe in her when he had no reason to ever believe in her again. Pressing a palm flat against the cold glass, she stared out into darkness. She squeezed her eyes shut.

Until she heard the animal roar of a powerful engine and they flew open.

As the Jaguar came to a screeching halt across the street from her pink door, she stumbled away from the window.

The headlights switched off; the driver's door flew open. Charlie jumped out, and strode across the street, disappearing from view beneath her window.

Downstairs, the pink door with the new hardware slammed back against the wall. He came pounding up the steps two at a time. Her heart swelled with fragile joy. Could it be that he—

Her apartment door flew open and he stomped his way inside. His skin was flushed, his eyebrows drawn down, his black eyes snapping with anger. "You were supposed to lock the door. After I expressly told you to lock it, you couldn't do that one thing? What maggot's got into your brain?"

Whatever the words she might have spoken died on her lips. Pulse pounding, her breath began to come in spurts. She took one step, two, then three into the warmth that radiated from his tense body. "Well, hello to you, too, your High-and-mighty, Pain-in-the-ass Majesty." She placed one hand on his chest, against his rapidly beating heart, and shoved.

He yanked her into his arms.

Her first reaction was to whack him a good one across his face. That notion lasted a nanosecond.

She wrenched herself out of his arms and stumbled back a step. Clasping her arms around her middle, she began to cry. Again.

"Annie." His breaths came fast. "Please don't do that."

If he took her in his arms… No way. It would hurt too much to have him hold her again, because yes, he was here with her. But only for now. "I'm not crying." She hiccupped as tears ran past the corners of her mouth, and dripped onto her shirt. "Crying involves sobs, and I'm not sobbing."

He laughed, a soft, sympathetic sound. "That's the kind of thing I expect you to say. It makes no sense. It's why I came back."

"You came back because I'm irrational?" She didn't need his sympathy and soft words. He was going to leave after he'd done what he'd come to do.

Explain what he hadn't last night. Why they could never be together because of what she'd done.

"No." He held his hand out to her. "I came back to apologize."

Her breath caught. Oh God, did he—? She wanted to believe. But there was a *but* coming. A shoe was going to drop. And *then* he would leave.

He held out a hand to her but let it fall back to his side. Sighing, he said, "As intimate as we'd been, it stunned me to think I was only then hearing about what happened to you in New York. I wanted you to have told me before." He stopped. "Before my mother blackmailed you."

Yes, but how cruel of him to speak of his mother. Next would come how he understood why she'd said those hateful things.

He sighed. "I was angry, furious really. Why didn't you tell me, I wondered? Where was your honor, your courage, your honesty?"

She lurched backward. She shook her head. "Please, Charlie. No more."

"I wondered why you let those things happen to you."

"I didn't let them happen." For a moment her voice was strong because this was true. But then she remembered. She was about to lose him. "Charlie, I know. I should be ashamed."

"Don't be. It's I who should be ashamed, deeply ashamed."

Her heart gave a big thud. The words... They confused her.

"How could I have told myself that I was the injured party?"

She stared deep into his eyes, as if there she would see the trap.

"Annie, my dearest girl." He took her by her shoulders and stooped down so their faces were level. "How you dealt with the insurmountable, how you've muddled through, all on your own your entire life, without help or advice or direction, how you weathered that storm that was not of your making—you are the embodiment of honor and courage. And there is no one more honest than you."

She wouldn't dare to think...

"You have beggared yourself to help people who three years ago were strangers. You planted that garden because you wanted to help Bisby's children better their lives. You want to fix Molly and Brandon and who knows how many others because you can and because it's the right thing to do."

She bit the inside of her cheek. She wanted to hurl herself into his arms and press her face to his chest, breathe in his Charlie scent. But should she trust—?

"If only I had remembered that part." He stroked her cheek and cupped her chin. "If only I hadn't been the man you accused me of being, so cocksure, so thickheaded, so damned arrogant."

She straightened away from him and looked up into his beautiful face. Swiping the back of her hand across her face, she said, "Charlie, do you think you could get to the point?"

His beautiful lips curved up into a genuine smile and the tension in his face lightened. "There. I would have missed that. How alone I would have been with my pride. How could I—"

Into his words she caught her breath. "Oh God… Please don't tease me."

"I'm not teasing you." He took her face in his hands, his thumbs brushing away her tears. "You have to let me finish. Those things that happened to you, that weakling who was your boss and his wife accusing you of stealing, you having to declare bankruptcy, there was nothing you could do. You cannot blame yourself for what happened. I won't let you."

"There isn't going to be a *but,* is there? The shoe isn't going to drop."

He leaned back. "What?" He sighed. "No, don't tell me."

She slipped her hands under his sweater, seeking his skin, finding, instead, the soft cotton of his t-shirt, and let the tears come.

Bending to her, he pressed his cheek against her head. "Even in the awful months after my father abandoned us, even as I struggled with my new business, I had entree to people who eased the way for me, who helped because there's a title in front my name."

"I have to stop crying," she wailed. "I'm going to get dehydrated."

He gave her a gentle squeeze. "Stop making me laugh. I need to complete my confession. Last night I acted just like that person you accused me of being. Distant, cool, the consummate aristocrat. I put an insurmountable distance between us, just as I'd been taught to do with people from childhood. I measured you without making the first attempt to understand you."

She smiled through the tears that refused to stop. "You don't have to confess another thing."

"I do." Pressing his lips against her temple, he murmured, "I should have believed you. More than that, I should have believed *in* you."

His words washed over her like peace. The hours of agony, when she'd thought she'd lost him became nothing. Feeling strong and centered again, she straightened and stepped out of his arms and gazed up at his beloved face.

Pulling a scrap of already wet tissue from her sleeve, she blew her nose to relieve her sinuses. Outside, the sky was lightening, and with it her heart. "The thing is, your aristocratic eyebrows."

They came together over a vertical line that formed above his nose. "I beg your pardon?"

"They say something about you, you know." She reached up to smooth down first one furrowed brow and then the other. "Not that. When you raise them."

"Ah." He raised them.

She placed her fingers over his lips. "And that 'ah,' too. Like you've heard something icky and are waiting for the jerk in front of you to confess to what they shouldn't have done."

She faltered, all seriousness again. "When you're really in judgment mode, you put your hands behind your back and keep them there. You did that last night. That's when I became petrified, because I knew I was going to lose you because of having to tell you what I'd done."

"Annie…" He reached for her.

"No, now let *me*. I have a confession of my own. I was at fault. I should have trusted you. I should have trusted us. I should have told you about Joe and Cindy and my bankruptcy. I should have told you the moment I knew that what was between us was more than sex."

"For me it was always more than sex." He took her hand in his, looked at the scar, and then ran his fingers over it. "The truth is, for me it was fascination with your brilliant, smart-mouth self before it was sex."

Annie gave in to a snicker, but it went away as quickly as it had come. "I thought you couldn't understand. Your life experience and status are so much above mine."

He took her in his arms again and drew her against his chest. "We're going to have to work on this Charlie-is-better-than-Annie business. And you're going to have to train me to stop saying 'ah' and putting my hands behind my back in that too-aristocratic way. I can't help my eyebrows, though."

Hope swelled further. She wound her arms around his waist and pressed against him. "I'm sorry, Charlie. I should never have let my foolish prejudice come between us."

"All these apologies are depressing me, and I'm beginning to wonder if I'm holding some other Annie besides my Annie in my arms."

My Annie. He was softening her up like sweet, melting butter. She thumped on his foot. Too bad the drama of it was missing since she had no shoes on. "Oh, it's me, okay."

"I thought about something on the way back here to Bisby," he added, swaying with her in place. "I'm not going to throw my Camville history up to you anymore. I don't want it to be a thing that comes between us."

"That would be a mistake because all those dead people made you who you are, and I'm proud of who you are." She gave him a comforting squeeze. "Sometime when you feel like it, I want you to tell me about them."

"And I want to hear about you, about your parents, what their loss meant to you because it must have meant a lot even though you pretend it didn't. I even want to hear about your witless grandfather."

"I'll tell you, but you better be prepared. I'm going to cry. I hate it, it scares me, but I will."

He put space between them so he could lean down from his great height and give her a look of blatant disbelief. "You? Annie Lukin, fearsome woman? Scared?"

"Yes, scared. Of emotion. I'm not scared of things," she said with defiance.

He bent to press his lips against her hair. "I'm guilty of that too. Not letting my emotions show. Perhaps we need to work on that together."

She sighed. "It'll be hard." And then softening again, she added, "I said I wasn't going to be so judgmental about rich and titled people. I meant that. I'm sorry now I thought you were one of them, snobby like the others, one more guy passing through my life, who had an inflated sense of himself."

Color stained his high cheekbones.

"I decided I might be wrong about you. Maybe it was when you offered to make things right with the garden. Or when you teased me about my cape."

His beautiful, mobile lips twitched. "Your alleged cape."

"I think I must have begun to fall for you then. You made me your slave, you and your handsome face."

He ran a finger down her nose and across her bottom lip. "You mean my serf."

She grabbed his finger. "Your willing serf." Taking his hand in hers, she placed a kiss on his palm. "Then you bowled me over with your sense of the ridiculous. We're matched that way. But what finally did me in was your warm heart. When you told me that little bit about growing up here in Bisby, about your sister and how you took care of her because she was your only family…" Her voice trailed off. "That's when I knew if I lost you, it would kill me because more than anything, I wanted you to be my family."

He closed his eyes, his eyebrows knitting in pain. "Oh, my darling. That's what all your generosity is about isn't it? Doing things for family."

"Because after my parents died, I didn't have one."

"And you wanted one."

His arms around her, her body molding to his, his body surrounding hers, he was all heady warmth, assurance, and rightness. Her head spun. She stood on tiptoes, wound her arms around his shoulders, and reveled in the joy of being held by him, in the goodness of it. "I did. I really did."

"Annie." He bent and pressed his lips close to her ear. His breath tickled. "I will be your family. If you will be mine."

She craned her head back to look up into his soulful, black eyes. His one eyebrow was raised. This time it spoke of anxiety. It came to her that Charlie—no, not Charlie but Charles, the Duke of Lindsey—

wasn't so sure of himself in this moment. "I can't think of anything I'd like more."

He took a deep breath and let it out slowly. "You do know there's more, though."

Her heart continued its acrobatic high jumps. "Spit it out, Your Eminence."

"The first time I saw you…" He was whispering.

She stared straight into his so dark eyes, smoldering now with passion. "Yes?"

His smile was slow and his eyes warmed to treacle. "I must have loved you then." He closed his eyes and bent to kiss her. "Now when I hold you in my arms, all the smooth and unsmooth pieces in me come together."

Annie sighed. "In case you got confused somewhere along the way, I guess I should tell you I fell in love with you pretty much at the same time, although I was too dense to notice."

"The violence. All that throwing dirt," he murmured against her lips. "That would stop anyone, even you."

"Not anymore. I love you." She kissed him back with everything in her. "I love every single one of your names. Charles." She stood on her toes to press a soft kiss to his lips. "David." Another kiss. "Hugo." One more. "Montagu."

"I love Charles the Duke of Lindsey. And I love you. My Charlie." Her cheek pressed against his chest, she heard the comforting beat of his heart and she knew she was where she needed to be—and where she wanted to be—forever.

323

CHAPTER TWENTY-ONE

Charlie took Annie back to Lincoln. Once they were on the road, she made a joke about how the Jag was going to be able to make the trip between Bisby and Lincoln without him behind the wheel. Then she promptly fell asleep. He didn't disturb her. Instead, driving slowly for him—no doubt a good thing for safety reasons, since he held Annie's hand the whole way—he let himself delight in the feeling of them being together. As they were supposed to be.

Pulling up to the hotel, he ushered a cranky Annie into the hotel lobby and checked them in with the same clerk he'd checked out with mere hours before. Once Annie was tucked up in his bed, he called Neil.

"I'm not that surprised," Neil said when Charlie told him about Tom. "The man's not got much going on upstairs. I'll track Stoughton down after I have a chat with Tom."

Who he would find in his hidey hole, the Strangling Duck, pint firmly in hand.

Annie refused to press charges against either Tom or Ross. Over a lunch for the three of them— Annie, Charlie, and Neil—in the Lincoln hotel's restaurant, she was adamant. "What's the point?" She took Charlie's hand, although she'd hardly let go of it since he'd awakened her a couple of hours before with some entirely satisfactory daytime sex. "I've got what I want."

Neil leaned forward. "Annie, you have to stop being so nice to people."

With eyes Charlie hoped were heavy from their lovemaking and not because of the grief he'd inflicted on her, she smiled. "Sorry, Neil. What you see is what you get."

Saint. That word Andy had used to describe Annie, Charlie had wondered then. Now he knew the word fit her to perfection. How lucky he was that she was his. Clearing his throat of emotion, he changed the subject. "George is gone. I rang up Viola and she interrupted her packing for London to tell me he took some things and disappeared."

"I can corroborate that he is nowhere to be seen around Bisby," Neil said. A tick of a smile at the corner of his mouth, he added, "Perhaps he's left the country. He might have gone to the other side of the earth for all we know."

Charlie said, "Perhaps as far as Australia?"

Neil shrugged. "It's possible."

"Too bad it's not a penal colony anymore."

Later that night Charlie met Andy and Neil—Annie, as well, since she relented and let Molly run things at The Ocular, for once—over a pint at the Strangling Duck. At some point Annie left the men at the bar and joined Maudie in the kitchen to teach her how to make a wicked sauce for wings Maudie planned to add to the Strangling Duck's selection of gastro pub food.

Bringing Andy up-to-date on the talk he'd been having with Neil, Charlie said, "It would have been nice, if Australia was still a penal colony, and I could have sent my mother there as well."

Andy raised his glass. "Cheers."

"You have to give it to your mum, Charlie," Neil insisted. "She's nothing if not resourceful."

"True," Charlie said. "She was able to blackmail Annie after she figured out that Tom and Clarice's son, Eddie, the one I gave a job to out of kindness to her—"

"No good deed and all that," Andy interrupted.

"And who I have now sacked, could research Annie's past in New York, and give that information to my mother. She, in turn, planned for Clarice to tell her friend, the editor at that scurrilous rag, the *Daily Prime*, to print it if Annie didn't do what she wanted her to, which was to give me up." He took a long drink and set his glass down on the bar with a thud.

"My mother is no longer in my life. I doubt she will care about that as long as I support her, financially, which I am honor-bound to do."

Andy raised his glass. "Here, here."

"Annie and I will be much happier without her malign presence."

"I'll drink to that." Neil followed words with deed.

"What will bother my mother the most, though, is this. I've cut her allowance by the equivalent of Clarice's salary. Going forward, if she wants to keep Clarice, she's going to have to spend less on herself."

"Knowing your mother as we all do," Neil said and looked from Andy to Charlie, "She'll complain."

With a chortle, Andy said, "But Clarice will have to go."

Much as he hated to, Charlie drove back to London for meetings he couldn't avoid. One that he actually wanted to take was the one with Lance Parrish from Stanford, Mellish and DeWart, the firm representing the consortium. He wanted to clear up any suppositions George had left standing about the Manor. He planned to leave London for Bisby when this meeting was finished since he hated being away from Annie for even an hour, let alone a day.

"We thought you might cancel things, Lindsey. We understand, certainly in light of our last discussions with Swynford," Parrish said, relaxing in the same Biedermeier chair Annie had sat in during their first dramatic—or was it traumatic—meeting.

"Oh?" Charlie had been fiddling with a pen, spinning it around on his desk blotter, thinking about what Annie had been wearing that morning, once he let her dress, and how she had left her hair loose because he'd asked her to.

"He wanted to be paid," Parrish said. "He made sure to tell us that would be part of the deal. We thought it would be a good investment and so a finder's fee seemed reasonable. But then Swynford started asking for more than we were willing to give him. That gave us the impetus to start looking at the property in Hampshire."

"As I've said, George is not part of any negotiation we might have going forward." Charlie stopped spinning his pen and sat forward. "How would the consortium feel about developing Melbury Manor other than as a shoot?"

Parrish tipped his head to one side. "Do you have something in mind?"

"In fact, I do." Charlie proceeded to show him.

Not long after, they walked to the elevator, Charlie feeling very much in accord with the man. Parrish offered his hand. "I must say, if I have to deal with a toff, I'd rather it be with someone like you rather than that lazy sod—sorry, I had to say it— who's your brother-in-law."

"*Was* my brother-in-law." Charlie stood back as the elevator doors opened. "I'll expect the more formal proposal within the week."

Parrish stepped into the elevator and turned. "It'll be a first draft, but you'll have it, Your Grace."

Charlie put his hand against the door to keep it from closing. "No need to call me that."

Parrish smiled. "All right, then. Lindsey."

"Not that, either." Charlie put his hands in his pockets. Before the doors closed, he said, "Call me Charlie."

Later that night, back in Bisby, long after dinner service was over, guests and staff gone, Charlie had his gypsy girl to himself. "I want you to see something." With a tug of his hand, he led her over to the VIP table. "Will you sit?" He held out a stapled-together sheaf of papers.

After one glance she took them. "What is this?"

"It's a proposal from the consortium."

"The one that's supposed to make the Manor into a shoot? Are they still?"

"That very one. And no, they aren't. But they've given me a new proposal."

She cocked her head to one side.

"From the beginning I had my doubts about how much benefit the consortium's original proposal would bring the people of Bisby."

He sauntered to the front of the restaurant and peered outside. "It kept teasing at me. The solution. We already have a garden on the property at the Manor. Why not make it bigger? Why not make it more useful?"

He heard the scrape of chair legs and her steps as she crossed to where he was standing. Hand on his forearm, she squeezed. "You mean make the Manor into a school of some kind?"

He took her hands in his. There was a glow in her eyes he'd thought, yesterday, he'd never see again. "No, Annie. Not a school exactly, lovely as that idea is. If the garden is bigger, it truly becomes a community garden. More of Bisby can participate, adults as well as children. You can teach the virtues of not only sustainable gardening but all the other lessons you think it important for them—especially the children—to learn. But there's more."

She bent a quizzical frown on him.

Charlie held up the sheaf of papers he'd worked on with Parrish earlier in the day. "Until you came along, in all the three hundred years since the Manor was built, have the people of Bisby ever enjoyed any part of the Manor's land? No. That's why I'm breaking the entail."

Her beautiful black-brown eyes that he'd been fascinated by that first day they met began to shine. She took hold of his shirt and levered herself up against him.

For a moment he allowed himself to be distracted by the feel of her body against his. "Except for one hundred or so acres I'll keep around the house, I'm going to deed all the rest over of the 16,000 acres to the East Lindsey District Council with the stipulation that the land be used in perpetuity as a public park."

She made a soft sound and stood on tiptoes to kiss him on the chin. "Oh, Charlie. You couldn't give me a better present if you tried."

"Well, I'm going to try to buy you another present, a car, if you would let me, so you don't have to walk to Nell Capes's house when you deliver her biscuits."

She squinted her eyes at him. "Charlie, have you ever been to New York?"

"You know I have."

"Why would anyone have a car in New York? Public transportation is way faster."

"True. But you live in Bisby now, where people actually need a car to get from place to place."

"I know." She bit her lip. "The thing is…" Her voice dipped. "I…uh…I'm afraid I never learned how to drive."

He began to laugh. "You mean that day you suggested you would drive for me it's a good thing I didn't let you?" He laughed some more. "Darling, no matter that you think it, you cannot always be in charge."

That crooked smile he loved so well made an appearance on her mouth. "If you buy me a car, you're going to have to teach me to drive."

He gave a mock shiver. "Let's hope we both survive the lessons."

She snickered and started to back away.

Tightening his grip, he said, "I'm not through. There's more." He put his hands on her shoulders and held her away from him. "I've bought the storefronts on either side of The Ocular."

He laid one finger over her mouth as she began to speak. "Before you say anything, please hear me out."

She rolled her eyes.

"I think I know what's in that wary mind of yours. You think I'm going to interfere in your business. Why would I? You've been massively successful. Buying the storefronts was another thing altogether. It was about us becoming partners and developing our medieval village. But that is the last high-handed thing I'll do. I promise."

Her mouth dropped open. "The last high-handed thing you'll do? Really? Have you met yourself, Your Highness?"

"Would it be better if I said I'll try?"

She patted his cheek. "Much better."

"When we get started with our project, we'll want the opinions of others. Andy, and Neil, even your Molly. There will be many thousands of people who will want to visit Bisby. One can easily imagine all the shops that will spring up on High Street."

She began to speak and then stopped. He kissed her and smiled against her mouth. "I'm enshrining this moment in my memory banks. I am fully aware that these few moments where I've succeeded in silencing you won't happen often."

He wrapped his hand around her braid and took a breath. "If you want to enlarge The Ocular into one of those storefronts, have at it. It's up to you. Or not."

As she tightened her arms around his waist, he felt her take a deep inhale. "Charlie, I can't let you do this for me."

"Why not?"

"Because we've got our own businesses that for all kinds of reasons we should keep separate. Separate but equal."

"Ah, an American thing. But may I remind you that we are in the UK, now. We don't do that separate-but-equal thing."

"And you never had a tea party."

They'd been having a spirited discussion about the differences between their homelands and the benefits—and detractions—of both. The discussions most always ended in equally spirited lovemaking.

In his loftiest voice he said, "We Brits do not throw our tea into the water. Ever." He grinned. "Unless it's a cuppa."

She laughed as he knew she would.

His answering grin faded. "I want you in my life. In my world. In my experience the best way for that to happen is to tie us together under the law. That way it would be more likely that when you were frustrated with me and my aristocratic ways that I failed to control one time too many, it would be harder for you to take off to the land of separate but equal."

"Charlie, what are you saying?"

He gave her a little shake. "It's not like you, my darling, to be so dense. I'm asking you to marry me."

She shook her head. "Charlie, you will never get rid of me, but you don't have to marry me. I'm not duchess material. Duchesses don't look like me or act like me, and they don't work in hot kitchens making dinner for people six nights a week."

"You're right. They can't make a risotto as spectacular as yours. They can't make a tonnato sauce like you can. And no one can seduce me as you do with your rhubarb tart or your vanilla ice cream or your Mt. Etna Cake—and if I didn't say thank you as many times as I should have last night, thank you for that."

She opened her mouth to speak. He kissed it shut.

"I'm not finished," he whispered against her lips. "They're also not beautiful like you, or as brilliant. And they're not fascinating like you in every way imaginable." He raised one eyebrow. "Besides, whether you're my duchess or not, you'll be my wife.

That's the designation I'm interested in. What do you say? Will you do it? Marry me?"

Her smile was slow in coming back, but when it did, he let go the breath he'd been holding. She stood on her tiptoes. "I have to marry you. Lynette has dreams of being the BFF of a duchess and I always try to please my BFFs."

"Am I one of your BFFs?"

"You're the chief BFF."

"And does that mean what I want it to mean?"

"Well, this serf always tries to give her lord and master what he wants. You know the answer is yes."

He snagged her braid and wound it around his hand. "Look at all these gyrations you put me through to get that particular answer. You're not a very good serf, are you?"

"If you think I won't work out, I can change the answer."

He clapped a hand over her mouth. "Too late. You've said yes. One thing you will learn. A duchess never goes back on her word."

She dived back into his arms and squeezed him. "I love you so, Charlie," she said in a fierce undertone. "I love you in spite of your title."

He kissed her hard and with possession, branding her with his mouth. "And I love you more than your title."

She stuck her tongue out at him. "I don't have a title."

"Yes, you do," whispered her Charlie, the duke of her heart. He kissed her. "You have a quite singular title. You're my..." He kissed her.

"Darling..." He kissed her.

"Lovely..." He kissed her.

"Gypsy girl..." And he kissed her.

The End

ACKNOWLEDGMENTS

I could never have written A Duke For Dessert without the help of some incredibly smart and generous-hearted people who helped make these pages believable. I include wife and husband, Melissa Vecchione Prideaux and Brendan Prideaux: Melissa for helping me understand how Annie would think as a chef who believes in clean cooking and running a farm-to-table restaurant; and Brendan who just happens to have lived part of his life in Lincolnshire near where my imaginary town, Bisby, is located. For what it's like to run a fine dining establishment my thanks go to two great chefs, Adam Greenberg, chef extraordinaire and winner of Chopped Champions, and Michael Lucente who helped me figure out how to set up a restaurant kitchen. For English slang and colloquialisms, my thanks go to Victoria and James Thornborrow. Any errors or misuse of said slang, which I am sure there are some, are mine. Much love to and appreciation for my critique partners, Jen Wilck, Lisa Verge Higgins, and Nancy Herkness and their unstinting love and support. This book would never have seen the light of day without them. Last but never least, much love to my husband, Andy, without whose patient cheerleading I wouldn't be an author today.

Oh, and one note…years ago, I discovered the very real Nicola de la Haye and her ne'er-do-well husband, Richard Camville in the genealogy room at the main New York Public Library on 42nd Street. I didn't know that one day I would be giving them centuries' worth of descendants, including Charlie, the swoony, very fictional duke of Lindsey…though very real in my heart.

ABOUT THE AUTHOR

Miriam Allenson is a believer in it's never too late to start something new. She's been writing her whole life but only recently published her first novel, FOR THE LOVE OF THE DAME. Her second novel, A DUKE FOR DESSERT, is the first in the Billionaire Dukes series. Miriam and husband, Andy, live in northern New Jersey, just off the Garden State Parkway, which means she can get anywhere from there.